BROKEN GROUND

Also by Joe Clifford

The Jay Porter Novels

Lamentation

December Boys

Give Up the Dead

Rag and Bone

Nonseries

The One That Got Away

Wake the Undertaker

Memoir

Junkie Love

Anthologies

Choice Cuts

Trouble in the Heartland (editor)

Just to Watch Them Die (editor)

Hard Sentences (co-editor)

BROKEN GROUND

A JAY PORTER NOVEL

JOE CLIFFORD

OCEANVIEW PUBLISHING
SARASOTA, FLORIDA

ISBN 978-1-60809-348-9

Cover design by Christian Fuenfhausen

Published in the United States of America by Oceanview Publishing
Sarasota, Florida
www.oceanviewpub.com

10 9 8 7 6 5 4 3 2

PRINTED IN THE UNITED STATES OF AMERICA

In Memory of Becky Murdock

ACKNOWLEDGMENTS

Thanks to my lovely wife, Justine. I'm running out of ways of saying thanks for putting up with me. I'd like to say it'll change, but I doubt I will. I'll probably always live in a fantasy world for half the year, growing out my beard in the winter months, wearing knit caps indoors, and drinking small-batch craft IPAs I don't really like to get in character. You make me a better writer. And a better man.

To my sons, Holden and Jackson Kerouac: whenever I question why God let me survive those crazy years, I find the answer in your perfect faces. I love you boys more than you could possibly know. In the words of my surrogate dad, "Big" Jim Petersen: you make it all worthwhile . . .

A well-earned shout-out to my sister, Melissa, and my brother-in-law, Anthony—and to the newest addition to the family, my niece, Sofia Antoinette Greco: welcome!

Thanks to my brothers, Josh and Jason, both of whom serve as inspiration for Jay Porter's world.

Thanks to my beta readers, Tom Pitts, Jimmy Soyka, and Celeste Bancroft. You guys have to suffer through the rougher, more unreadable versions. It's a tough job but somebody's got to do it.

A special thanks to my agent, Liz Kracht, who pushed me harder on this book than she ever has before, and I think you'll see the result on the page.

ACKNOWLEDGMENTS

To *all* the writers and readers in the crime community: you are why I do what I do. Thanks for your endless support. I love you all.

To Oceanview Publishing: Bob and Pat Gussin, Lee Randall, and Autumn Beckett—you've given my little mountain a home, and I'll keep doing my best to reward that faith.

Thanks, David Ivester at Author Guide, for all your hard work. And lastly, Pam Stack, whom I feel the special need to single out. You have been a tireless advocate from the get-go; you've been by my side through the good times, and you've picked me up when I've been low. Your support has never wavered. Next round at Bouchercon is on me.

BROKEN GROUND

CHAPTER ONE

"HI. MY NAME IS JAY and I'm an alcoholic."

Even after all this time, the words felt funny coming out of my mouth, unnatural, forced, like reciting a prayer in church long after you've stopped believing.

The small basement crowd stirred. Someone coughed. No one said hello or repeated my name. I tried not to take it personally. It had been a long meeting. Everyone was tired. The coffee finished percolating with a final burb. I heard the far-off creak of doors opening and shutting, followed by the hollow shudder only the cold invites. A moment later, a woman walked in. Black hair, pale skin. About my age. Something about her was familiar, but I knew I was mistaken. I didn't know anyone in this town anymore.

"I started coming here last year after my best friend, Charlie died," I said, leaning into the mic. "The doctors told him he needed to stop drinking. Pancreatitis. One drop would kill him. Last time we spoke he was sober and coming to these meetings. He sounded happy, like he was working the steps. I had a lot of things going on in my own life. I'm not making excuses for why I didn't check in on him sooner. When I found Charlie, he'd been dead for days. Sitting in a chair, blue and board-stiff, watching *Rocky* on repeat. He'd stocked up on a bunch of liquor, the hard stuff, whiskey and bourbon, gin, which he seldom drank—he was a beer guy like me—so I know it was on purpose. No one came looking for him. Nowhere he needed to be so bad he was missed."

I watched her settle in her seat and did my best not to stare, shifting my gaze, evenly distributing my attention across the crowd. There were a couple dozen people at tonight's birthday meeting, but the harder I tried not to look at her, the more it became like trying not to think of pink elephants.

"I never considered myself an alcoholic," I said, forcing myself to slow down and enunciate. When I spoke in public I tended to rush, mumble. "It was just beer. How bad could it be? But it was a lot of beer, and after Charlie died, I guess you could say I hit rock bottom. Except I'd been falling for a while, and no matter how low I got, I managed to keep digging. And I know my attitude and decision-making turned a lot of people off, my being too morose or too cynical or whatever. But you have to understand, in my head, I didn't view myself as pessimistic. I saw the world the way I saw it. Some people call that bleak, dour. But it's hard not to have a negative worldview when so much goes wrong."

I began to sweat. People looked bored. I felt stupid. I wanted to say "fuck this" and get out of there, but saying "fuck it" and running away had caused most of the trouble in my life. If ever there were a time to make a stand and face the music, it was now. That was the whole point of this ceremony, my confession, owning up to the mistakes I'd made. I was holding onto more than this chip.

"My older brother, Chris, was a drug addict. He was a pain in my ass, but I loved him. He died, too. Five years ago. Ran out of a house, high, waving a gun around till the cops had no choice but to shoot him. I had a wife, Jenny. But I pushed her away. Everyone who's ever loved me, I've pushed them away. We have a son together, Jenny and me, Aiden. He's six. He's my whole world. I want to be a good dad. Jenny and her new husband, Stephen, recently moved back to Pittsfield, couple towns south, so I get to see my boy more. Which is great. But for a long time, I couldn't see him because they were all the way in Burlington, and these hits took a toll. I didn't realize I was drinking so much to cope. Push my emotions down, put them on hold, give me another day to figure shit out. Except I never figured shit out. I'm not blaming everything on my drinking. I'm not rationalizing how I behaved. I know I hurt people—I own that—but drinking wasn't helping. Getting used to this new way of living, not cracking a beer at lunch or the end of a long workday hasn't always been easy. It hasn't made me rich. But I think it's making me a better person."

I thought someone was starting to clap so I paused. But they were just shifting in their seat.

"It's been nine months since I had a drink," I said. "Every night I come home to an empty apartment—even my cat got sick of me and ran away. I'm in bed by nine o'clock most nights, up at five in a meat locker every morning because I can't afford the high heating costs. I don't have any friends, no social life, don't do much for fun, no hobbies. No girlfriend. My only joy is seeing my son. And I know this all sounds depressing as hell. But here's the weird part: this is the best I've felt in a long time. At least since before my folks died, which was over twenty years ago. I still get panic attacks, and I don't smile a lot, but I also don't feel like I'm shouldering the weight of the world either. All those little things that used to be able to sideline me for days, gouged rotors or losing electricity? They're no longer major catastrophes. I fix the brakes. I pay the bill. I deal with life on life's terms." I presented my coin, hoisting it high, overheads catching metal and making it shine. "Holding this chip, it means something. It means a lot. It means everything. Because I know if I don't pick up a drink, just for today, I'll be okay. Thank you."

I'd practiced at home for days in front of the mirror, pausing at the right moments, inflect and project, make eye contact, go with the "less is more" approach, tweak facial expressions for maximum effect, act normal and put together—but when I got up to the lectern, all those eyes on me, I spewed my entire history. Like auto-dumping on a school essay, it all came out. When I finished, the small crowd in the church basement clapped politely and then everyone bum-rushed the coffee maker and ashcans upstairs. When you take away the drinking and drugging, all you have left is caffeine and nicotine. And I was kicking cigarettes, too. Or trying to. The problem was after she walked in, I lost my focus; I couldn't take my eyes off her. She was a magnet. I'd force myself to look away, but each time her face drew me back; and there I'd be, listening to my own stupid voice, spewing nonsense, gawking like a dipshit.

I've always noticed pretty girls. Can't help it. Even when I was happily married for all of five months, like moth to flame. It's not like she was *that* pretty. She stood out though. There was something about her, something that touched on an old, forgotten memory, like a song lyric you can't quite remember, can't move on from until you get it right. Whole thing made me feel like a fraud. There I was talking this big game about being a better person and the benefits of sobriety and reiterating my pledge to personal growth, and I meant it, but the entire time I kept stealing glances at her, thinking the things men think about women they find attractive. It didn't help that she was staring at me. I was talking. That part made sense. When I'd look away, though, I'd feel her eyes burn into me, rapt, engrossed, invested, conveying interest deeper than a woman merely paying attention to tonight's speaker, which didn't help me streamline my speech any better. The rest of the room, pruned-up old people sporting gin blossoms, with abysmal posture and ugly fleece coats, receded into the background, making her stand out all the more, a spotlight cast center stage. That's what happens with certain women. No matter how big the crowd, the bright lights shine on them and them alone.

After a few back pats, which made me uncomfortable—I felt like an idiot for oversharing—I was standing at the coffee station, doctoring this shitty, watered-down brew with powdered creamer that never fully dissolved, like tiny marshmallows in tepid hot chocolate at the county fair.

"Congratulations." She was talking to me but glancing around the dispersed room as if trying to locate something precious she'd left behind. Aside from a couple discarded pews upturned in dusty corners, metal chairs stacked like an uneven deck at the casino, I didn't know what she hoped to find. Maybe the same thing we were all looking for in these dank basements.

I nodded thanks and returned to poking the bobbing balls.

"It's a huge milestone," she said. "You shouldn't brush it off." She pulled a chip out of her tight jeans pocket. Brassy, glossy, gleaming. "The Holy Grail." She smiled. "One year. Free and clear."

"Good for you." I stopped playing with my coffee. "I'm not undermining the accomplishment. I'm just not sure—"

"You really have a problem?"

"No, I can admit I have a problem. Plenty of them. I just don't know what came first." I courtesy sipped the swill. I was itching for a cigarette, making me fidget more than usual. With February's frigid bite, I was in no hurry to head out into the icy black night. I didn't want to stop talking to her either. Dating is frowned upon in AA—thirteenth-stepping they call it—not that I gave a shit what these old-timers thought about me. I wanted to do the right thing for once. I wasn't ready for a relationship. I wasn't planning that far ahead, but I was lonely, could use the touch of a woman, and I liked being near her. She smelled nice. The way she stood there, nibbling her lip, twirling a finger through her hair, she couldn't make it any more obvious. When you stop drinking, you stop going to bars. You don't meet a lot of women at the Gas 'n' Go. Plus, if you aren't lubed up, conversation is as awkward as a middle school dance.

"When I first saw you in the rooms," she said, "I wasn't sure you'd make it."

Seen me? I'd never seen her before. Despite that fleeting familiarity, I wouldn't have forgotten a woman who looked like that. Not among this crowd, which hardly teemed with runway gorgeous. I can be oblivious but I'm not blind. Then again, maybe I was doing something right, focusing on their bumper sticker advice, eye on the prize, waiting for the miracle to happen.

She thumbed up the stairs. "You mind if I grab a cigarette while we talk?"

I still didn't know her name.

*   *   *

We ended up in my truck because neither of us could say a word through the teeth-chattering shiver of the St. Paul's parking lot. Not that the inside of my cab was much better. The heater in my truck had blown, again, and my resolve to lay off the cigarettes ended with the first whiff of her Camel in the enclosed space. Then I was digging in my glove compartment for my emergency pack of Marlboros. Eight days this time. Not bad.

The parking lot glistened with a slick sheen of ice, the moon's lamplight splashing down. Flurries drifted, remnants from the latest storm.

"What's wrong with your leg?" She'd seen me limping up the stairs and across the lot.

"Accident on the ice. Few years ago. Hurts worse in the cold."

"It's good to see you like this, Jay. Sober, working the program."

Jay? Like we were old friends. I'd never been to this particular meeting. I'd only come to get my chip. It's not like I went to *that* many meetings, period. When I made the decision to quit drinking, it wasn't easy. But it wasn't that hard. Cut intake in half, then half the half. The first few days sucked. I sweated out a handful of sleepless nights, tossing, turning, but that was it. Which made me wonder why it had been so hard for Charlie. Presented with an either/or option, he'd opted to die instead. I still had antianxiety meds to stave off the panic attacks. The boredom got to me most. Since I stopped drinking, my life had become one dull, long, uneventful day blending into the next.

Not that I didn't have plenty to do. After my old boss Tom Gable fled for Florida, I'd started my own estate clearing business, working twelve-hour days. But it all felt perfunctory, like I was killing time until I could see my son again. This was what early sobriety was supposed to be like, I reminded myself. One day at a time. Don't try to do too much. Keep it simple, stupid. Boring, sure. But a helluva lot safer.

"I'm sorry," I said, "but have I seen you around the rooms before?"

"You don't remember talking to me . . ." She trailed off, before coming back with what was an obvious lie. "A couple months ago. Meeting upstate. In Berlin, I think."

I'd never been to a meeting in Berlin.

"Anyway," she said, not waiting for confirmation, reaching over for a stiff handshake. "My name is Amy."

I should've known then. I'd never met a good Amy in my life.

CHAPTER TWO

WE SAT IN silence, staring out the window, like the last stanza in a Dan Fogelberg song. I waited for the snow to turn to rain, a tearstained send-off accentuated by bittersweet saxophone. The "let's-get-to-know-each-other-better" vibe upstairs was gone, replaced by rigid unease. I sensed there was a question she itched to ask me, something personal. Each time I thought she was about to ask it, she'd turn away, panning around grounds like she'd done downstairs, searching for external answers that didn't exist.

I enjoyed sitting near a pretty woman as much as the next guy. At thirty-six, I'd also gotten a better handle on when I was being played. And I was being played. I might've been laying off the beer, and Amy had me beat by a few months—but I knew a junkie when I saw one. The longer I sat with her, the more I recognized the telltale signs. It's not about physical appearance. Although that was evident, too. The eyes. My brother had that look. The perpetual shell shock, trauma that never fully fades. But it was more than that. Junkies always have an angle, are always searching out ways to manipulate, even when it's unnecessary. You can feel it. Doesn't matter if the question is straightforward and the request reasonable. They can't help it; it's in their blood. If my junkie brother taught me anything, it's that they're all liars. Say they had an apple for lunch when they had an orange. In the rooms, they say a drug is a drug is a drug. But that's bullshit. Beer isn't the same as meth or heroin or crack. You drink too much, you get angry or overly affectionate, nostalgic. The hard drugs, they change you. Even when you're done with them, they aren't done with you.

"So, you're an investigator?" Amy said.

And there it was. A few years back, I'd gotten sucked into investigating. Mostly due to Chris. It all centered on a hard drive my brother had gotten his hands on, incriminating evidence involving this one prominent family in town. But I was done with all that. It had led to nothing but heartache, costing me my wife, son, and everything I loved.

Amy waited for an answer.

"No. I'm not. I used to investigate claims for an insurance company. Ancient history. These days I work in estate clearing. Someone you know dies and you need their house cleared, I'm your man. Otherwise, you got the wrong guy. I haul junk for a living."

"I heard you do a lot more than that."

"Yeah? And what did you hear?"

"Stories." Amy glanced out the cold glass. Frost spread across the windshield, tiny Arctic armies invading, infiltrating my defenses. "Like how you helped expose that kids-for-cash scandal in Longmont, were the one who brought the hammer down on that steel CEO in Boston a couple Novembers back. What's his name?"

"Ethan Crowder."

She was right. Once I got sucked into that hard drive business, I was exposed to a world I wish I never knew existed, webs of lies, each thread designed to ensnarl and frustrate me more. I'd exposed Ethan Crowder, revealing him to be the affluent, abusive piece of shit he really was, a monster who preyed on young, lonely women, and in the process, I helped emancipate his teenage son,

Phillip. And I'd helped put Judge Roberts away, it was true. Not that my involvement made the papers. I didn't get as much as a thank-you card. "How do you know about any of this?"

"Ashton is a small town. What? You don't want the money?"

"I have a job. Clearing estates."

"And you do investigating on the side. Everyone knows who you are, Jay Porter. Why do you think I'm sitting in your truck?" Amy traced a lazy finger on the glass, drawing out this next part. "And, of course, there's the Lombardis."

"What about them?"

"Nothing." She swirled a heart in the dew before wiping it away. "Just that you hate them."

Whole town knew about my junkie brother, Chris, the town basket case, how he'd run out of an old farmhouse five years ago, waving a gun, begging the cops to shoot him. Few knew the Lombardis set that wheel in motion.

"Why do you hate the Lombardis so much?"

"Let's say, I did a lot of digging, and that family is seriously fucked up." I didn't need to evoke the hard drive found at a Lombardi Construction site, the grainy photos that may've proven their father, Gerry, was a pedophile. The old man died long ago. My real ire was reserved for his sons, Adam and Michael, politicians down in Concord. The brothers had used the drug problem up here as their own personal piggy bank, funneling the crisis into privatized prisons and for-profit treatment centers.

"What do you know about that new rehab Adam and Michael built?" she asked.

"Anything you want to know about those two or their rehab you can find on the web, same as me."

"Michael's a state senator down in Concord," Amy stated with authority. "Adam used to own the family construction business, which built half of Ashton, until he sold his interests to join his big brother's campaign." She paused, making sure I was taking her seriously. "Word on the street is Michael's eyeing a run at governor."

"Good for him."

"Together they pumped a lot of money into the Coos County Center."

"No shit." There wasn't a move the brothers made I wasn't aware of. No one could ignore that monstrosity if they tried. The recently erected rehabilitation clinic, built on the grounds of the old TC Truck Stop, rose tall above the Turnpike pines, a constant reminder of my failures. "What exactly are you asking me?"

Amy pulled a picture out of her pocket, passing it along. A wave of déjà vu washed over. Like last year with the missing Crowder boy. Only this time it was a girl, a younger, prettier version of Amy. Five years erased by age, another five subtracted by not making terrible life choices. Had to be related—features too familiar to be anything but. Amy had managed to hold onto her looks. Not by much. About my age, she had miles on her. The lifestyle will do that, and recovery doesn't necessarily bring those years back.

"That's my baby sister, Emily. I want you to find her. She has the same problem I do. Did. Drugs. I know she's in town. She's avoiding me. She's supposed to be in rehab but she split."

"Let me guess. The Coos County Center."

She nodded. That was why she was coming on to me, what felt off, the roundabout approach, buttering me up, in through the back door. Make it personal, draw me in.

"I told you. I'm out of the missing persons business." I punched the dashboard lighter again, scratched my scruff, tried to turn away. A drug addict sibling in trouble hit a little too close to the bone.

Amy fumbled around her purse. "I don't have much money—"

"Maybe you want to go to the cops."

"People like us can't go to the cops."

I knew what she meant by "people like us," and I hated that that genus now included me.

"Please," she said.

It was the *please* that got me, the desperation touching tender memories. My brother had been dead five long years, but it didn't take much for the cut to bleed fresh as yesterday.

"What's your sister's last name?"

"Lupus."

Amy Lupus. Of course. It had been a long time. High school parties by Paper Goods Pond and Silver Lake felt like a lifetime ago. She used to be blonde. She used to be younger. We all did. I didn't let on that I just now recognized her. She'd been one of those wild stoners, the kind that would smoke cinnamon sticks if they thought it would get them high. Not surprising she'd end up a junkie. Once I made the connection, she looked a helluva lot better. Euphoric recall, all right. I was with Jenny back then, but Amy Lupus was the kind of girl every guy wanted.

She still had her purse out, waiting for me to name a price. It was funny. Last year, I'd turned down over ten grand to find Ethan Crowder's kid. Because Crowder was a prick. I found the boy to spite him. An ex-junkie, Amy wasn't rolling in dough.

"We can worry about that part later. Why don't you tell me what happened and we'll take it from there?"

"I don't want to owe more than—"

"How's two hundred sound?"

She looked at me like I was missing half a head. Who knew? Maybe I was. Maybe I was a bleeding heart. Or just a lousy businessman.

At that point, a junkie who'd bailed on treatment? Dollars to donuts, she was holed up at one of the dumpy motels along the Turnpike, getting loaded. That's where my brother would run off to whenever he'd fled rehab. I figured I'd spend a couple hours on the Desmond Turnpike, dangle a twenty spot, and make a quick two hundred dollars in the process.

I reached over for the picture and cash. "When was the last time you saw your sister?"

"Few weeks ago. When I brought her to the CCC."

Maybe it was the cold February night in a church parking lot after an AA meeting, or the fact that I was supposed to be completing one of those goddamn steps, the one about an honest and fearless moral inventory, a process I'd been putting off. I hated that term. An inventory was what I did after I bought items at auction and stashed them in the back of a U-Haul. I started to stew, conflicted, tearing my own insides apart. Because I knew what the right call was, which made making it that much harder.

"Are you sure she was admitted?"

"Of course. I drove her there myself. What kind of question is that?"

"But you didn't do the actual intake." Most places let family members enter the facility. I knew for a fact that the Coos County Center did not.

"I dropped her at the gate. I watched the staff escort her in."

"How do you know she's not there anymore?"

"The first few nights she called, like she promised she would. A recorded voice announced the call was coming from the center. So I know she was there. Then the calls stopped. I phoned the CCC patient pay phone. Emily was always at dinner or a meeting. Then a patient tells me Emily hasn't been there for at least a week. The hospital wouldn't tell me anything. Confidentiality. Emily was supposed to sign a release so her doctors could talk to me, but she never did. I finally got a sympathetic nurse who gave me enough hints."

"Hints?"

"Emily checked out. AMA."

Against medical advice. Rehabs are not like prison. Unless you are court-ordered, you can walk out any time you please.

"How bad was her habit?"

"That's the part I don't understand," Amy said. "I was the junkie in the family, the black sheep, the bad one. Emily was the good girl. I didn't know she had a problem until she called asking if I'd bring her to the hospital."

"Drug of choice?"

"Prescription pills."

"Parents?"

Amy shook her head.

Another orphan.

"You got an address?"

"For where my sister lives?"

"That's what people use addresses for."

"She had an apartment up by that college."

"White Mountain Community."

"That's the one. But she wasn't spending much time there. I don't think she was taking classes."

"You don't . . . think?"

"We weren't close, okay?" Amy snapped, unable to hide hostility. "I was surprised when she called and asked me to bring her to rehab. I figured she must have friends from school, other people she could hit up. She's always been popular. We don't exactly get along. After I got clean, she still harbored resentment."

"You have names of any of these friends?"

"Yes, and I've called them all. They said Emily cut herself off years ago. I found out she has a new boyfriend, this drug dealer. Calls himself G-Money."

"G-Money. You're shitting me."

Amy shrugged.

"You have an address for . . . G-Money?"

She handed me a Post-It note where she'd already jotted down both addresses. I wasn't sure how much I liked her preparedness. "I've talked to him, too," she said. "He swears he hasn't seen her. I've been by his place, sat outside for hours, gone back every day. Seen him come and go. Went up, peeked in the windows. No signs of her living there."

"He some sort of badass or what?"

"G-Money?" Amy laughed. "Hardly."

"And her apartment?"

"I told you, she hasn't been there in a while. She'd dropped out of school. I think she was evicted from her apartment."

I checked the dashboard clock. "Okay." I passed along my number. "Call me in a day or two. I'll see what I can do."

"How long before you—"

"I don't know. Soon. I have to go now."

If I hurried, I still had time to catch my son, Aiden, before my ex put him to bed.

CHAPTER THREE

JENNY'S NEW HUSBAND, Stephen, was out of town. Even though it had just been my weekend, my ex-wife arranged this special visit. On the drive over, I didn't smoke. Jenny hated it. I chomped gum, watched the frost crackle across the glass. It was such a pretty night. I'm not a city boy. Closest I made it to the big city was growing up with my aunt and uncle in the Concord suburbs. Sometimes living in a rural mountain town got to me, what felt like perpetual winter on this slab of stone. We got a summer, it didn't last long, and the lack of sun exacted its toll, slathering the landscape in shades of gray. But on nights like this, the skies above the range so clean and clear, I couldn't imagine living anywhere else.

Heading south, my mind started to drift. I tried to shut off the crazier parts. Which was hard. Especially after a conversation like the one I'd had with Amy Lupus about her missing sister. These triggers brought up my past and could send me spiraling. There were a lot of similarities. Sibling. Drugs. Dead parents. Both of us in recovery. I began getting nostalgic for a girl I didn't really know. After I made the connection I could picture Amy Lupus, bleached blonde, tattered flannels, big earrings, ripped jeans, fuck-me eyes, leaning against the Ashton High brick wall. I didn't go to Ashton High—I went to school in Concord. Maybe my memory wasn't so good after all and I just made up shit. If so, I should start elaborating better fantasies, ones where I came out on top.

No cigarettes to quell my nerves, I didn't pop a single lorazepam to settle any jitters. I'd picked up tricks in therapy, imagining colors, humming soft, soothing tunes. These techniques helped keep the worst of the anxiety at bay. More than that, though, I focused on going to see my wife and son. I knew they weren't *my* wife and son anymore. But pretending for a couple hours produced a calming sensation. I imagined, workday over, I was returning home to my family. My loving wife would be waiting at the door to ask how my day was before making for the kitchen to finish dinner that wasn't pasta out of a can. My son would leap in my arms with enthusiastic shouts of "Daddy's home! Daddy's home!" I knew it was bullshit, that I was choosing to remain willfully ignorant, but maybe I needed that.

Jenny greeted me at the door, all smiles. Since I'd stopped drinking, I saw the change. The light in her eyes had returned. She never made a huge deal out of me quitting—my ex-wife understood how uncomfortable effusive praise made me. I didn't think I was acting *that* different. I'd never missed a day of work, regardless of how much I drank the night before. Unlike drugs, beer doesn't gut your bank account. Not that I had much of one to speak of. I didn't like admitting that stopping a lousy six-pack or two a night impacted jack. Maybe these meetings were getting through this thick skull of mine. Either way, I liked earning her respect. The warmth in her smile brought me back to those sandy shores on the riverbanks, being seventeen again, holding her trembling body close to mine, a return to sunnier days when everything seemed possible. Like a character in Springsteen's "The River" before it all turns to shit. I wanted to believe I was still a young man. And though thirty-six is hardly anybody's ancient, my body parts were breaking faster, slower to repair, and no matter how optimistic I got, I'd never be seventeen again.

I'd never been in their new house. Since moving back, Jenny almost always did drop-offs and pickups at my place. The couple times I drove up to their glorious three-story mansion—okay, it wasn't a mansion but it had to cost three quarters of a million—Jenny met me in the driveway, a long way from the front door. Anything to prevent me from interacting with Stephen. Understandable. I *did* try to break the guy's jaw last time I saw him. I may've been sober, but my fuse still burnt fast.

Knowing Stephen wasn't there made walking inside easier. I'd never be the guy's biggest fan. He'd played a part in moving the family from Vermont to New Hampshire. For that I was grateful. Stephen had a good job in Burlington. Investment banking. Easily six figures a year. Someday I'd thank him. I was glad I didn't have to do that tonight. There's only so much personal growth a man can take for one day.

The interior design was glorious, elegant. This was what I did for a living. It's a talent to size up décor, make an educated, informed estimation of value. That's what estate clearing's all about, an ability to calculate, at a glance, risk versus reward. At an auction, the rooms packed with bidders, you don't have time to search your smartphone. Can't access the Internet in the sticks anyway. You have to look with your own eyes, draw from your history, trust your gut.

It was a classy space, with original paintings and unique wainscoting, a huge upgrade from living with me. If I had to guess, I'd say the dining set alone would fetch four grand. Swallowing the humble pie, I felt happy for her, even if the bite tasted bittersweet to me.

I heard my son's voice. Aiden bounded down the stairs from the second floor, jumping in my arms from at least five feet away with squeals of "Daddy! Daddy!"

At almost seven, my son had his own style, and it killed me. Ripped jeans and a knit cap over a little-kid fauxhawk, that's what Jenny called it, like a Mohawk but with hair matted on the sides instead of totally shorn, and a tee shirt of a punk rock cat. Jenny had relaxed tonight's bedtime for me. She told me on the phone Aiden was starting to backtalk. When she'd tell me the stuff he'd say, though, I couldn't help but crack up. The kid had an edge to him, a real personality. When I was his age, I didn't know what planet I was on. He was already cooler than I'd ever be. He clung to me like one of those old-school koalas on a pencil. Not that I minded. That's the unspoken parental secret they can't explain before the fact—the physical need for your child's touch. We need them more than they need us.

"Daddy!" Aiden said, sliding down. "Guess what we learned at school today!"

My son proceeded to tell me about today's lesson, which involved ships. A famous accident on the Great Lakes, forty years ago, a freighter running into an unexpected storm. He said a lot of men drowned but it wasn't too bad "because there are no sharks" in the Great Lakes. Having spent a few minutes beneath the ice of Echo Lake, I didn't want to shatter his sunny worldview. Getting eaten by a shark would've done the poor bastards a favor.

Being near my boy was wonderful. The touch of his skin. The smell of his hair. His smile. He showed me the drawings he'd done. I listened to him talk, getting all excited, telling me about friends I didn't know he had; and yeah, this was not my beautiful house, and no, this was not my beautiful wife. But fuck it. We all lie to ourselves to get through the day.

Then it was Aiden's bedtime. Jenny let me tuck him in. After I read a couple stories, one about a smelly dump truck and the other that Dr. Seuss story, *Oh, the Places You'll Go*, which can depress the shit out of you if you think too much about the words,

I joined Jenny at the kitchen table, where she'd taken the liberty of preparing me coffee. She knew I drank a cup before bed most nights. And she remembered just how I liked it.

"You look good, Jay," she said.

I nodded and hoped she stopped there.

"I don't know how to say this. I mean, without sounding condescending. But . . . I'm proud of you."

I waved her off. I hated this part, the congratulations for giving up a few Michelobs or Miller Lites. It wasn't that big of a deal. I swirled the sugar into milky clouds, clanking metal against rim.

"Don't do that," she said.

"What?"

"Pretend like it's nothing. Like you haven't made great strides—"

"It's a backhanded compliment. Saying I'm doing a good job now. It implies what a shit job I was doing before. Like telling someone how great they look since they lost weight. What you're really saying is they were a fat ass before."

My ex scoffed and rolled her eyes but couldn't help smiling. "Same ol' Jay." Christ, she was as beautiful as when we were kids.

"When's he back?"

"See? Even that is progress. Using the proper pronoun and not calling my husband 'the jerkoff.'" She laughed.

I did, too. It almost felt like we were grown-ups, conversing like normals, teasing, flirty with witty repartee. A goddamn cocktail party, sans cocktails and other people.

"Stephen agreed to move down here so you could see Aiden more."

"I know." I also knew it had to be, at worst, a sideways move. Stephen was in banking, and those guys don't do anything without consulting a bottom line. If he hadn't been able to match salary, work out the math in his favor, he wasn't helping me foster a relationship with my kid out of the kindness of his capitalist heart.

"I can see what you're thinking. That Stephen didn't give up anything. Not true."

"I said I appreciate it."

"An option presented itself. He got to leave Morgan Stanley for another investment firm, one that handles annuities for insurance companies. Alliance Life. It's less cutthroat. Payouts for victims of accidents, dealing with structured settlements, financial planning."

"A real Samaritan."

"He's helping people manage their lives after tragedy. He's also home more. Tonight notwithstanding." Before I could jab, she conceded, "And, yes, the money is good. I get to be a stay-at-home mom. But he'd been with that company since he got out of grad school. He had to say goodbye to old friends, start over. He did it for me. For you. Us."

"How many different ways can I say thanks? Want me to write him a card? Paint him a picture?"

"I just know you, Jay Porter. You can snatch defeat from the jaws of victory."

"What happened to being proud of me?"

"I am. But you'll always be skeptical. Stephen is doing his best to include you in this new arrangement. He knows it's not easy, and he's making concessions to help make this work. He's not trying to replace you. You know that, right?"

I nodded. Didn't seem like my words were helping much.

"How's the business?" she asked. "How's it feel being your own boss?"

"Since when have you been a fan of estate clearing, Jenny?"

My ex-boss Tom Gable had been like a second dad. Last year someone beat him with a pry bar on the side of Lamentation Mountain, put him in a coma. When he woke up, he and his wife moved to Fort Lauderdale. With all the old people, the swap shop business is booming down there. Tom gave me a chance to buy the business. I didn't have the money, or the credit, to secure a loan with the bank. I got to keep the name at least. Which was only fair. Everything Under the Sun was my idea.

"I'm happy to see you happy." Jenny sipped her tea. "I was wrong to try to make you be something you're not."

My job had always been a source of contention when we were together. Part of the reason I tried my hand at corporate.

"You didn't make me take that nine-to-five job at NorthEastern Insurance," I said. Yeah, I'd felt the pressure to man up after we got married, be a better provider, get health insurance, take care of my family. But I knew what I was. "Being on my own, freezing my nuts off in the subzero. What can I say? It's where I belong."

"I know 'happy' is not an easy emotion for you to embrace."

"I didn't say I was happy."

"You don't seem as miserable, how's that?"

"I like having my son nearby. And you. I like . . . this. Spending time together, talking, if only for a few moments."

I thought I caught her blush. I almost asked, "How did I ever let you go?" But I wasn't doing that to her. I had my shot. I blew it. We'd tried our best, we'd run out of time, but Jenny Price would always be the love of my life. Didn't matter who her new husband was. Didn't matter how much more money than me he made. Maybe Stephen agreed to the move; maybe he wasn't as big of a greedy, money-grubbing prick as I assumed. But Jenny had pushed for it. For me. And having her and Aiden so close was making me . . .

Goddamn, she was right. I was happy.

* * *

Like they say in the rooms: sometimes your Higher Power does for you what you can't do for yourself. I had taken a risk being my own boss. When Tom Gable moved and sold his company to his rival, Owen Eaton, I had two options. I could work for Owen, who offered me the gig, along with a big bump in salary and room for advancement. Plan B: I could take a chance and venture out on my own. The first choice was the safe play, the conventional move, like protecting a lead in the fourth quarter with the prevent defense. And the only thing the prevent defense prevents is winning. Plus, I despised Owen Eaton. He represented everything I hated about estate clearing. An asshole, the guy bilked his clientele, lying about what an antique was really worth, then turning around and selling it for a king's ransom. There was a reason he was among the most successful dealers in the state. If that's what it took to win, I'd rather lose. To work for him, I'd be a hypocrite, a phony. I had a lot of flaws. But I wasn't full of shit. Owen was a dirtbag. Drinking or not, I'd throttle the sonofabitch within a week.

And my risk had paid off. Business had been good. Being Tom Gable's second in command had its perks. The healthy inventory may've gone to Owen Eaton, but many of our former clients stuck with me. Or at least a good chunk of them, enough to keep me going. I had a reputation as an honest, fair appraiser. I had houses to clear, goods to sell, nice warehouse space. Okay, more shack than warehouse, and I could use more regular customers, steadier work. But I was building something good. And when I was finished, it would be all mine.

Driving back to my dumpy apartment, I thought about Amy Lupus and what she'd hired me to do. More than most, I knew the hard row addiction leaves to hoe. Still, something felt off in the way she'd approached me. I didn't like it. Ties to the Coos County Center and the Brothers Lombardi? The missing sister, easily substituted for my own dead brother, history repeating itself? I lived with a ghost. Always would. I didn't want to forget Chris. I made sure to send letters to my nephew, Jackson, who lived with his mother, Kitty, in California. My nephew was around Aiden's age—I didn't know if Kitty, Katherine, was reading my letters to him—I don't know any right-thinking mom who would. But it kept my brother's memory alive. I wondered if that was a good thing.

When is it time to bury the dead?

CHAPTER FOUR

BEING MY OWN boss, coupled with the seasonal lull, meant I could take time off when I wanted to. The summer had been kind to me. Meaning a lot of people died. Shitty for them. Good for estate clearing. More people die in the winter, but by the time families hire you to clear out the house, it's often months later; I was always playing catch-up. I had a couple houses on the docket but no firm deadline. First thing I did next morning was look for Emily.

There was no point bothering with the Coos County Center. It's easier to get into a prison than it is a rehab. Without a release, no doctor or counselor would talk to me. I headed for Emily's apartment instead. I'd already spent the two hundred Amy gave me on this month's child support, supplementing with the emergency cash I kept in my closet, a shoebox savings account I'd dipped into way too much of late. No, Jenny didn't need the money anymore. She told me that. Once. I was paying for my kid.

The drab brick apartment complex squatted behind a short brick wall, sides swallowed in hard, mud-colored snow. Five compact units. Not nice. Not all that run-down either. I could see a college student living here. Or a poor person. Then again, on the Ashton outskirts, those two were often the same thing.

White Mountain College operated beyond town limits. Students frequently rented in Ashton because of its close proximity to campus and lower cost of living. But it was still a community school. They didn't have a lacrosse team or colorful mascot.

There were no names on the metal mailboxes. I had an apartment number, but Amy hadn't given me a key. If Emily had been tossed out, maybe the new tenant could tell me something. I knocked. No answer. No one was around, no cars in the tiny lot. The day blustered gray and cold, surrounding area barren, save for the cemetery across the street, simple stone tablets peeking out from seas of rolling white. If residents weren't at class or their factory job, my money was on the local bar. I could get inside the apartment easy enough. Spending my life in estate clearing, I had acquired a skill set. Picking a lock is not like the movies. You don't need two paperclips with your ear pressed to the tumbler. Nine times out of ten a simple credit card did the trick. When I tried the handle, I was surprised to find it unlocked.

I called hello. No response. The apartment dark, I kept the lights off. No reason to draw unwanted attention. Enough gray filtered through the bent plastic blinds that I could see where I was going. I'd expected to find it bare, but the place was furnished, very much lived in. I found mail on the small end table, stacked neat, addressed to Emily Lupus. I had the right apartment.

My first thought: a setup. The door was open, mail left where I could find it. Why would anyone want to set up a junkyard dealer? I told most folks I dealt in antiques, because that sounded more impressive. "What do you do for a living?" "Estate clearing." Which was just a fancy way of saying I collected the leftover crap no one else wanted. You're not a garbage man; you're a sanitation engineer. You're not a stewardess; you're a flight attendant. I could face the truth, though. I was a scavenger, like Sanford and Son, minus the dad.

It was a dismal little place. Not crack-house or drug-den skeezy, and it beat all hell out of the places on the Turnpike where most drug addicts crashed. It looked like the kind of place where a college student would live. Plywood furniture you had to assemble yourself; requisite "We Can Do It" Rosie the Riveter poster and Tibetan peace flags tacked to the wall; Che Guevara tee shirt in the hamper. I'd hooked up with enough college girls back in the day to recognize the calling card.

I saw the textbooks by the bed. I picked up one. *Ethics of Journalism in the Twenty-First Century*, 12th ed. Fanning through the pages, I found a syllabus. Advanced 300-level class. This semester. I noted the professor's name. Dr. Steven Ostrowski. I hated that first name, for obvious reasons, but at least he spelled it the right way without the soft, feminine "ph." Maybe I should pay Steven a visit. The school was just up the road. Unlike rehabs, confidentiality was not a factor, but there was no reason for him to speak with me either. I had a friend, an acquaintance, a guy I knew, Fisher, who'd taken journalism classes at White Mountain. Dr. Ostrowski might be more forthcoming with an alum. Why create the extra headache for myself? I'd already begun regretting doing this favor for Amy, and for two hundred bucks, this had started feeling like favor.

I checked the rest of the textbooks on the bedside. There were several, all nonfiction, all about journalism. *Sound Reporting*; *Truth Needs No Ally*; *Understanding Media*. Emily took her studies seriously, a real bookworm. No one reads that dry-ass shit for fun. I picked up each, flipping them over, scanning for notes in the margins, initials, maps, cryptic codes. Anything. But there was nothing. Nada. Pages pristine. Then I found an odd number in the even set. The book on the bottom: *Toxins in the Soil*. I thought at first it might be a play on words, like the media euphemism for exploitation, "dirty laundry," the title to a crappy Don Henley song; nothing moves product like death and consumption, tune in at eleven for sex and the salacious. But, no, it was an actual book about dirt, like the kind you find in the ground. Soil, mud, earth. This wasn't an academic text.

I knew dudes in high school who'd get stoned and watch the Nature Channel all night, devouring pints of Ben & Jerry's, scarfing packages of Oreos, watching gazelles get maimed by lions. I could understand that. Who the hell reads books about dirt in their spare time? I don't care how high you get. I pored over that one, too, scoured, page by page, but found no hieroglyphs to decode. It was just a book about dirt. Like reading the history of salt or codfish. People are weird.

Walking out, I heard the purring. A tuxedo cat lurked in the corner. There was an alcove with a litter box by the bathroom, water, food. Both bowls were full. Cats aren't known for their ability to regulate portion control. Which meant either a neighbor was stopping by daily or Emily had been here recently.

The apartment complex didn't strike me as the sort teeming with eager beavers happy to help, but I checked anyway, pacing the landing, knocking on each door. Four more in total. No one answered.

As much as I was dreading it, I headed back into the heart of Ashton to talk to Emily's drug-dealing boyfriend, G-Money.

I recognized him as soon as he opened the door. G-Money's real name was Curtis Michaels. He used to work as a bagger at the local grocery store. It's not politically correct, but dude was one of those white boys who tries way too hard to be black. With pants slung below his ass, exposing his boxers and bony butt, he had on an A-tee shirt, despite the frigid temps. A buck ten soaking wet, he looked ridiculous puffing his pigeon chest, his pencil-thin neck bogged down by layers of gold chain. He'd grilled his teeth, too. How about a little discretion? You want to deal drugs, go with a sweater and vest, sensible footwear, a haircut that doesn't look like you used glue for conditioner. I had a hard time believing any girl would slum it with this clown, even for free pills.

"Yo, what you want, holmes?"

I didn't point out that we lived in Ashton, New Hampshire, population white as fuck. His address was on Fairview Drive, which was the worst section of town, not including the Turnpike or trailer parks. Duplexes with dehydrated lawns populated the turnabout, houses in dire need of new paint. Single-family homes had been split in two to double the rent for landlords. But the neighborhood still landed a long way from Harlem. The Dairy Queen and Mommy and Me boutique were still within walking distance.

"You know a girl named Emily Lupus?"

"What's it to you, dawg?"

"Hey, Curtis. I remember you, okay? You used to bag my groceries at the Price Chopper before you started dressing like Skinny Pete. So I'll do you a solid, okay?" I ran a finger, gesturing up and down his goofy getup. "I won't tell my friend Rob Turley, the town sheriff, that you're dealing drugs. You return the favor by answering a few questions about Emily without giving me attitude. Deal?"

Curtis G-Money guffawed, snorted, spewed weasel-like sounds through his tough guy front, but he left the door open when he turned to strut away like one leg was longer than the other.

I lit up. Didn't bother asking. Place stank like a bar before clean-air acts. A thin blue haze hovered like wisps of morning cloud ghosting the winter lake. I spotted the hallmarks of addiction, bongs on the table, scraps of scorched aluminum foil, the popped tops of cheap disposable lighters. Crackheads buy the cheapest lighters possible. They can't wait long enough in between hits for the lighter to cool down, and the springs in these cheap pieces of crap overheat, popping like buttered corn at the theater before a matinee. I didn't give two shits what this drowned rat did in his spare time.

"Want a beer, yo?" he asked, heading for a mini-fridge. Why his apartment didn't sport a regular-sized box, who knew?

"No, thanks. I'm cool." I waited. "Emily."

"Yo, I ain't seen that bitch." He cracked the tab. The fresh smell of cold hops wafted over, distracting me for a second.

"I heard she went to rehab."

"Wouldn't know shit about that, yo." Curtis G. leaned against the dingy countertop, rubbing his finger along the sink edge, then on his teeth to savor the numbness of cocaine. At least I assumed that's what he was licking.

"When was the last time you had any contact with her?"

"I'll tell you same thing I told her bitch sister when she come barging in here, gettin' all up in my bidness. I don't know where Emily is. Why you care? You a cop or somethin'?"

I glanced down at my dirty jeans and untied work boots, my secondhand flannel, gray work coat, deciding whether the question deserved a response. I decided it did not. I was getting sick of playing nice.

I stepped to this wannabe, but before I could tell Curtis to get his fucking shine box, he said, "A month."

"A month what?"

"Last time I seen her."

"Her sister thinks she left rehab and has been living with you."

"Yo, I don't know what to say, man. Yeah, she crashed here a couple nights. But that was a month ago. It's not like Emily was into partying. Met her through a friend, and then she's hanging around. But she don't buy nothin'. She don't do nothin'. I offer to kick down. She won't put out. Then she starts asking questions. Like all interrogative. Do I look stupid, bro?"

Yes, G-Money, very much so.

"Bitch was prying into my personal life, sounded like vice or a reporter."

"What kinds of questions?"

"About other junkies 'n' shit. The drug problem up here. That new treatment center they built. I don't know, man. Ask her. I ain't no rat. I tossed her skanky ass out. I ain't going back to lockup."

Like this joker ever saw the inside of a prison. He'd be sold for a deck of playing cards before chow. At worst, he'd done a night in county for possession before Mommy bailed him out.

"Already told her sister same fuckin' thing."

"Amy."

"Yeah, that's her." He wound a finger around his ear. "*That* bitch the one who needs rehab. I know *her*. She been partying up on this mountain for years. She don't remember but she copped from me at a party before."

"She's in recovery."

"Recovery," he spat. "Ain't no one recover from heron."

He said it like that, too, "heron," you know, like the bird.

Whipping out my wallet, I plucked a business card. I'd finally gotten around to having new ones printed. Used to have these goofy things with a cartoon character in a hard hat giving a thumbs-up. My old boss had them made for me, and I felt like a tool whenever I passed them out. Since branching off onto my own, I'd taken the time to look more professional. Hence the new cards: simple, elegant. My name and number in sleek black font against bone-white background. Jay Porter. And underneath: Estate Clearing and More. About summed it up. Although I was growing less certain what that "and more" meant. Besides trouble. For me.

CHAPTER FIVE

I HEADED OVER to my little warehouse on Alling Street, a gutted garage not all that different than the one I lived above. But it was *mine*. I'd spent my whole life working for someone else. Even if he'd treated me more than fair, Tom Gable was still a boss. If I wanted to bid high on a particular item, I had to clear it with him. I couldn't take flyers. Tom was great at what he did, and I didn't regret the years I spent working under him—he taught me everything I knew about estate clearing—but there is something to be said for being your own boss. Win, lose, draw, it's all on you. Someday I hoped to be big enough to have people working under me. That day wasn't here yet, but as I walked up the alleyway to my fledgling business, I saw the possibility on the horizon. I was building something good. A future. Finally, I was moving in the right direction.

Everything Under the Sun was spelled on a sandwich board out front. Since I hadn't opened the showroom for walk-ins yet, that gesture was mostly for the mailman. Inside, I had a computer set up for inventory and storage for all my winning bids. Working for Tom, I'd gotten used to having three hundred thousand dollars' worth of merchandise stocked and ready to go. Working solo, I'd acquired about a tenth of that. Still not bad. Plus, those numbers were skewed because items are only worth what you can get for them.

I spent a few hours rearranging and restacking stuff that didn't need restacking or rearranging. It was important to stick to my routine. Another tool I'd picked up in AA: healthy routines are your friend. Move a muscle, change a thought, which often meant staying out of my own head, and when you are new at not drinking, your head is not somewhere you want to spend a lot of time. Stocking knickknacks and bric-a-brac, my mind wandered. I couldn't stop thinking about Amy Lupus or her sister. Why did it eat away at me so much?

Dropping in the chair, I lit a cigarette and reached for my landline. Ashton had terrible cell reception. Where I was, way down in the ravine of Chamberlin Highway, which wasn't a highway as much as it was two lanes that nobody used, forget about coverage. I found his number in my contacts, though I didn't recall putting it there.

"Oh boy," the voice on the other end answered, deadpanned. "Jay Porter. To what do I owe the pleasure?"

"Knock it off, Fisher. I need a favor."

"No shit. Why else would you be calling?"

He was right. I didn't call Fisher unless I needed something. He'd been Charlie's friend, not mine. Since Charlie died, I had no reason to call him. Except he was a whiz at digital research, a top-flight cyber nerd. Having attended White Mountain, he could speed along this process with his hacking skills and all-around knowledge of the World Wide Web. My electronic acumen was limited to hunting and pecking search engines.

I'd been meaning to call before now, apologize for not having been nicer to him in the past. It was one of the steps I was supposed to complete. Making amends to those I had harmed. Hadn't found the time. As soon as I heard his grating, nasal voice I was reminded why I hadn't found the time. It's rotten to say, but I just didn't like the guy.

"You're right," I said, attempting to make peace. "Listen, man, I want to say I'm sorry—"

"Let me stop you right there, Porter. I know how AA works, okay? Apologizing for being a dick and all that crap. Save it. You're not drinking beer? Good for you. But I never thought that was your problem."

"No? And what's my problem?"

"You're an asshole. A self-absorbed asshole."

"That's what I'm trying to apologize for."

"Yeah. Before you ask for a favor. Don't you realize that makes you a bigger asshole? Jesus, man, at least have the common sense to call a day earlier, do your Step Five or whatever the fuck it's called. Offer a half-assed, insincere apology. *Then* call and ask for the favor. Wait twenty minutes in between the two. Sure, it's transparent, but, fuck, dude, at least feign making the effort."

"Never mind—"

"Hold up. What do you need? You're catching me at a good time. I don't have anything else to do. It's pissing rain down here and I'm bored anyway."

"Down here" was Lakeland, New Hampshire, half hour southwest of Concord, a couple hours away. I think that's where he still lived.

"Which means it'll be snowing up here soon."

"That's what you get for living on a mountain, numbnuts."

That's how it worked on Lamentation this time of year. Heavy rain down south spelled a blizzard up north, bucketloads of the wet white stuff. High on the hill, the snows lasted deep into March. I'd be digging my way out of this mess long into April.

Through the window I watched the tops of Lamentation Mountain pierce the cloud cathedral, charcoaling skies, churning darker, thick gray smoke roiling, ready to unleash its fury, throwing shade down the backs of deep-packed ice.

"Spit it out," Fisher said. "You're gonna ask anyway."

"You got your degree in journalism from White Mountain, right?"

"No. I took a few courses at White Mountain. Finished up down here. Why?"

"Just trying to have a conversation, man." I attempted to change tack, redirect questions not directly related to my immediate needs, be social, talk about what he was up to. Be less "internally focused" as Jenny used to call it. "Still writing that conspiracy rag of yours? What's it called? *Occam's Razor*?"

"Adorable. This new you. Pretending to give a shit about other people's lives. Keep it up, Porter. Might get you laid. Ask what you need to ask. I said I was bored. Not desperate."

"You still in touch with any professors up there?"

"White Mountain? I know some names. Why?"

"I'm looking for a girl. Emily Lupus. Journalism student. Supposed to have checked in to the Coos County Center."

"Emily Lupus? Any relation to Amy Lupus?"

"Little sister."

"She was hot as fuck," Fisher said. "A year younger than us, right? Stoner. Blonde. Wild child. There was that story of her showing up drunk in, like, the seventh grade, and her friends having to sneak her home." Fisher paused. "She still hot?"

"Amy? What's it matter what she looks like?"

"Nothing, Porter, I'm sure you're helping out of the kindness of your heart."

"She's paying me."

Fisher spat a laugh. "Stick to finding lost pets, dude. You don't have the greatest track record with missing persons. Not to mention, Turley finds out you're playing intrepid private eye again and he'll haul your ass in."

"I'm not worried about Turley." Our local sheriff had given me grief about investigating in the past. "It's different this time."

"Isn't there a step about being honest with yourself?"

"Finding my brother was a special case."

"And then finding that missing kid in rehab when you were at NorthEastern? And then finding that other missing kid in rehab last year? And now . . . you're looking for a girl missing from, where's it again? Right, rehab. Face it, Porter, you're an SJW."

"SJW?"

"Social Justice Warrior."

"Thought I was an asshole."

"Sometimes they're the same thing. In fact, most of the times they are. Hey, if I gave more of a shit, I'd point out how this is all about you trying to fix the past and save your dead brother." He stopped. "You didn't answer me."

"What?"

"Amy Lupus. Still hot?"

"Jesus. She's all right. I don't know. I guess. Yeah, she's good looking. But the drugs took a toll."

"Junkie?"

"Ex."

Fisher busted a gut, and I couldn't figure out what I'd said that was so funny. "You want me to ask my old professors about a girl?" he said, laughter trailing off. "Sure. Got the professor's name? No promises. It's a small school and they have a high turnover."

"Ostrowski."

"You're in luck. Dr. O. I know him well. Nice guy. Bit of a square bear but earnest, good dude. He's the one professor I've stayed in touch with since I moved. He owns a house across the street from campus. He isn't going anywhere. What are you looking for exactly?"

"I'm not sure."

He laughed again. "Don't quit your day job, Porter."

I hung up the phone. Yeah, I wanted to be a better person, was trying real hard to be the shepherd. But that didn't mean I had to get insulted by a five-foot-one runt who thought he was an e-Hunter S. Thompson.

I squashed the still-good half smoke, lit another, feeling my heart race, tapping the pills in my pocket. No, I hadn't been the nicest guy when I was drinking. But I hadn't been that awful either. Only Jenny really seemed willing to give me a chance. Other people treated my recent sobriety with either skepticism or outright contempt. It's hard to move on when people won't let you forget.

The phone rang.

Ripping it off the hook, I started off with a loud and clear "Fuck you, Fisher—"

Only to be interrupted by Sheriff Rob Turley.

"Were you over on Fairview Drive visiting Curtis Michaels earlier today?"

"You've got to be kidding me." Fisher was right. If Turley found out I was doing any investigative work without a license again, he'd get pissed. He'd warned me off several times. But I'd *just* been at Curtis' house. How could Turley possibly know? Little shit must've phoned it in. Wasn't like I'd pressed him that hard. In fact, I thought I'd been downright pleasant. And since when do drug dealers call the cops?

"Neighbor got your license plate number," Turley said.

Was everyone part of a community watch these days?

"Jay, get in your truck. Meet me. Now."

"Where?"

"Curtis Michaels' apartment. Or do I need to send a squad car?"

"What for? Dude, I got shit to do—"

"Someone stabbed Curtis in the neck with a screwdriver."

CHAPTER SIX

PULLING UP TO the duplex I'd left not five hours ago, I absorbed dusk sinking into the countryside, that foreboding February gloom hinting at Northern Lights and hardship, where every step feels like you are trespassing in a graveyard at midnight. Ashton PD and the EMT were pulled on the curb, strobing the block, calling nosy neighbors to stoops. This strip of Ashton, Fairview Drive, may not have been the skids. But it wasn't Park Avenue, either. In the spring, melting snow would yield chewed-up clumps of dirt and cheap, secondhand toys, faded plastic cars and busted trikes. I tried not to be a classist, even though I harbored prejudices against certain rich people. Still, I'd be the first to admit there was something about thrift-store toys that broke my heart, the teddy bears missing an eye, chewing gum stuck to its mange. I dealt with junk all day long. Most of my apartment was recycled crap. But when I gave my son a Christmas or birthday present, I always made sure it was new, still in the box, shrink-wrapped in original packaging. I didn't know why that was so important to me. I'm sure, like my psychiatrist suggested, it traced back to my childhood. Then again, what *doesn't* trace back to your childhood as far as psychiatrists are concerned?

The flashing lights. The commotion. Twisted metal poking out of filthy snow. The residents cinching cheap wool coats and threadbare, dingy robes, gawking from their porch. It was all too much. I toppled a pair of lorazepam in my palm and ground them to dust.

One of the cops tried to hold me back until Sheriff Rob Turley motioned for them to let me through. When we were seventeen, Turley had been a joke to me, the dork we dunked in the pond. As the years went on, our fortunes had changed. Back then I was more, I don't know, arrogant? Cocky? Cool. Confident. Now in my midthirties, I was a junkman picking up the pieces of his fragmented life, and Turley was the law. I resented him for the power play. But maybe that's what I needed. Perspective. Grounding. To be put in my place. At a meeting the other night, someone said you learn humility by being humiliated; it forces you to surrender your ego, choke down the humble pie. It's tough to feel cool in church basements surrounded by old drunks who reek of the early bird special.

Even though I had Turley by several inches, he seemed to stand taller than me. A man sure of himself, brazen with bravado. He'd slimmed down since last year, which erects a spine, but he was still overweight. Didn't matter if I stood six feet and carried close to two hundred. Being broken down in order to build myself back up had rendered everyone around me bigger. This wasn't an accurate reflection, I knew, it was all projection, but perception is nine-tenths of the law. Walking inside, I struck a defiant cigarette.

"Put that out, Jay. You're contaminating a crime scene."

I flicked the burning butt into the driveway and followed Turley into the middle of the kitchen, where Curtis and I had just been talking. A pool of blood glistened the linoleum, shining slick with flashing emergency vehicle lights streaming through the open front door.

"What were you doing here, Jay?"

"How you doing, Turley? Good to see you as well. What you been up to?"

"Boss," one of the deputies said. "You want me to bag that stuff in the bedroom?"

"What stuff?" I asked.

"None of your fucking business stuff."

"What's crawled up your ass?"

Turley panned from the blood to me, me to the blood.

"You don't think I had anything to do with this. Don't start with that bullshit." Last year when my former boss Tom Gable was attacked, I was initially a suspect. Though Turley would later say I was never *really* a suspect, that he was covering his bases, being thorough, doing his job. Of course, he waited to say all that until *after* Tom had woken up and exonerated me.

"No," Turley said, equal parts bored and agitated. "Curtis told us who it was as the ambulance guys were carting him out. Some lowlife he owed money to. But you *were* here. Right before this happened. You care to explain that?"

I shrugged. I didn't have an answer. Lousy timing? Shit luck. Born under a bad sign. "Is he going to be okay? Curtis?"

"Yeah. Fine. Missed the jugular. Clean through his neck, come out the other side, like a funky piercing."

"This woman I met at AA asked me to find her sister," I said. "Checked into the Coos County Center couple weeks ago. Signed herself out. No one has seen her since. Curtis was her boyfriend, feeding her pills."

"Fuck, Jay. Didn't I talk to you about this? You are not licensed to investigate. It is illegal."

"Spare me the lecture. I wasn't investigating. I was doing a favor. A woman was worried about her sister. I was trying to help."

"Trying to help." It wasn't a question. Turley kept his gaze locked on the red, shimmering sheen. "Back when Steve Earle was a junkie—"

"You know who Steve Earle is?" I hadn't taken Turley as the kind of guy who listened to outlaw country.

"I'm not as big a hick as you think I am. In the middle of Earle's addiction, I read an interview with him in *Rolling Stone*, or one of those magazines, where he said something like, 'We aren't bad people. Bad things happen to us.'"

"I own Steve Earle records."

"So do I. Always liked *El Corazón*."

"What's that got to do with me?"

"You figure it out." Turley skulked around the crime scene.

"Turley, you know I didn't have anything to do with this. You said—"

"I know what I said." Turley shook his head, stalking past his subordinates, me on his heels.

Outside, the start of a storm lazed on shifting silver plains, light snow falling. I could feel the rage through the back of his brown sheriff shirt. I was trying to keep my cool. Like with Fisher, I'd often ridden Turley hard in the past, and I was trying hard not to do that. AA encouraged talking less and listening more. I'd made a lot of mistakes, and maybe this was part of the process, my penance, taking the same shit I'd dished out.

"Curtis was real scared," Turley said. "Gave up his attacker quick. Name that ain't in the system, guy could be anywhere."

"And?"

"And I think he's making it up. I think it was someone else, and he doesn't want to say who."

"You already said you don't think I had anything—"

"I don't. Cool your jets, Jay. Curtis is lying, but I know it wasn't you. Your truck was seen leaving here hours before he was stabbed, another vehicle ID'd. But I *do* find the timing strange, you showing up, meddling when I'd explicitly told you not—"

"What is your problem, man?"

Turley spun around. "You, Jay. You're my problem."

"I already told you. I was doing a favor for a friend." I pointed back at the dumpy apartment. "You saw the rigs and paraphernalia. Kid was playing with fire."

"But you don't deny being here?"

"So? I didn't have anything to do with someone jamming a flathead in his neck."

"Who said the screwdriver was a flathead?"

"It was either a flathead or a Phillips. Lucky guess?"

"I don't care that you didn't stab this kid. Wouldn't care all that much if you did. Little wannabe turdburgler. We'll process him for distribution, send him back to prison. He's already done three months. He's looking at a year now. Town's better off without him. But you're sure as shit in the middle of it. Every goddamn thing that's gone wrong in this town for the past five years, you're in the middle of it. Soon as the neighbor reported the license plate was for a Chevy, I knew"—Turley clenched his eyes tight, jaw locked, head tremoring—"I *knew* it would come back yours. Doesn't matter if you didn't know this guy. Doesn't matter that Curtis gave up the guy who did it. Where there's trouble, there's Jay Porter."

"I told you, I was doing a favor—"

"For a friend. Yeah, yeah. This friend have a name?"

"I met her at a meeting. There's that whole 'anonymous' part." If Rob Turley wanted to find out who Amy was, he could do that on his own time. I wasn't helping him do his job.

Turley whipped out his little police pad and starting scribbling, writing frantic and angry, tearing off the sheet with vengeance, passing it along.

"What's this?"

"A citation."

"For what?" I wasn't giving him the satisfaction of reading whatever nonsense he'd scrawled.

"For conducting an investigation without a license."

I laughed.

"I'm serious."

I crumpled up the paper and threw it at him. The wadded ball bounced off his chest.

"Pick that up."

"Screw you, Turley. You pick it up. You can't give someone a citation for that. That's not a real ticket."

"Yeah, well," he stammered. "I can arrest you. Take you before the judge. Explain you're impersonating a cop—"

"I never told anyone I was a cop."

"I can spin things a lot of ways. Want to take your chances?"

"Go ahead." I clasped my wrists together.

Turley made like he was reaching for his cuffs, but I'd called his bluff. Police hate unnecessary paperwork. There was more of a chance of my dead brother coming back to life than Rob Turley taking me in.

I fired up a smoke. We were outside. Nothing he could do about it now. I nodded back at the property. "You should get back to your job. Go arrest whoever really hurt poor G-Money."

"I don't know what game you're playing."

"I'm not playing any game. I told you the truth."

"Right. A woman. Whose name you won't give me. Wants you to find her missing sister. Who happens to have been a resident of the Coos County Center. Gee, who owns that again? That's right. Your good pals Adam and Michael Lombardi. The girl's boyfriend gets stabbed with a screwdriver in his kitchen. Hours after you were here. Today of all days. How stupid do you think I am?"

I swallowed my comeback. I was more curious about the other part. "What do you mean 'today of all days'?" What was so special about a random weekday in February?

"Like you don't know."

"I don't."

"Stop. You know damn well what's going on at the CCC or else you wouldn't have picked this ridiculous cover story. Girl missing from the Lombardi place?" He okayed his sausage fingers. "Can you stop yanking my chain? For one minute. What happened? Someone at a meeting tell you Curtis owed them money, you stop by, make sure your truck's seen? You think this is the best way to get my attention? You know I'm not doing anything with a phone call. You want to give me your pitch now? Your crazy theory about Adam and Michael Lombardi? What nefarious treachery are they planning this time?"

I'd heard bizarre ramblings in my day—my junkie brother was the king of them—but Chris' string theory followed a perverse, logical sense, if you were willing to plunge headfirst down rabbit holes. In fact, compared to Turley's nonsense, Chris' ruminations passed scientific peer review. I didn't know where to begin or how to respond.

"I'll tell you this right now. Whatever wrench you're planning to throw, whatever ax you got to grind, whatever sand in their gears—"

"Enough with the tool metaphors. I'll say it again, speak slow and calm as I can. A woman at a meeting asked me—"

"To find her sister. Yeah, got it. And you can shove it. You step one foot near hospital grounds, I will have your ass arrested. Think I'm kidding? Try me."

"I already know I can't get information from the CCC. Confidentiality laws." If I thought I could get answers from the Coos County Center that would've been my first stop.

"I'm talking about the ceremony tomorrow morning," Turley said. "The press is going to be up there. It's a big deal, been in the works a while. I'll have my whole squad standing patrol. Ashton's entire force. And we will be on the lookout for you. Whatever happened back in that apartment, however you heard about this scumbag, however you thought you could use Curtis as leverage to disrupt festivities, you can forget about it. Sorry you wasted your time. But you got too clever for your own good. The dedication is going off without a hitch." Turley stabbed his stubby finger at me. "If you bother either one of them. I'm talking a text, a dirty look from across the street—you think one bad thought—I *will* arrest you and I will curry every favor I have with the courts to teach you a lesson you won't forget."

"What are you talking about? What dedication? Bother who?"

Turley huffed and puffed, furious I was making him say it. But I didn't know what "it" was.

"Adam and Michael Lombardi are back in town to dedicate the new wing at the Coos County Center. Been plastered all over the news for weeks, Internet, papers, television, the new legislation Michael's backing, part of his campaign promise to combat the drug epidemic up here. Adam called me a couple days ago, then Michael himself, warning me you'd try to cause trouble." Turley glanced back at the apartment. "And lo and behold . . ."

Adam and Michael Lombardi back in Ashton?

"I mean it, Jay. Stay away."

CHAPTER SEVEN

So, THEY WERE back, the brothers, my bane. It had been almost five years since Adam Lombardi moved his family out of Ashton, five years since I'd had to see the sonofabitch in person. Then again, no one in town had seen the photos of their father with little boys; no one knew what we knew. Charlie, Fisher, and I wrestled with whether to go to the press. We decided there wasn't enough evidence. No one would've believed us. It was our word against theirs. Pictures blurry, evidence circumstantial, copies of copies, theories speculative, conjecture. The best I could do was threaten Adam, get him to make his father step down from coaching his youth programs that granted the old pervert easy access to kids. A minor consolation. Didn't matter that Gerry's heart gave out a few months later. Didn't matter that Adam split town shortly thereafter. I'd forever question whether I should've at least tried going to the mat.

What are you chasing, Jay? This sense of justice and retribution will run you down . . .

I dropped in front of my computer and clicked open the *Ashton Herald*, online edition. There it was. Front page. Ashton's Kennedys. Tall, dark, handsome, corrupt as fuck. The Coos County Center was Adam and Michael's baby, make no mistake about it. Adam may've outsourced the actual construction of the treatment center to Tomassi, one of the oldest outfits in the

Northeast, but he'd purchased the land, and Michael wrote the policies, greased the requisite palms to speed along the process. The TC Truck Stop sale hauled in a pretty penny. There had to be more to it than that. No way the Brothers Lombardi weren't getting points off the top, benefitting from the packed-house enrollment. I never got how that part worked. Shareholders? Silent partners? No idea. But they were making bank off the CCC, that was for damn sure. And here they were, conquering hometown heroes, back to smash another champagne bottle off the skulls of the suffering, have a good laugh at the downtrodden's expense. I powered down the computer. I couldn't read another word.

I was grateful Adam moved away, whatever his motivation. I couldn't stand seeing his stupid face around town, the fake smile he'd force outside the Price Chopper, his two ugly popped-collar kids and goddamn trophy wife, who I used to like. But I couldn't separate parts from the whole. Lombardi was my problem. Brother. Father. Family. There's something to be said for out of sight, out of mind. I can't say I ever forgot, and it didn't take more than driving by the CCC or hearing Michael's name on the television to draw my ire. But knowing they were back in town? Dedicating some new wing, like nothing had ever happened, felt like a smack in the face and kick in the nuts.

I hit an AA meeting but ducked out early. I couldn't take all the lumps and louts whining about poverty and failed relationships. Never had I been more aware of the empty promise that self-love could heal what we internally lacked. I headed back to my place to read more about this dedication Turley was talking about.

I hadn't heard a word about it. Then again, I hadn't been keeping up on local news or current events, keeping it simple, staying stupid. At the crime scene, Turley and I had been carrying on two separate conversations. I couldn't entirely blame Turley for his support of the brothers. He only knew half the story, the half that made me come across stark raving mad, and to go back now and explain the whole situation after the fact would only make me seem nuttier. It's not like my stock had gone up since then. To Turley, Adam and Michael were two local guys who'd made good, and I was at best jealous of their success, and at worst as crazy as my dead junkie brother.

Turley's hard-ass attitude at the crime scene made sense. In hindsight. I'd just misinterpreted the source. I kept waiting for him to pin Curtis G's flathead mishap on me, like last year's attack on my boss, Tom Gable. Wrong place, wrong time, you have your patsy. But that wasn't why Turley was so pissed. He'd been warned. About me. By Adam and Michael Lombardi themselves. Turley's pump had been primed for disruption, so all I had to do was be me.

Funny thing was, I hadn't obsessed about Adam or Michael Lombardi in a while, except when blindsided by network news or geography. The name didn't eat away at me like it used to. It was more like an annoying discomfort, heartburn after a spicy meal, fitted sheets you are too lazy to straighten, the middle seat. Hitting meetings, staying the course, focusing on immediate tasks at hand, living in the moment, I was starting to learn to let go, move on, leave the past where it belonged. God grant me the serenity and all that shit. But now? Now the assholes were shoving that shit right under my nose, ordering me to take a good, long whiff and say how much I liked it. Soon as Turley told me those two sonsofbitches were back in town, I was back to five years ago and my brother finding that hard drive, what that sicko Gerry Lombardi did to those little boys. I was beyond finding solace in the Big Book or leaning on the Twelve Steps and Traditions.

So much had happened to me since Chris passed along those photographs. He'd died. I'd gotten divorced. Fell in lust with a college student named Nicki who screwed me over; developed a wicked crush on a recovering alcoholic named Alison who deemed me damaged goods. My boss moved away and my best friend drank himself to death. But these tragedies paled in comparison to the cost of my own private war, where I raged like hell against the mechanizations behind the scenes. Each time I believed I was taking on individual instances of injustice—falsely imprisoned teenagers, trumped-up drug charges, abuses of power—but I was wrong. It was all part of the same miscarriage: the rich and mighty manipulating New Hampshire's courts, circumventing due process, turning addiction into a profitable business model where vultures feasted on the needy. And when you pulled back the curtain, you found the same two charlatans pulling the levers: Adam and Michael Lombardi.

I powered my computer back up, ready to dig in. I wanted a beer. Crack open an ice-cold one and get back in the fight, because I felt that itch growing stronger, overtaking, starting to consume. Once I gave into the scratch, I knew I wouldn't be able to stop. I'd pluck loose a string that begged to be pulled, and I'd have to oblige, compelled by faith that through the process of unraveling I would finally be able to tie it all together. University journalism student and recent resident of the Coos County Center, Emily Lupus, now missing. Adam and Michael Lombardi back in town because of said rehab. Curtis the Grocery Bagger with a flathead jammed into his neck. Me poking around. These events weren't random. They had to be related.

Unless I was wrong and thinking crazy thoughts again.

Over the past few years, I'd come to accept I had an anxiety dis-order. When I got riled up—and I was fucking riled right now—I could fly off the rails, and that's when shit got scary. I could see things that weren't there, hear people who weren't there. I became my own worst enemy.

I popped a pair of lorazepam and the meds helped bring me back to Earth. Pulse and heart rate slowing, I accepted there was no conspiracy. That's what Chris would've thought. That's what the old Jay would've bought into, too. How did I know Emily hadn't checked into rehab to get help? How did I know she didn't have an actual problem? Because her apartment was neat? The testimony of Bag Boy Curtis? I was projecting. College kid, cramming too hard, popping pills to stay awake and study, she didn't have to be a scumbag addict. If AA had taught me anything it's that addiction doesn't discriminate. If Emily *did* feel like she had a problem, it made sense she'd go to her sister, Amy, who was in recovery, and of course she'd check in to Coos County because that was the new detox hot spot in town. The Lombardis called Turley because I hated their guts, and I had a reputation for being a troublemaker. They were being proactive. That scenario added up. That was the most logical and reasonable explanation.

Except . . . where was Emily now?

* * *

I tried her apartment again, and then the Turnpike and more well-known junkie hideouts. After bribing occupants and employees with twenty-eight bucks' worth of cheap beer and fast food, I was seriously cutting into my profit margin, and no closer to finding Emily Lupus.

I hit the same late AA meeting as the other night, hoping to see Amy. She had my contact information. Dumbass that I was, I'd been in such a rush that night, anxious to catch my son's bedtime, I'd neglected to get hers. I didn't want to sit around and wait for her to call me, since I now had a hundred more questions and a helluva lot more at stake than I did two days ago.

Of course, Amy was nowhere to be found. People are never around when you want them to be. Drove me nuts. When they want to find you, they pop in, seek you out, bug you, call at all hours when all you want is to be left alone. You need to get ahold of them, and everyone is David Fucking Blaine, pulling a disappearing act.

I hung around to listen to tonight's speaker, but again lost patience. It was a Step Meeting, meaning they go through the Twelve Steps, one by fucking one. Sitting in that depressing basement, I wanted to kick my own ass for thinking I could ever find faith in these rooms.

A haggard woman was yammering about how hard it had been since her cat died. Six years ago. And that was before she became homeless. I wanted to scream, "Get over your dead cat!" Worry about finding a place to live, a job, money—prioritize—but she kept going on and on about this fucking cat, Mr. Whiskers, and how much she missed him. Made me want to pull my hair out.

As this woman prattled on in her St. Vincent wool, the loss of her cat somehow turning to gratitude for having a place to stay at the woman's shelter, a decrepit old converted nunnery, I kept thinking: Why stop? I know it sounds shitty. But there was a reason for me to get sober. I had a kid, some skills, was still young, relatively speaking. High floor, low ceiling, so what? If drinking too much was getting in the way of me having the life I wanted, I was willing to try something else. But this woman? With her dead cat and ugly coat, pushing sixty, sleeping in a women's shelter in Meriden? Shit, just keep using, man, keep drinking. What the hell else did she have going on?

I split before the Serenity Prayer. I couldn't stomach holding anyone's clammy hand, bowing my head in solemn obedience, the meek parishioner in the hands of a merciful God who might turn angry if I didn't do what He wanted. I didn't want to be reminded about all the things I couldn't change. The only thing I wanted to do less was go home. I didn't want to pull into the gas station, didn't want to see the dark lot, feel the cold air that hurt my face, slough through the significant snow that had started to accumulate. I didn't want to open the door to my meat locker apartment, choke down another bland, soft meal because I needed to eat despite not having an appetite. I didn't want to watch TV or read a book or search out a movie I'd seen a thousand times. There's an AA slogan: Stinkin' Thinkin'. It means when you've been drinking and drugging for so long, your brain has a way of tricking you into focusing on the negative instead of the good things, because then you'll give up on your sobriety. But even *that* realization was making me angry. Where were the good things? Instead of giving myself props for self-awareness, I was livid at myself for embodying a fucking bumper sticker.

When I pulled in and saw Fisher's hatchback waiting in Hank Miller's filling station lot, I gnashed my teeth so hard I thought I'd crack a crown.

"What the hell are you doing here?" I jumped down from my truck, slamming the door. "It's almost midnight."

"You called me, remember?"

"Yeah, and you could've called me back. I didn't ask you to drive all the way up here and pop in unannounced. What did your old professor have to say?"

"Hasn't called me back yet."

"Then I'll ask again: Why the fuck are you here?"

Fisher didn't answer right away, staring up at me, cross-eyed through the glasses he didn't need. "Turley called me. He was worried. Suggested I check in on you."

I let him follow me up the well to my second-floor apartment.

"He said he saw you earlier." Fisher glanced around uneasily. "Lombardi's back in town. Thought it might be a good time to take a trip."

"I don't need any hand-holding. And I'm not in the market for a houseguest. I've got a lot of shit going on. So, yeah, great to see you again and all that. Sorry for being a prick, thanks for the information you didn't get. I'd offer you a beer but I don't have any. Help yourself to a cup of coffee." I pointed at the cold pot I hadn't finished from this morning. "Heat it in the microwave. Then you can see yourself out. I'm going to bed."

"I'm not here just to see you," Fisher said. "Timing happened to work out. Had to come up and see my mom anyway."

"I thought your mother moved to Florida."

"She did. Then she moved back."

"Old people don't move from Florida to Canada."

"She doesn't like flamingo and turquoise. What can I say?"

I pulled my cigarettes, running fingers through my mussed-up hair, then down my scratchy, unshaven face.

He helped himself to a seat at my kitchen table littered with the red-lettered bills, nameless, faceless corporations threatening to turn off my lights, my heat, my power. No matter how hard I fought to do the right thing, I was still falling behind. I lit a smoke off the stove.

"What are you doing here, Fisher?"

"I told you. Turley called me—"

"I mean, why do *you* care?" I drew hard on the Marlboro. "I'm not trying to be a dick. But Charlie was our connection. Last I checked, he was dead. It's not like we have anything in common. Why are you so concerned about me? I'm fine." Soon as I uttered that word, "fine," AA's mantra for the acronym rose up: Fucked-up, Insecure, Neurotic, Emotional.

I was angry; I was also being cruel. But I didn't care, either. I couldn't be bothered to be a bigger man. Fisher didn't take the bait. His compassion and empathy were sincere. I never hated that little runt so much.

"Porter, you're doing good."

"Oh, yeah, I'm crushing it." I spread my arms over my shit pad. "Divorced, broke, thirty-six. I got a warehouse full of garbage. See my kid every other weekend. Haven't been laid in ages. I quit drinking. I'm waiting for the miracle." I glanced down at my imaginary watch, then up at the water-stained ceiling. "Where's my fucking miracle, Fisher?"

"It wasn't your fault," he said.

Christ, I wanted a fucking beer.

"Charlie. His death. It wasn't your fault. You did the best you could."

I felt the wall of tears threatening to crash through the dam. And I'd be damned if I was losing it in front of Fisher.

"Please, man, leave me alone," I pleaded. "I don't want your company. I don't want your absolution. I don't need your forgiveness. You were Charlie's friend, too. Yeah, I didn't check in on him. I should have. I had a lot going on, okay? I'd just been cleared of suspicion I bludgeoned my boss. I had that woman, Alison, sending me mixed messages. I was trying to find that missing Crowder boy . . . My life wasn't all roses and picnics either. How was I supposed to keep Charlie afloat? I could barely keep myself upright. Jesus. Can't you see I'm not up for company? How can I make it any clearer? We're not friends, man."

"You don't have to like me. It's all right. But Charlie loved you. And he wouldn't want to see you like this." Fisher stood up from the table, sighing with that resignation I'd become a master of eliciting. "I'll be staying at my mom's for a few if you want to talk. Don't piss away the progress you've made."

"Dude, I don't have a drinking problem. Never did. I leaned too hard on beer. I stopped because it was a waste of money and wasn't making me any happier, and I wanted to try something different. Big fucking deal."

"Don't pick up, okay?"

"Pick up?" I sneered. "I'm not a junkie."

I waited till he walked out the door, before slamming it shut behind him and popping another pair of lorazepam.

Then I stalked around my kitchen, chain-smoking, grinding my jaw, ripping fingers through my hair, powdering enamel, kicking random crap on the floor, pushing over chairs.

I never wanted a drink more.

CHAPTER EIGHT

I WOKE FEELING hungover. Which was funny because I didn't get hangovers when I drank. I hadn't had a real hangover since I was twenty. Your body adapts. My head blazed, belly burned, that relentless throbbing where it feels like a midget's clamped onto the back of your neck, stabbing your temples with tiny daggers, tap dancing on your last nerve. For a moment, I had to wonder if, after Fisher left, I'd gone somewhere and gotten so ripped I'd blacked out. Of course, that wasn't true. I'd gone straight to bed. But I was hungover, all the same. Drunk on the real drug that had fucked me up most of my life: all-consuming, fiery rage.

What are you so angry for, Jay? You act like you got it so bad. You don't. You have a son and wife who love you...

I used to.

I rummaged through my fridge for something with protein, coming up empty. I'd meant to go grocery shopping yesterday. I kicked shut the door, settling on stale mixed nuts in the cupboard.

After washing back the bitter taste with day-old cold coffee, I made for my phone. I had to call Fisher and apologize. I had asshole tendencies, and Fisher got under my skin, but he didn't deserve any of that. Guy had driven up at night, in the falling snow, trying to help, standing in my kitchen, taking it as I berated him, insulted him, emasculated him. His only crime? Giving a shit about me.

When the knock sounded on my door, I was glad. Sometimes you have to look a man in the eyes when you apologize. And my regret was genuine this time. Fisher had hit the nail. It resonated, obvious in the aftermath. Adam and Michael being back in town was the excuse I'd used to get ready for a fight. Not having done enough to save my best friend's life was the monster I wasn't prepared to face. Charlie's death underscored everything I was experiencing right now, the guilt I felt for failing him. I could rationalize I'd been too busy, that it wasn't my responsibility. But the truth was I'd let him down when he needed me most. I had to give myself some credit, though. Yeah, I'd acted like a douche toward Fisher. But it used to take me weeks, months, sometimes years to see that. Progress, not perfection, right?

When I opened the door, I didn't find Fisher.

"Sorry to drop by like this," Amy said. "I called, but you didn't pick up."

"No reception." The number listed on my card was for my cell since I spent most of my time working outdoors. I didn't even know where my cell was. I seldom had the ringer on anyway. I wasn't big on texting. I liked talking on the phone even less.

"Can I come in?"

This was my problem. The other night, at the meeting, Amy had been good-looking enough that I'd noticed her. But it wasn't like I hadn't seen a lot of pretty girls in my life. Now? I couldn't stop thinking of that girl in high school, the blonde-haired hellion with a reputation for being bad news. Amy stood in my kitchen, and I wanted more. Where was the ex-junkie with the hard life I'd assigned? Like soft-filtering the camera lens, the way they did with Hollywood starlets in the 1940s, I knew the reason behind my reassessment. Because she *was* trouble, and in my mixed-up, muddled, screwy brain that made her more desirable. Treat me well and I think less of you—what's wrong with you for liking a guy like me? But be a headache, cause me aggravation, thorn in my side, be a pain in my ass, or better yet treat me like shit, and I fall in love. Every fucking time. Fucking self-awareness. Amy Lupus had lied to me at the meeting. Or, at best, misrepresented the truth. Curtis the Bagger was hardly trustworthy. But he'd had no reason to lie to me, either. He claimed Emily didn't do drugs, never accepted kick-downs. He said she was only there to ask questions. A journalism student. Anyone could see where that story went.

Amy peeled her winter gear. It had stopped snowing, but her shoulders and head were dusted with ice and flakes because even when the storms abated and the heavens parted, the residual and reminders remained.

I told her to make herself at home, and went to brew a fresh pot of coffee. She sat at my kitchen table like it was the most natural thing ever. Nothing about what was going on was natural. I'd reconnected with this girl, woman, whom I barely knew, and already she was fucking with my head. On second thought, maybe it was completely natural, my life a never-ending cycle of trading one step forward for two steps back.

No one spoke until the coffee was done brewing. Talking first felt like losing leverage. I sat at the table with a couple mugs and milk and sugar and anything else someone would want to put in there, and I waited. Amy had come here. She had something to say. I'd play it cool and wait for her to reveal whatever was going on. From the occupied apartment, to the well-fed cat, to Curtis G., the grocery bagger with the screwdriver in his throat, Amy's story had more plot holes than *The Empire Strikes Back*.

Instead, all she said was, "Any luck finding my sister?"

I must've waited a good ten seconds before responding. "That's it?"

"Is what it?"

"I went to see her boyfriend, the one you told me about."

"G-mon—"

"Please. Don't call him that. I recognized the little shit from when he bagged my groceries at the Price Chopper. His name is Curtis. Curtis Michaels, wannabe gangsta fuck."

"Did he tell you anything?"

"Before or after someone stabbed him in the neck with a screwdriver?"

"Stabbed him? Are you serious?"

"Yup. Couple hours after I left his place."

"Oh my God. Is he okay?"

"He's fine. He'll be spending the next year in New Hampshire Correctional for dealing. Who cares? He owed someone money." I watched for a reaction. She had none. "What's this really all about, Amy?"

"What do you mean?"

"Why did you hire me?"

"To find my sister." She reached in her purse, pulling out an envelope, sliding it along. "I know that two hundred was a retainer—"

I pushed the envelope back.

"I don't want any more of your money. Call it a day's wages. We're square. But I changed my mind, okay? I don't want anything to do with your sister. Or you."

"I don't understand. I paid you."

"You want the two hundred back, no problem." I got up, making for the back closet, stopping to turn over my shoulder. I'm good at reading people. At least I thought I was. Either Amy was oblivious or she had a real future in Texas Hold 'Em.

"The other night," I said, returning to the table, "after the meeting, you mentioned my history with the Lombardis."

"So?"

"So, guess who's back in town, dedicating a new ward or wing at that rehab your sister went 'missing' from?" I did the air quotes thing, which I hated, total poser move, but in this case, I felt justified. "She was a journalism major, right?"

"I don't know. I think so. I told you. We weren't close."

"Then why call you to bring her to rehab? I'll tell you why. Because people know *you*. People know you have a drug problem. Every junkie in Ashton should have a scarlet J stamped on their forehead. You bringing her in lent credibility."

"I don't understand."

"Your sister didn't have a drug problem."

Amy's face fell. Disappointment? Confusion? Pity? She pushed herself up and came around to my side, a move reminiscent of what Jenny used to do when I was getting worked up, pushing logic to its fringe. I found myself mixing them all up—my wife; other women I'd been involved with over the years; that college girl, Nicki; that radical recovery woman, Alison Rodgers; and now Amy. They all blurred together. When she reached for my shoulder, I slipped her grasp and hopped up.

Amy stood, perplexed expression frozen in place, waiting for my response. I didn't have one. What felt so strange just a few moments ago no longer did, and I didn't know if that was because the meds were working or I was seeing things clearer, or if I'd been wrong all along. These feelings of mine, that something was "off," were just that. Feelings. I'd had a recent history of . . . breaks . . . with reality. I couldn't always trust my reasoning. When I got stressed—and the events of yesterday had me stressed—my thought processes got scrambled.

"I'm not lying to you, Jay," Amy said.

"Take your money back. It's not worth the headache."

"Wait. I can try to come up with more—"

"You're not listening. I don't want anything to do with Emily or the Lombardis or the Coos County Center. Your sister wasn't on drugs."

"Who told you that?"

"Her dealer buddy, Curtis."

"And you believed him? He's a lying sack of shit. Emily needs help. And now she's signed herself out, and I can't find—"

"How did you know about my brother and the Lombardis?"

"Everyone knows your story, Jay."

"Well, I don't know you. The first conversation we ever had was the other night. What was that bullshit about meeting me in Berlin three months ago? I've never been to an AA meeting that far north. I rarely leave Ashton."

"My feelings were hurt."

"Why?"

"We know each other," she said.

"I know who you are. But we don't *know* each other."

"I've lived in Ashton my whole life. I remember when your parents died in that accident. I was one grade behind you, but I remember it just the same. I remember when you left town. I remember when you came back to visit and the keggers by Paper Goods Pond and Silver Lake in the summer." She laughed, a forced, fake one. "I used to be better-looking back then. I liked you, but you were always dating Jenny Price—" She stopped. "I'm not flirting with you."

"I didn't say you were. But you're playing me. I don't know why. But you are."

"You're a strange guy, you know that?"

"Yes. But I can't help you. Sorry."

Amy dropped her purse on the table, pulled out a scrap of paper and a pen, and scribbled info, pushing along the slip. "That's my number and address. Please. If you reconsider—"

"I won't."

Amy left. I watched from the window, through the ice-speckled pane. My landline rang. I plucked it off the wall, watching her walk to her car, answering blind.

"It's me."

"What's up, Fisher?"

Amy got in her car and pulled down the snow-packed street.

"Let's meet at the office," he said. "I got information for you."

CHAPTER NINE

THE "OFFICE" WAS our nickname for the Olympic Diner, the twenty-four-hour dinette on the Desmond Turnpike where Charlie, Fisher, and I used to hang in high school, pigging out at two a.m., soaking up booze with greasy fried foods after those parties by the water where Amy Lupus apparently clocked me from a distance.

I hadn't been back to the Olympic since Charlie died of pancreatitis last year. Felt wrong. I would've put up more of a fight with Fisher, suggesting a different meeting spot, but I was busy watching Amy walk away. How many women had I watched leave me like that? The sound of shoes creaking down wooden stairs, the backs of their head out the window, cold penetrating glass, footsteps beating a path through the ice and snow in the opposite direction, climbing into rides to somewhere far from here, somewhere far from me.

As soon as I stepped in the diner, a pervasive sadness overtook me. Losing Charlie was like losing a brother all over again. That was the worst part about not drinking. Beer kept the snarling wolves at bay. Now emotions had free range, an open invitation to come and go as they goddamn pleased. They call it "the ins and outs." One minute you're brimming with hope over a blue jay perched on a telephone line, the next you're on the verge of tears because of a fucking Nationwide commercial.

Fisher was already there, but I needed a moment to find him. He was sitting in a different booth. When the three of us got together back in the day, we always sat in the same booth. Through the door, hard left, rear wall. A permanent reservation just for us. Without Charlie, there was an unspoken understanding between Fisher and me. We'd never sit in that booth again.

"I'm sorry," I said, slipping opposite him. "For the other night."

"Don't worry about it."

"You didn't deserve that. I was, I don't know, fucked in the head."

"Jay," he said. "Don't worry about it." He never used my first name. I was always "Porter."

The pretty Greek waitress brought us coffee as Fisher dug around his leather satchel, retrieving a notepad, flicking back a couple sheets of paper.

The waitstaff was one of the selling points of the diner. An endless parade of gorgeous young women. Daughters, sisters, cousins. It was like that line in *Dazed and Confused*: I got older; they stayed the same age. Young, twentysomething, perfect. Didn't used to depress me so much. At what age is ogling twenty-year-old girls creepy? At thirty, I didn't feel so bad. Thirty-six? I'd crossed a line.

"You asked me to call my old professor," Fisher said, snapping his fingers because I'd turned around to watch one of the waitresses bend over and fetch a muffin for a trucker.

"Yeah, about that," I said. "Don't bother. Waste of time."

"Emily Lupus was enrolled at White Mountain," Fisher said, ignoring the moratorium. "Dr. Ostrowski said she was a straight-A student, way too smart for White Mountain Community Tech. No way a druggie. He'd picked her for an internship with a local paper."

"What paper?"

"Didn't say. But Ostrowski only picks the best and brightest for internships. This new wing at Coos County has been getting a lot of press. I got the impression that was her assignment."

"Covering the dedication?"

"Not necessarily that. The drug crisis up here. In general."

"What makes you say that?"

"A few things Ostrowski let slip. About the way lawmakers and politicians make money off addiction. More of a liberal slant. Rehabilitation over incarceration. That kind of thing. Doesn't matter. She bailed. Quit."

"The internship?"

"The school. Requested an incomplete for the semester."

"When?"

"Few weeks ago."

"Right around the time she went into treatment."

"That would make sense. Needs help. Can't go to class or work if you're strung out."

"Except her professor says she's honor roll material, straight edge. Curtis G-Money, whatever the fuck his name is, also said she never touched any drug."

Fisher shrugged.

I started thinking. She pretends to have a problem to get admitted, have to look around.

You're reaching, little brother . . .

Fisher sipped the coffee the pretty Greek waitress refilled. "That's the story I got for you anyway."

"Could've told me all this on the phone."

"Yeah, I could've." He stared across the table, too sincere for comfort. "How you holding up?"

"Don't."

"Don't what?"

"Be nice to me after I acted like a prick. Treat me like some wounded bird. I hate that shit."

"I miss him, too, y'know. Charlie Finn was the best friend I ever had." Fisher looked as pained and conflicted as I felt. "We tried. The doctors told Charlie he had to quit drinking or he'd die. He chose to keep drinking. That's not on me. And it's not on you, man."

I studied the traffic zipping along the Turnpike, spitting snow and sludge, wanting to believe that. But I couldn't. Fisher didn't live here. I did. I should've checked in on Charlie. I got wrapped up in my own bullshit and I didn't make the time. And now he was gone. And it was too late to do anything about it.

"Hey, man," he said, laughing. "Remember when you and Charlie got caught trying to unscrew that license plate from the bar wall?"

"You heard about that?"

"Charlie told me."

"I was crushing hard on this girl—me and Jenny were going through a rough patch—and this girl, I can't remember her name, but she liked chickens, wanted to raise them. I don't know how you raise chickens in this Arctic wasteland. But that was her dream, build a coop, get fresh eggs, hippie chick, and there was this funny sign about chickens." The Dubliner, Charlie's favorite bar, had unique license plates and kitschy signs from all over the country covering the outside smoking porch. Route 66. The Rattlesnake Speedway. All the places we'd never get to see. "After a few pitchers, Charlie suggested we steal it, so I could impress her. It was summer. Hot, muggy. And we were blotto, falling-down drunk. Charlie pulls his Swiss army knife, plucks the little screwdriver, gets to work. The owner, Liam, caught us, tossed us out." I couldn't help but laugh. "86'd. Fucking Charlie. We were back the next night."

Fisher hopped up and pulled his wallet. "Just because you quit drinking doesn't mean you don't get to still be an asshole. From time to time." He knocked on the table twice, his signature move. "You want to do this again, I'll be at my mom's house for a few more."

Making for the door, he stopped and clasped my shoulder in an awkward show of affection. "Give yourself a break, okay? You're doing good, Porter. Keep it up. Charlie would like to see you happy." He pointed down at the table as if he were leaving me with something invaluable. "You going to do anything with that?"

"With what?"

"What I told you about the girl, Emily?"

"No, man, I'm going to forget I ever heard the names Emily or Amy Lupus. There's a house over on Four Rod I'm supposed to clear out. Time to make money. I have no idea what's going on with the missing sister, but the last thing I need is to get mixed up in any more drama."

And at the time, I meant it.

*　*　*

The storm struck earlier than projected, pinning me inside the old farmhouse on Four Rod Road, cherry-picking the castoffs. There's a creepy element to dealing with the dead, especially when you work alone. You don't have to believe in the supernatural or ghosts. You're sifting through a man's life, his history, legacy. A part of him is left behind, and you can feel that presence looming, a harbinger of the bell waiting for us all.

These houses were surrendered to me to scavenge because the previous occupant either didn't have any family, or what family he did have didn't care enough to stake a claim. Never mind if your family hates you, if they think there's something valuable, they'll ransack the place. Which meant I wasn't sifting through a dead man's leftovers; I was sifting through leftovers deemed worthless by vultures.

This house belonged to a man named Mathis. Owned a flower shop in town. Didn't leave behind much. There were a couple vases that might fetch a few bucks at auction. The real score was a hunting knife. Steel blade, foreign, kept sharp. Left in a random drawer. An odd artifact for a florist. But a cool find for me. I slipped it inside my coat.

I spent most of the day throwing away shit. That's what the family hired me to do. To clean the fucking house so they could sell it off. Let the kids squabble over who got what percentage of blood, sweat, and mortgage.

It was around five when I wrapped up. Usually I bring along a U-Haul. But I'd already scoped the house out and knew pickings were slim. Vase, hunting knife, and a cleaning fee for all the crap I had to haul out to the dumpster in the driveway. A glorified janitor.

The snow had stopped by then. Not too much damage, five inches maybe, but a lot of ice, power lines and branches weighed down. The totals didn't merit bringing out the plows, but the number of felled limbs detoured routes. To get back to my apartment, I had to go over the Ridge, hit the Desmond Turnpike, circumvent the impassable, narrower roads, then peel off onto Orchard, a desolate stretch that traced the mountain, its jagged, craggy peaks disappearing into rapidly descending night. Still dusk, what little light lingered wouldn't last long.

Out of nowhere: a panic attack.

It could happen like this. I'd had a fine day. Nothing had me stressed, I'd worked all day without worry, and then boom, my heart starts racing double time, and I'm left fumbling for my meds and smokes. Was it always going to be like this? Like I were a deer on the boulevard of life? I took a double dose, the attack so swift and strong. Was it this stretch of road? I'd taken this same route the night a man masquerading as a detective snatched my brother from the Ashton jailhouse. That was five years ago.

I hoped that was it. If I had tangible, concrete reason for my anxiety, however irrational, I could work toward finding a solution. But if this panic attack were totally random, my brain a haphazard patchwork of crisscrossed, jangly wires commanded by happenstance, a slave to no reason or rhyme, I'd be forever on edge, waiting for the next ambush. There *had* to be an inciting incident. Was this it? A fucking stretch of road where bad stuff happened, like, half a decade ago? Was that all it took?

I needed to get out of Ashton. If everything in this town reminded me of misery, maybe it was time to move. This whole region, this entire mountain, was one big trigger. I couldn't relocate too far because this was where my business, my boy, was. I'd finally gotten my son within reasonable driving distance. I couldn't bail now.

After four lorazepam, my heart was still racing, the night lacquered black. The sharpest edges had been rounded, but I remained jittery, on heightened alert. Took a while to calm down to my normal high-strung and wound-too-tight baseline.

That's when I came upon the truck.

CHAPTER TEN

IT WAS PARKED helter-skelter, right in the middle of the road, big blue tarp tied down and rippled over the bed, blocking passage, forcing me to either turn around or get out and see what was going on. This section of Lamentation led up to Gillette Gorge, a popular hunting spot, where dozens of cabins spread out between blinds. I wasn't surprised to see the man in the orange hunting vest. Even though the Gorge was a ways up the mountain, and we were still in the foothills. I rolled down my truck window, losing patience for the inconvenience.

The man in the reflective orange hunting vest trudged up from the culvert, waving. "Thank God you stopped," he hollered above the rushing winds. "I'm sorry, mister, I've been out here for a half hour."

I could've tried steering around him, maneuvered past on the shoulder, dipped into the ditch, which ran the risk of spinning wheels and having to call for a tow. He seemed desperate. And young. He was still a good distance away, but I could see he was just a kid, not much older than those high schoolers manning the till at Hank Miller's garage. I was betting dead battery. That meant digging out the cables, lining up the engines. Wouldn't take long, but I wanted to get home, eat dinner, go to sleep. I couldn't leave a kid out here in this weather. A tow truck wouldn't show before the boy's nose and toes blackened with frostbite.

"Thank God," he repeated, holding up his cell, walking over. "I can't get any service." Which wasn't uncommon for this stretch. The tall peaks of Lamentation Mountain blocked tower reception.

As he came closer, I saw he wasn't a boy. He was older, a lot older, one of those creepy men who retain a baby face regardless of their age, like Truman Capote or Matthew Broderick. He pulled off his hunting cap, revealing wisps of receding hairline.

"It's my cousin," the man said. "We were hunting. He had an accident." He wasn't holding a rifle. And that baby face made him look like such a rube; I couldn't envision him firing a popgun at squirrels. "We were climbing Lamentation, tracking a bull. Stupid, right? I know. Should've waited till we got up to the blinds. But the moose was *right* there. My cousin slipped. Fell about twenty feet. I think he broke his leg."

I brought out my cell, and he reached for my hand. "I told you, man. No service. Can you help me get him loaded in the back of my truck? I was able to slide a board under him and stabilize the leg, but the terrain—I can't carry him on my own. Please. He's too heavy. I covered him with blankets, but he won't last long if I don't get him to a hospital. Carl is a big guy. It'll take both of us to lift him."

"How far in is he?"

"Not far. A hundred yards? But it's over the ridge, up the hill, which is the problem."

I smelled beer on the guy's breath. Part of AA's credo involved helping others. I should've kept driving, let this be AAA's problem. I was already regretting my good deed. I'd put in a full day and was tired. Why was it my fault a drunk fell while hunting?

I pulled my keys and jumped down. "Let's take off that tarp and drop the gate so we can slide him up there."

"I got it," the man said. "Can you tell Carl you're gonna help? He's gotta be scared shitless."

While he went to his truck, I headed into the forest.

Fifty yards in, I heard him fall in line behind me.

"What's your name?" I asked, cloud cover and jungle covert making it tough to see, howling winds hard to hear.

"Carl."

"I thought that was your cousin's name."

"It is. We're both named Carl. But he spells his with a 'C.'"

"How do you spell yours?"

"With a 'C.'" He started laughing. "Sorry. Trying to be funny. I laugh at stupid shit when I'm worried."

I smelled the beer stronger now, or was it bourbon? I wondered if I made stupid jokes like that when I was drinking, if I thought I was being funny when I was really being obnoxious.

Carl had his flashlight out, panning over the snowy forest floor. We walked a while, what felt farther than a hundred yards. I led, he followed, the shine over my shoulder guiding passage.

"Are you sure we're going the right way?"

"I'm sure. He's up the hill, past that boulder."

The boulder rose up like a leviathan on a rough sea. Huge. As boys, my friends and I played in these woods. We'd have snowball fights, chuck stones at random cars driving by. I knew this landscape. Getting a body—a heavy guy—over that rock? There was no room to the right or left, mountain walls rising up, all passages blocked. Only way out was up and over.

"Carl?" he called out. "You okay?"

"Yeah, Coz," came back the weak reply. "But this leg hurts like hell."

"Don't worry. I got help."

"We're going to need rope," I said. "You got rope?" To extricate someone over that boulder, we'd have to tie a strap around a stout, sturdy trunk and use serious physics.

Carl shook his head.

"Go back to my truck," I said. "I have canvas gunnies in the bed. Grab both pair. We can tie them together to create a pulley."

"That'll work?"

"I move heavy furniture all the time. Trust me. Hurry."

Carl clomped off, and I started to scale the rock to get a better assessment of the situation, come up with a rescue plan, planting soles wherever I could gain traction, slipping more than scaling.

"Carl?" I called out. "You still with me?"

"Yeah, I'm here." He moaned in agonizing pain. "Not sure how much longer though. I can't feel my leg."

"Hang tight," I said. "Your cousin went to get gunny straps. We're going to fasten a makeshift conveyor belt."

I couldn't get over the boulder. There was a tall tree nearby. At least I'd get a visual. I pulled my phone, opening the flashlight, following the stream. Branch by branch, I hoisted up alongside the big rock, searching out a break, a crevice, anything wide enough to squeeze a body through. But there was no straight path, not that I could see, and trying to navigate those slick, icy limbs, I had a hell of a time staying on two feet. I turned over my shoulder, back toward the road I could no longer see. Then my cell died in the cold. Like that. Had eighty-seven percent battery in the truck. Now nothing.

"Hurry up with those straps," I shouted.

I'd climbed high enough in the tree that I could see over the peak, peer down into the valley below. Squinting, trying to get my eyes to adjust to the darkness, I couldn't see shit. No body, no board, nothing.

I called Carl's name. No response. I prayed the dude wasn't dead. I already dreaded having to explain to Turley how, yet again, I'd found myself in the middle of a clusterfuck.

Then the branch snapped and I fell, face-first into the abyss.

I was able to stand, the deep snow breaking my fall, luck sparing me a split skull. Stumps and shards of stone jutted out all around. Tweaked an ankle, nothing broken. Everything hurt. My bum leg, the one permanently damaged from falling through the thin ice of Echo Lake, responded like I was getting electroshocked anytime I applied pressure.

"Carl?" I called.

No answer.

"Carl! Carl!" Didn't matter which one I was calling. Neither answered. I could track the Ashton wilderness as well as anyone. During the day. The vegetation out here grew unruly, rife with wild bramble and thorn bush; seeing anything at night proved a fruitless cause. Even if there were streetlights on the road—and there weren't—nothing could penetrate the tall wall of evergreen. I stood in a black void, this senseless vacuum of space. A man lay dead, dying, or subdued by a severe bout of hypothermia. I couldn't leave him there. Getting back to my truck and driving for help wasn't an option. Not enough time. Maybe that's what the other Carl had decided to do? I listened to the wind, tried to use the bounce-back off trees to gather bearings, recalibrate my internal compass, triangulate position based on rates, distance, time. I hadn't dressed for an extended trip.

Feeling my way, toe-tapping ice, weary of creeks and pools, because small rivers ran everywhere out here and rushing waters never fully freeze. I stuck to boulder and bark. I couldn't differentiate wildlife calls from footsteps crunching snow. Staring up at stone walls and towering pines, I succumbed to vertigo. I'd just staved off a bitch of a panic attack. Now she'd returned like a pissed-off ex. How did I end up in the middle of the woods? Lost, no cell, totally unprepared. I steadied my breath, stood statue still, focused all energies to will myself back to reality. I resisted ridiculous notions that the Carls had lured me out there, two psychos hunting humans for sport.

I kept calling their name. *Why isn't anyone answering?* Someone had to hear me. Why hadn't he returned with the gunny straps? I kept shouting. Then something told me to shut up. I felt like an animal tracked via Buffalo Bill night goggles, the defenseless prey in the sites of a determined, cunning predator.

In the middle of the forest at night, on the steep, craggy hills of Lamentation, terrain an inhospitable alien topography, the atmosphere drained thin and just breathing presented a challenge. The wind patterns on the range streamed stronger the higher you went, unpredictable, hitting from the left, right, up top and underneath all at once. I hadn't double-socked or layered in thermals. I already couldn't feel my hands. I had to get back to my truck and call 911, hope my fingers still worked well enough to plug in the phone charger, never mind circling till I found a pocket of reception.

A loud crash sounded inches from my ear, a heavy clod falling from above, carrying its echoes deep into the jungle. My heart jammed in my throat. Above the slashing winds, I thought I heard the cock of a shotgun. Night, clouds, and trees swallowing any light or stars, I made to run, but prickers tangled my feet. I kept trying to convince myself that wasn't a gun blast I'd heard, just the night sounds of the countryside.

You're in the grips of an episode. Everything will be okay.

Footsteps approached, slow, precise, gun muzzle scraping ice. A low whistle taunted, menacing, mocking me. I sensed a stock hoisted, poised, leveled. Slow and easy, I slid the hunting knife out of my coat. I couldn't see him. He couldn't see me. I transferred handle to mouth, trying to extricate myself from the briar patch, each movement ensnarling me more. Fuck it. I gripped the blade and ripped my leg though dead blackberry brush, thorns gouging calves and thighs, leaving tips embedded in flesh.

Blinded by the darkness, I didn't move, didn't breathe. Couldn't have been more than ten seconds, but time hinges on circumstance, circumstance plays with time, and I stood there a lifetime. Semantics don't matter when there is a price on your head. The wind stopped. A twig snapped. Close enough for me to take my chance. I jumped out swinging, the sharp edge slicing through extra thick winter padding, going deep enough to puncture vital organs.

The high-pitched shriek, like a pig stuck, wailed through the woods. I lowered my shoulder, knocking over a mass of meat. I heard something thud to the black forest floor. Unsure of what I'd hit, I wasn't sticking around to find out. I ran, trusting my gut, this tangle of thatch my childhood's end, losing faith by the second but clinging to what little religion remained. Stumbling and staggering, I felt a slick sludge drip from the tip of my knife, smelled the sweet metallic tang of blood above the clean scent of freshly fallen snow.

I managed to turn myself all around, bouncing off bark, tripping on twigs, falling forward, smacking off stone. I crouched behind a boulder. I didn't know if it was the same boulder or a different one. Stone all feels the same.

Behind me in the black, I heard a horn bleating. Car horns. I stumbled toward the source. Slowly, light dappled through the copse of Orchard Road. Then I heard, "Move your fucking truck, asshole."

When I emerged from the forest, two cars were parked behind my Chevy I'd left blocking the road. The other truck was gone.

A woman sat behind the wheel of the first car, window rolled down to better scream at me. "You're blocking the goddamn road! You stupid sonofabitch!"

A guy stuck his head out the driver's side behind her. "What the hell is wrong with you? How long's it take to piss? People need to get home!"

I waved them off and limped up into my truck.

There were no other tracks on the windswept road.

CHAPTER ELEVEN

"OKAY," TURLEY SAID, bringing me a cup of coffee. I was in the interrogation room, a place where I'd been so often over the past few years, I felt like I should have my own desk with nameplate and personalized, ironic mug by now. "Let's go over this one more time."

"How many fucking ways can I say it? A guy lured me into the woods to shoot me. I mean, I think he planned to shoot me. One of them at least."

"And you stabbed him with that?"

The bloody knife lay bagged on the table between us.

"I told you. I didn't stab him. I swung at whatever knocked into me. Sliced. I don't know how deep I cut him. I couldn't see. It was dark. But, yeah, I hit something."

"In self-defense?"

"They were trying to kill me!"

"You stabbed one of them?"

"I didn't stab! I swung that knife before they shot me. Swung. Not stabbed."

"Why did these men want to shoot you, Jay?"

I didn't appreciate the condescending tone, but I couldn't mention Emily Lupus or investigating the Coos County Center, White Mountain Tech or internships at newspapers. I sure as hell couldn't evoke the Lombardi name. I regretted reporting this at all.

Turley pulled his little policeman pad, repeating my words. I knew what I'd said. And so did he. It was a dirty, rotten cop trick.

Like hearing a recording of your own voice played back, how irritating and stupid it sounds. "And you say you heard a squeal 'like a stuck pig,' that right?"

"I didn't say 'squeal.' I said 'shriek.' From a man. The sound *a man* makes."

"But like an animal. That's what you said. The sound was like an *animal*." Turley closed his notepad. "A pig. Your words." He paused, unable to hide the skepticism. "You know it's rare to find wild boar on the mountain?"

"It wasn't a pig. I'm not crazy." I pointed at the knife. "See the fucking blood? Test it if you don't believe me."

"Don't worry. We will. But that takes time. In the meanwhile, I'd like to go over your story again."

"We've gone over my story ten times!"

"Calm down, Jay."

"Why would I be hunting with a fucking knife?"

"Yet you admit carrying a hunting knife?"

"Because I found it at the house I was clearing out. I told you that."

"The house." Turley glanced down at his policeman pad, pretending to read. "Mathis. The dead florist. Not the kind of cutting utensil you expect to find at a floral shop." Turley rubbed the pudge under his chins. "What did these men say there were hunting?"

"Moose, I think. What difference does it make? Why . . . why would *I* be hunting? Have you ever known me to hunt?"

"People on the mountain hunt. People pick up new hobbies all the time. Except here's the thing, Jay. It's not hunting season."

"There you go! They were lying. That proves they were trying to lure me out there. See?"

"Moose season is October."

"How the fuck would I know that?"

"Everyone up here knows that. And why, if these men planned on killing you, did they give you a weapon to defend yourself?"

"Maybe they were planning on picking me off from the trees. Or jacking me up at the gas station if I took a different route. Wanted to claim self-defense. Needed just cause. How the fuck should I know?"

"And you said this all took place after they blocked your path on Orchard Road?"

"Yes."

"Until some cars scared them off?"

"They started beeping, yeah."

"Can you give me a physical description?"

"I only saw the one guy. He had an old man baby face."

"I mean of the cars."

"Did I, like, get a license plate? No. I was a little preoccupied with not dying."

"Old man baby face? I don't know what that means."

"Remember Ferris Bueller?"

"The movie?"

"The character."

Turley shrugged. "Sure. I guess."

"Well, he looked like that."

"Like Ferris Bueller?"

"No, I mean how the actor who played him never got older. Still looks the same. His face. Like the Karate Kid."

"I'm sorry, Jay. I don't know what you're getting at."

"The man. He was older. Like in his forties. At least. But he had the face of a teenager."

"And you're sure he wasn't a teenager?"

"He was going bald. How many teenagers you know going bald? He had wrinkles, man, was older, but with a baby face."

"During hunting season, everyone's up at Gillette Gorge . . ." Turley had stopped listening to me, talking to himself.

I didn't understand what he was getting at. If it wasn't hunting season, there was no reason for the orange vests. It was all a ruse. Why was I, a man who'd never been hunting in his life, supposed to be an expert on when moose hunting season ended?

"Send a patrol car," I said. "If I got him, he's not getting far. Follow the blood trail in the snow. He also said—"

"He? Carl?"

"Yes, that's the name he gave me. He said his cousin was hurt—"

"This is the second Carl? The one you never saw?"

"Yes. They were both named Carl. That's what they told me. Dude, I didn't think about hunting season. Because I don't fucking hunt! Send a cop car—"

"Then they just let you go? I mean, if you stabbed one, where's the other one? How did he get away?"

"Maybe he's still out there. Our trucks were blocking the road. Some motorists couldn't pass and starting laying on the horn. Scared them off."

"How long were you out there?"

"Twenty, thirty minutes?"

"Thirty minutes is a long time to wait to pass a truck blocking the road. No one called the station."

"Send out your men to do a search."

At this Turley sighed and leaned back. "We did, Jay. There's no body. No blood. No truck. No tire tracks. Except the ones belonging to you."

"I'm not crazy."

"No one said you were." Turley closed the book. "This sounds like a matter for Fish and Game. If these men *were* hunting outside of season"—the way he stressed "were" betrayed his doubts— "it's their ball game. The gates up to Gillette Gorge are locked this time of year. I'll give 'em a ring, make sure no one has been using the blinds illegally."

"What about someone trying to kill me?"

Turley's expression told me all I needed to know.

"Fuck this." I stood to go. Light-headed, I lost my balance, taking a forearm on the table, dropping to a knee.

"Jay, you're bleeding."

I hadn't felt it till then. I'd been running so hard on adrenaline. It was so cold. When Turley mentioned the blood, I felt the sticky wet pain. I stared down at the red splotch spreading through my flannel like an oil slick. Disoriented, I swayed, slipped. My head smacked off the table and I dropped to the floor. I was conscious, but, Jesus, my face hurt. Turley had already dashed out of the room, barking for an ambulance. I peeled up my shirts and saw the gash, a nasty flay of flesh, deep below the ribs, angry organs bulging, pulsing, trying to break through the thin layer of sinew, aching for their first taste of light.

When the EMT arrived, I told them I was sober and didn't want any painkillers.

"Sorry," the medic said. "But you need morphine." He loaded up a giant syringe, and in that moment, I understood what got my brother so hooked. A soft, warm pillow of winds caught me, carrying me off, taking away all my pain.

*   *   *

I woke in the Pittsfield ER with a nice nurse named Ann who called everything a "watchamadoodle," as in "Let's get you some more watchamadoodle." I had a good idea what that watchama-doodle was. I sure as shit felt better every time she injected me with more of it.

I replayed what happened in the woods. How did I not feel getting cut? Did we stab each other at the same time? Like the punches thrown at the end of *Rocky III*? The doctors confirmed it was a knife wound so it's not like I'd run into a jagged branch or landed on a sharp rock when I fell. Why a knife? Guns are a lot more effective, and a bullet made more sense in terms of a hunting accident cover story. Then again, the fastest way to make God laugh is to make plans. I didn't know what their plan for me was. Maybe I'd thrown a wrinkle in it. I wasn't getting an opportunity for a follow-up Q&A.

When the medics cleared away the matted fabric and flayed skin, the doctors said it wasn't that bad of a cut. Sure looked nasty. A few inches lower, though . . . I was lucky. If my intestines met the business end of that knife, all the shit I was full of would've seeped into the bloodstream, and I'd have gone septic, saddled with a colostomy bag, which I'd have to hide in a fucking fanny pack. I already had the permanent limp from severing the saphenous, a screw in my knee, pin placed from an earlier fracture, busted and bruised joints, a collarbone that jutted out from cracking up my truck and never getting it set right. The day I had to start toting around a bag of shit everywhere I went was the day I gave up living. I already had a tough enough time getting a date.

Maybe it was a slow evening for trauma in the boondocks, but Ann returned to keep me company. Nothing like spending time with a kind, older woman to make you realize how much you miss your mom. Every boy needs a mother.

We spent half her shift talking, about how much she missed her adult children and vegetable garden back home—she'd grown up in Texas. I was grateful for the distraction. I didn't want to dwell on what had happened in the forest. There was that sick part of me chirping in my ear, suggesting Turley was right and I'd made up the whole thing. I didn't know what scared me more: that two strangers were trying to kill me or that I might really be crazy.

"They had me up in Oncology," Ann said, southern twang on full display. "Seeing a lot of cancer cases lately. Been a real outbreak. Such a sad sight. Watching a man's body waste away like that. Ain't nothin' much you can do with the Stage Fours but make 'em comfortable."

I remembered reading somewhere how it took twenty years for cancer to grow, one of the reasons I could justify smoking. No one in my family lived past fifty anyway.

"More than cancer," Ann continued. "Respiratory illnesses, too. Seems to strike manual laborers most, construction workers. Such tragedy. So hard this life, ain't it, Jay?" She snapped the IV line, spurring fluids to drip into my vein.

Out the window, sinister winds scraped dead branches against the glass like a witch's fingernails.

"Probably that burning underground dump we have," I said, through an opiate-aided chuckle. Ashton had this long-standing rumor about a burning underground dump, a fire deep within the earth that would never go out. An urban myth. Or rural legend.

"There's something going on with this town," Ann said, dead serious. She leaned at my bedside. "Something . . . unnatural. I'm not trying to scare you, but in the last six months, we've treated a rash of these respiratory illnesses, fast-spreading tumors, stuff I've never seen. Comes on quick, kills quicker." Ann pulled up, straightening her stiff nurse's uniform. "Listen to me prattling on," she said, fixing my pillow for me. "You're looking peaked. Let's get you more watchamadoodle."

She got more watchamadoodle, and I felt right as rain. Lying in that hospital bed, talking to a nice lady, conversation effortless for hours, I enjoyed one of the more peaceful moments I'd had of late. The painkillers didn't hurt either. Freed from the shackles of guilt and shame, I drifted off to sleep on downy wings, dreaming of sweet, swirling colors, sunny-side-up skies, and boundless cotton candy fields.

Until Turley showed up at the crack of dawn and told me they'd tested the blood on the knife.

It wasn't animal; it was human.

Mine.

CHAPTER TWELVE

THEY KEPT ME through midmorning for monitoring. The blade, which apparently I'd used to eviscerate my own guts, had gone deep but not deep enough to be life threatening. A head-shrinker dropped by to make sure it wasn't intentional. I rolled my eyes until he was satisfied. After a final check of the hot-glued gash, they bandaged me up, said to take it easy for a few, and sent me packing.

I had no choice but to accept PTSD had gotten the best of me. I heard something that wasn't there and panicked. I'd swung a knife in the dark, missed a ghost, and stabbed myself on the follow-through. Before running off like a lunatic, weaving through hobblebush and snowdrifts, dodging tree limbs waiting to snatch me up.

The hospital wouldn't discharge me without a ride. My truck was in Ashton. I didn't have anyone to ask. I wasn't calling Turley. Wasn't up for dealing with Fisher. I thought about calling Amy but decided it was too pathetic. You need to know someone longer than a week before you start asking for rides from airports or hospitals. The staff allowed me to hitch a ride north with an ambulance. I'd been in that ER enough over the years, riding shotgun felt like cashing in frequent-flyer miles.

Back at my place, I wandered empty room to empty room, feeling gusts breach the seals. The doctors said to stay off my feet, but I couldn't stop pacing.

Most of this life is manageable. When you are sane. Yeah, it gets hard. Bills need to be paid, food put on the table. You blow chances left and right, like losing the love of your life for being a hardheaded sonofabitch who can't let go of the past. We get older and body parts don't always work. So we patch them up with solder, steel, staples. My body had taken such a beating of late, I'd begun to feel like Darth Vader, more machine than man. My one respite from this world, beer, had been taken from me. I had my pills. But, fuck, I could use a cigarette.

I lit one off the stove. Freezing rain pelted the glass, like BB pellets fired from a bully's tree fort. The raw winds picked up. The thought of stepping outside right then filled me with dread. I had nowhere to be, but I felt like a shut-in. I wasn't ready to add agoraphobia to my list of maladies.

As long as you have your wits about you, you can weather the storm. But when your own mind turns on you, sanity declaring *you* the enemy—when you can't trust your version of events? Goddamn, sometimes all you can do is stagger from the stove, crash on the sofa, and stare at the water stains on the ceiling.

Last year, a man named Vin Biscoglio tried to hire me for a job. That was my last break with reality. After a five-figure promise on the back of a blank business card and several unanswered phone calls, I wondered if I invented Biscoglio, a perverse need to wage battle with my own inner dark side. Sounds nuts when I put it like that. But Biscoglio had come by late at night, was seen by no one except me, offering more money than I'd ever earned in my life, a good chunk of what I needed to buy the business from Tom Gable—how could I not be suspicious? Every effort to find the guy yielded a cypher. I uncovered no trace of him online or anywhere else. I started to believe I'd written that note to myself. Until they found Biscoglio's body at the base of the mountain, identity verified by the expensive suit he wore. Which was good because he didn't have a face left.

Wasn't much of a leap to say those two men weren't really named Carl. Unless I was getting lazy in my paranoia. I knew a hunter had flagged me down on Orchard Road. A man was injured and needed help. After that, things got fuzzy. I'd lost my footing in a tree, taken a spill, my head hit the ground hard. At what point did narrative lines diverge?

Could've knocked myself out, given myself a concussion. How long had I lain there? It was dark. They wouldn't have been able to see me, either. The more I thought about last night in the forest, the less certain I grew about what happened. Did I hear a gun shot? Or had a snow-covered bough broken in the gale? Were two killers sent to silence me? For what? Asking a few questions about a missing pill-popping college student? Reading a couple articles online? Talking to a dope dealer? None of this warranted murder.

Don't let them get to you, little brother. You can't doubt the things you're sure of.

No, I could get confused and misread situations. I had a panic disorder. But I wasn't nuts. Something wasn't adding up.

I needed to talk to Amy.

She didn't live far from the Landover, the bar where Jenny used to work nights as a cocktail waitress. It hurt like hell my ex-wife shared her bed with someone else now, and having my son call another man Dad killed me. But I was also happy Jenny lived in the nice part of town and didn't have degenerates grabbing her ass for an extra buck tip. My family finally had the life they deserved. All it had taken was getting rid of me.

Stuck between the end of the workday and the start of nightly AA meetings, I wanted to talk in person, not on the phone. Then again, I didn't know if Amy had a job, didn't know much about her life, period, beyond her career path charting the exact course you'd expect, from out-of-control teen to drug addict.

The address was for a dismal house in a dreary part of town. The house had been divided up into three or four tiny units. I pictured an under-furnished apartment with a few plants that needed watering, dirty dishes, maybe a cat. I didn't expect him to answer the door.

There was no reason Amy wouldn't have a husband or boyfriend. I assumed if she had been married, she'd be divorced by now. A first marriage is like a starter house; no one stays long. You live there a while, don't invest too much, then move on to something better. I wasn't sweating a boyfriend. With the tattoos and long hair, he reminded me of Jenny's ex, Brody, this piece-of-shit biker.

"What you want?"

"Is Amy home?"

"Who is it?" I heard Amy call from the other room.

He clutched a beer in one hand. I smelled the pungent aroma of marijuana wafting through the room. I wondered if Amy had backstepped. Walking up, she looked good, clear-eyed and -headed. It was none of my business, but it'd be a shame to piss away all that clean time for this clown. Why put herself in jeopardy? Or more to the point, what kind of asshole gets high in front of someone fighting to remain sober?

"Babe," she said, turning to her husband, boyfriend, whatever he was. I'd deduced they were together before the term of endearment. The way he closed ranks, his close proximity projecting possession, ownership. "This is the man I hired to find my sister."

"Oh, yeah. Right. Emily. How's that working out?"

I shook my head. Few places made me feel better about my one-bedroom above a gas station. How I'd let Jenny and my son call that dump home was a constant source of shame. But it beat fuckall out of this rattrap. Cramped, cluttered, reeking of glued-together meats bought at the dollar store and fried in cheap pans.

"This is Dan. My boyfriend." She announced it like she'd just figured out what that funky smell in the fridge was.

"Everyone calls me Hooch," he said, offering a fist bump.

I might've said it was good to meet him. I might've half-assed a courtesy fist bump. But no way in fucking hell was I calling him Hooch. What was it with the whitest mutherfuckers in the whitest state in America and their need to adopt gangsta nicknames?

I did not know Amy. I barely remembered her from high school. I owed no loyalty, no debt. I didn't know fuckall about her life except that she was an ex-junkie, poor, and worried her best years were behind her. Yet I felt this pressing need to protect her, keep her safe, because this dude was bad news. Maybe it was Dan's resemblance to Jenny's biker ex. Maybe it was knowing Amy was trying to stay clean and this cockknob was getting loaded six feet away. Maybe it was a deeper desire, some piss-marking male dominance. Didn't know. Didn't care. But I hated that mutherfucker.

Dan the Hooch was another wannabe like Curtis G-Money but bigger, stout, solid, older; unlike Curtis, he was a man. A douchebag. But a man. And he wasn't letting another man walk into his place and front. So he opted to vacate the premises, give me the floor. On his terms. He abandoned dinner, fatty scraps in congealed blood, and swiped his leather jacket off the chair. Asshole didn't bring his plate to the sink, leaving his half-full beer on the table for his girlfriend to bus, like she was his maid.

"I'm going to the bar." He nodded at me. "Later, Ray."

"Jay."

"Yeah, that, too." He slammed the door behind him. I listened to heavy boots stomp down the hall. A moment later, a truck engine rumbled to life, tires crunching snow, motoring off to whichever bar had the cheapest beer on tap and most pretzels in tiny bowls.

"You okay?" Amy asked, pointing at my ribs, which I favored, the bandages under my shirt evident once I'd taken off my winter coat.

"I'm fine. Accident at work. Cut myself on some molding. Your sister was still at White Mountain Tech. Taking a journalism course. Up until three weeks ago."

"Probably to get the student loans. A lot of addicts pull that one. Get the money, drop out."

I stared down at the beer and joint in the ashtray. "How do you let him do that?"

"What? Huh—" She followed my gaze to the party remnants. "It's his life. He's free to make his own choices."

"It doesn't bother you?"

"I don't know, Jay. Sometimes."

"Okay if I smoke in here?"

Amy panned over the run-down, smelly apartment. Stupid question.

"I don't think it's healthy," I said, picking up the lighter Dan left between the beer and pot. "You shouldn't be around this shit."

"And where am I supposed to go?"

"Kick him out."

"Hooch is my boyfriend."

I cringed at the nickname. "You call him that?"

Amy shrugged.

"You're not going to last—"

"Besides, the lease is in his name. Why are you here? I appreciate any help finding Emily, but you told me the other day you wanted no part of my sister. Or me. Now you show up and tell me I should leave my boyfriend?"

"I've been known to change my mind. And your boyfriend is an asshole."

"Excuse me?"

"Dan. You're trying to stay straight, and he's getting high right in front of you. That's a dick move."

"I'll take your relationship advice under consideration. Do you have any more news about my sister other than she was taking some stupid writing class?"

I pointed for her to grab a seat. I cleared the table and poured the beer down the drain. The joint had already self-extinguished. "I have a friend," I said, joining her at the table. "Knows professors up at White Mountain. He made calls. Your sister was working for a newspaper."

She wasn't getting it.

"Emily didn't have a drug problem. She wanted access to the rehab. I think she was working on a story."

"A story? About what?"

"Not sure. But my guess? She was trying to blow a whistle on the heartless bastards cashing in on the drug problem up here. She's a college student. Their hearts still bleed." I ashed in an empty beer can. "What if she got admitted to the Coos County Center to have a look around?"

"Have you talked to the newspaper?"

"I don't know which one she got assigned to. Hard to get a school to disclose student records."

Amy shook her head. "Shannon warned me about you. Said you were off. I didn't believe her. I'd seen you at meetings, remembered you from back in the day. You looked good, on the right path. I overheard someone saying you did amateur investigating. I took a chance because I didn't know where else to go. I'm starting to think Shannon was right."

"I don't know who Shannon is."

"She's my friend."

"What do I care?"

"She said you were obsessed with the Lombardis, and that their connection to the CCC would make hiring you a waste of money."

"I said I'd give you back your money."

"I don't want it back." Amy studied me. "What's your deal? Two hundred dollars ain't a lot of money. Real private investigators charge that an hour."

"I'm not a real private investigator. Why do you stay with him?"

"Do you have like ADHD or something? You jump from one topic to the next. Can you stay focused on any one task or conversation?"

"I don't believe ADHD is real. I think the doctors made it up so the pharmaceutical industry could pump kids full of drugs, get them hooked, bilk gullible parents. Do you want to discuss my political views? Dan is a bum, a loser. You can do better."

"The other day, you didn't even remember me." Amy turned away.

"I remembered you."

"I lied," she said. "We talked at those parties by the lake, we hung out."

"Hung out?"

"You kissed me once."

"Bullshit."

"You were drunk. But you did. No big deal. It was high school. I don't know what to say, why you don't remember me."

"I said I remember you. But we never—"

"Hooked up? Yes, we did. Once. Some lake party Jenny didn't show at. You guys had a fight or something. You downed a twelve-pack and started chatting me up. And you kissed me." She turned away, as if to conceal the hurt. "When I saw you at the meeting, I thought . . . I mean, fuck, I was something else back in the day. I never lacked for attention." She glanced down at her body, which still looked good to me. "Ten years pissed away on dope, I guess I'm not what I once was."

"None of us are."

"You've always been a good-looking guy. You know how many girls had crushes on you? But you lived down in Concord, were always with Jenny Price." The way Amy repeated my ex-wife's name carried all the disdain reserved for an underserving celebrity. "Even when you weren't." She hopped up, leaned against the counter, lighting her own cigarette, acting cooler with the distance between us. "Can I ask what happened? With you and Jenny? Why it didn't work out?" Amy stared through the window at the empty spaces.

I didn't know how to answer that. "I fucked up? Drank too much? Couldn't grow up fast enough. Pushed her away. Held onto grudges. Wanted someone to pay for what happened to my brother."

"Is that the reason behind your sudden reinterest in my sister?"

"I don't know if anyone will ever pay."

"That's not what I mean."

"Let's just say stories I once believed were separate are looking like they're all part of the same—"

"Conspiracy?"

"I don't like that word. My brother, Chris, found dirt on the Lombardis. Only he didn't understand how muddy it got. Neither did I. What if your sister did?"

Amy brushed a wisp of hair from her eyes. For the first time since high school, I caught that fuck-me stare. "Why did you really come here?"

I stubbed out my cigarette, stood up.

"Run my man out of his own house? Rambling about this bull-shit. Reminding me of when I was young." She looked ready to cry. "Damn you, Jay Porter."

"You can do better."

"Ha!"

"I'm serious."

"What? Who? You?"

"Fucking-A right."

Amy pushed off the counter. The moon shone through the dirty window, shining a brilliant beam though the pane, split-ting the light into four even squares. I wondered in which one I belonged.

We moved toward each other. Maybe with a beer, I would've been smoother, maybe with a beer I wouldn't be here at all. Either way, I should've had the common sense not to get involved with another man's girl. But lack of common sense never stopped me before. Funny how being drunk can make things clearer, how being sober can make life more confusing. We both ached, hurt, and when you don't have drugs and alcohol, your means of escape are limited. We met in the middle; there was no discussion. Our mouths mashed together like teenagers knocking teeth, hands fumbling to belong, like when the audio and video aren't quite synced in a film. Took a moment. And then it clicked.

I don't want to say time stood still, and I don't want to paint erotic scenes culled from romance novels. I won't oversell what happened or use words like love or fate, lust or desire, because it wasn't like that. But when we made it to the bed, and Amy had slipped out of her jeans and peeled off her panties, when I un-buckled my belt, got naked and climbed on top, I can say this: I never fit inside a woman better.

CHAPTER THIRTEEN

I DIDN'T SPEND the night with Amy, obviously, our goodbye as fast as the sex, which left me dizzy, disoriented, like I'd taken a new drug. I know I called Jenny on the way back to my apartment, and that it was late, and she didn't answer. I warned her. I couldn't remember what I said exactly, just that something bad happened in the woods, how two hunters named Carl may've been trying to kill me. I expressed concern for their safety and suggested now might be a good time for her, Aiden, and Stephen to take a vacation to one of his myriad vacation homes, make sure the security was turned on, and to sit tight; I'd call her when I figured out what was happening.

I tried to remember this party Amy was talking about where she said I'd kissed her. Was she fucking with me? Did she have me confused with someone else? We were going on almost twenty years. Or was I already a blackout drunk in high school? I didn't consider myself an alcoholic back then. I wasn't comfortable with the term now. But if I was drinking so much beer that I'd forget something like that, what else had I been wrong about? I prided myself on never cheating on Jenny. We had plenty of fights, break-ups, took a lot of time off. I could spin it however I wanted. Still made me feel like shit. Thinking about this made me unsure of everything, like my entire life had been a lie.

* * *

The next morning, I heard Hank Miller, my landlord and the owner of the gas station below, shoveling snow. I was surprised to see the unexpected, significant accumulation. Hadn't heard of a blizzard in the forecast. When I glimpsed out the window, there had to be a solid foot, the telephone wires slagged down by the wintry elements. I helped Hank, who was in his seventies, clear the lot. On my way back up, I grabbed a copy of the *Ashton Herald* from his mini-mart, a prewrapped pastry and protein bar, and made coffee upstairs at my place.

There they were. Adam and Michael Lombardi. The paper had done one of those obnoxious now-and-later side-by-side shots. On the left, the two brothers as scrappy, shaggy-haired kids, juxtaposed against the two strapping successful businessmen on the right. Amy and Emily Lupus reminded me of Chris. When I saw Adam and Michael, I didn't think of brothers or bonds; I only saw monsters.

The front-page article highlighted the new wing at the Coos County Center, which would be used to treat dual-diagnoses, meaning addiction and mental illness. Those two went hand in hand anyway. The part that got under my skin? They'd named it the Gerry Lombardi Ward. Which I swear they did to piss me off. The rest of the article was a nauseating love letter to all the good the Brothers Lombardi had done for the community. What a joke. Drugs were as present in Ashton as they'd always been. Town officials had managed to clear the riffraff from the TC Truck Stop. By steamrolling the place. Like flipping a switch and watching the roaches scatter. Dan the Hooch, Curtis G-Money, and the rest of the vermin on the Turnpike were still around. They were just hiding in new crevices.

The ceremony was set for ten o'clock this morning.

I showered, found clothes that looked least like the ones I normally wore, meaning a brighter-colored flannel, darker jeans, and an older jacket. Instead of my knit hat, I grabbed an old Red Sox cap from the closet and pulled it low, plucking a pair of wrap-around shades from the junk bowl by the door, the kind used for skiing, which I never wore. I didn't ski. I downed the last swig of cold coffee and set out for the circus.

The scene at the CCC presented a strange hybrid and cross-section. TV crews and reporters were there, but there was also a big crowd of regular townsfolk as well, residents who'd ventured out on this blustery winter's morn to see the closest thing we got to celebrity in our small mountain town. Supply a vat of fat babies, and the Lombardi brothers would be kissing chubby cheeks till their lips chapped.

A yellow ribbon gift-wrapped a doorway, which killed me, since the door had clearly been open and shut several times by now. All for show. The smiles and laughter, the goodwill and sickening cheer made my blood boil. A pair of oversized, ceremonial scissors rested against the wall. In a few minutes, the brothers would join hands in a show of solidarity, ushering in another revenue stream.

The CCC wasn't a prison. The treatment center was designed to help, probably did a lot of good, in fact. If Adam and Michael helped get it off the ground, they deserved props. But those two didn't fool me. These positives were by-products, the flipside of collateral damage, a necessary good to facilitate evil. They'd seen a way to profit on sickness, and each junkie, addict, crackhead, speedfreak, drunk who signed up for their services only added zeroes to the Lombardi coffer. The Brothers wouldn't piss on a burning bum unless there was a photo op in it for them.

I excused myself from the festivities. Back in my truck, glitter and pomp receding in the distance, I drove up the Turnpike, on my way to White Mountain Community Tech. I needed to talk to this Ostrowski. Straight-A students don't drop out and ask for an incomplete. Unless Emily did have a drug problem. Or really was some hotshot, up-and-coming reporter. I had no definitive proof one way or the other. Amy and Curtis G-Money weren't impartial observers. Given a choice between an ex-junkie and a drug dealer, I was going with the higher education professor.

I'd never been on the White Mountain campus. When I was in high school, my aunt and uncle had pressed me to go to college, offering to help offset the cost. I checked out a couple schools. But I didn't spend much time socializing. I breezed through administrative offices, never sent in materials or followed up. I wasn't the college type. I wanted to start making money. I also needed to get back to Ashton and take care of my brother. By then Chris was a full-blown junkie, homeless, and beyond saving. Not that that stopped me from trying.

I didn't know why this thought, lodged in my lizard brain, decided to make an appearance now, but it bothered me, like I'd missed out on some important developmental milestone. College parties, getting fucked up, sex without strings. I'd never been good at one-night stands. For as much pride as I took in living an unconventional life, there were plenty times where I wished I fit in. Then again, as Amy pointed out, my heart always belonged to Jenny. Last night I had some of the best sex I ever had, and my first thought when we were done? Disappointment that it hadn't been Jenny.

White Mountain Community Tech wasn't like the universities I visited. Most of the classrooms were housed in temporary pop-up trailers. There was an actual administrative building and a couple bona fide halls, but there were way more of these little pods. I didn't know where to find Ostrowski. Didn't know if he was here today, what office hours he kept, his class schedule. That information was available somewhere on the WMCT website, if I wanted to dig around. But I doubted it would be any faster. White

Mountain was low rent, underfunded, the type of place you landed when you goofed off too much, either by underachieving or shooting too high and not leaving yourself a safety school. Faith in a reliable web master seemed misplaced.

The school was small enough that it didn't take long to navigate on foot. I spoke with a couple secretaries, students working off loans, who pointed me in the right direction.

The Journalism offices were in one of the aforementioned pods. Stepping up the makeshift stairs, I felt embarrassed, like arriving at an underattended surprise party someone is throwing for themselves.

"Can I help you?" Fiftysomething, glasses, *Brady Bunch* perm. According to Fisher, Ostrowski had been at the gig a while; the least the college could do was give the guy an actual office. The trailer, while big enough to fit a couple classrooms, played low rent and claustrophobic. Heat coughed weakly out the vents, but it was still cold enough that Ostrowski wore his winter coat inside.

I introduced myself, explained what I did, as fast and generic as possible. It is not easy to combine estate clearing with part-time, unlicensed private investigator. I hated the term "PI." Sounded cheesy. But I wasn't a cop, either. I had zero authority and no grounds to be here. I needed answers, labels be damned.

Ostrowski told me to take a seat, and when I called him "Dr. Ostrowski," he insisted I call him "Steve."

"You want to talk about Emily Lupus?"

"She's missing."

"Missing?" He said it like I'd confessed to ordering green beans on pizza.

"Hasn't been seen for a couple weeks. Could be laying low." I paused, trying to figure out how to word my next question without sounding accusatory or disrespectful. "I don't know how to ask this,

Dr. Ostrow—Steve—but when Emily was your student, did you sense any issues with drugs? Pills?"

"Drugs? Emily?" Ostrowski laughed. "God, no. She's as strait-laced as they come. Great student, hard worker, terrific kid. I told her she was too bright for this place. Emily has an older sister who *does* have a drug problem. Part of the reason she stays in the area, I think." Dr. Steven Ostrowski sipped coffee dispensed from a machine. "Although," he added, "in all honesty, I'm not sure how much good it does. I don't think she and her sister speak."

"Her sister asked me to look for her."

"Interesting." The word wasn't uttered in surprise or as an expression of doubt, simply a statement of fact.

"Amy said Emily came to her. Confessed to having a pill problem and asked for a ride to the Coos Country Center."

"I don't know what to tell you. I spent a lot of time with Emily. I'd be shocked if that girl took anything stronger than a morning half-caf latte."

"Was she close with any of her classmates? Any friends you might be able to put me in touch with?"

"Not that I know of. She didn't open up about it much, but I got the impression that after her parents died, and her sister turned out the way she did, Emily wasn't willing to risk being hurt. I don't think she has *any* friends."

"Did Emily drop out?"

"Not exactly," Ostrowski replied. "A hiatus. She got a job with a newspaper."

"Can you tell me which one?"

The professor scratched at his Mike Brady curls. "The *Berlin Patch*. Emily started as an intern there. A couple months in, they offered her a full-time position. She took it. Don't blame her. It's a great opportunity for someone with her abilities."

"She's that smart?"

"Emily Lupus is the sort of student you dream of as a professor."
Dr. Ostrowski looked around the cramped confines of his dismal
quarters. "You don't get many of them here. White Mountain
isn't Yale or Dartmouth. We don't have the resources to recruit
top-notch talent. Part of the reason I signed off on the indepen-
dent study, which isn't something I often do. She was working on
a compelling case."

"Can I ask what that was?"

"Sure. But I can assure you that it doesn't have anything to do
with drugs or rehabilitation clinics, if that's what you're thinking."

"What does it have to do with?"

"Soil."

"Soil? Like dirt?"

"Do you know any other kind?"

Outside of calling addicts dirtbags, I failed to see how dirt and
drugs related. Maybe I'd gotten it wrong. Maybe Emily was just a
hardworking student turned reporter who was burning the candle
at both ends. If people like Ostrowski didn't recognize the signs
of drug abuse, just meant she hid it well. Amy was the junkie.
If anyone were an expert on the subject, it would be her. Emily
had this new high-pressure gig with deadlines and commitments.
Tough-as-nails editor riding her hard, she's trying to make a good
impression, so she starts popping pills to keep going . . .

*Doesn't feel right. Outside of Amy's word, where are the signs of
addiction? Look at the evidence you* do *have, not what you* want
to see.

I recalled the book on toxins in the soil at her apartment, bur-
ied among the stack of journalism texts, one of these things not
like the other.

"Dr. Ostrowski, do you have any idea what was so special
about dirt that Emily bailed on her degree to study it? Seems
weird to me."

"She was going to give me a full write-up at semester's end. I didn't require her to check in after she asked for the incomplete. You'd have to call the *Patch*. Not sure how much they'll tell you. Reporters and sources, ongoing investigations, etcetera. I'm not sure they'd tell me much more, and she was my student." He drummed his fingers off his office rotary. "You've tried her cell and checked her apartment, I take it?"

How incompetent did the guy think I was?

"Of course you have," he said, answering himself. He spun his chair around, plucking a folder from a lower tray on a rollaway cart. "I can tell you what she told me when she outlined the project. Toxins were discovered in soil up here and some construction workers got sick. Emily was working on an exposé, showing how the companies knew the soil was contaminated and chose not to clean up the spill, deeming such actions cost prohibitive, placing corporate profit over employee safety. It was a very intriguing project."

I flashbacked to the night I stabbed myself in the forest and that nice nurse, Ann, in the Pittsfield ER who told me about her time on the Oncology ward, the rash of construction workers who'd contracted fast-acting cancers and respiratory illnesses.

"I'm proud of her," Ostrowski said. "Emily is going to make a heck of a reporter one day." He tucked the folder away. "Give the *Patch* a call," he said, perking up. "They might not be able to get into specifics, but I'm sure they can tell you she's okay. My guess? Emily's moving around the state, working on this story, compiling data. Soon as you talk to her, she'll be better able to explain."

Yeah, I thought. If we can find her first.

* * *

I called Amy but didn't get through. Rang Fisher. Also, no luck. I then tried the *Berlin Patch*. I couldn't get anyone to even answer the goddamn phone to leave a message let alone ask whom Emily was working with. Damn thing kept ringing and ringing. No outgoing message, no prompt, nothing. Berlin was a haul north, around Lamentation, the town not much bigger than Ashton. I doubted its paper featured major players. I contemplated traversing the mountain but didn't want to deal with the ice, risking rollover, only to find an understaffed office keeping odd hours. Instead, I made for my warehouse to work on my fledgling business, which I hoped someday would earn me real cash. I planned to spend the rest of the day moving shit around that didn't need to be moved. Stay busy, stay out of my head, avoid trouble. Maybe a call would come in and someone else would've passed into the good night, and I'd get another sale. That's how I got paid. There were worse ways to earn a living, although in that moment, I was hard pressed to think of many. Perhaps one day I'd move off this mountain for good.

I hadn't made any headway into finding Emily, and walking into my storage space, I should've been feeling down or at least frustrated. Except I wasn't. In fact, I was feeling better than I was used to. Took me a moment to realize what that emotion was: hope. Everything Under the Sun was all mine. Fail, succeed, better, worse. It was up to me now. I liked that.

And getting laid last night didn't hurt.

I didn't feel great about sleeping with another man's girl, but I didn't feel that guilty either. Dan the Hooch was a drug-abusing douche. I had a tendency to justify my bad behaviors. I wasn't going to lie to myself and say what I'd done was something to be proud of. But I liked Amy. And she liked me. And she deserved better than that prick.

Clearing bids and stacking boxes, I sweated and wrought muscle, grunting as the skies turned darker. Every time I twisted or stretched, it felt like I was getting stabbed all over again. The sun never went down because it had never come out, washed-out gray fading to black like the end of a Wim Wenders film. Every once in a while, I'd flash on images of Amy's naked body, the way we fit together, two pieces of the same incomplete puzzle, and the thought made me smile.

Workday wrapping up, I remembered my panicked phone call to Jenny, the impulsive demand that she leave town, take the family and go on the run. And the fact that she hadn't returned my call did not bode well. I was making for the landline, mentally spinning damage control, when the phone rang.

"Jay. It's me. Turley." Tone authoritative, all business, ready to read the riot.

My first thought was someone had spotted me at the Lombardi rally, and I was about to get chewed out like a little kid caught pilfering sweets from the pharmacy. Turley couldn't do anything to me—the ceremony was public—and his demands that I stay away didn't hold any sway. Before I could offer a defense or polite fuck you, he hit me with something much harder.

"They found Emily Lupus."

The way he said it, I knew there was no point asking if she was okay. He put any hope to bed anyway.

"She's dead."

CHAPTER FOURTEEN

EMERGENCY LIGHTS SPLASHED off the rocky ice and snow. We were halfway around the mountain in the clouds. They call it Lamentation Mountain, but the range runs for endless miles, and we were far north, beyond Coal Creek and Silver Lake, past the turnoff to Crimson Peak, high enough up the cliffside that oxygen was growing thin. This was a part of the mountain folks seldom ventured to. Chevreport County. Though I couldn't say if this was Chevreport proper. In certain sections of New Hampshire, much of the countryside went unclaimed, like the old frontier. But it was no-man's land, scree and other shit you didn't want to deal with, fifteen feet of snow. Earlier I didn't want to trek to Berlin because it was such a haul, and Chevreport was a helluva lot farther than that. Great place to dump a body. Who would ever find it?

We were a long way from Ashton. With Emily's being from town, they'd called Turley, who greeted me after I slammed my truck door and started walking up the shelf, my untied work boots punishing layers of cleared snow.

Turley had that same expression on his face as he did the other day, like he wanted to tear me a new one, but he'd called *me*. Unless he was going to try and get creative and blame me for this, too. I hadn't made his life easy of late, my charges of hunter hitman not helping my cause. Turley had dealt with my PTSD in the past, my short fuse and bouts of mania. But I was on the uptick, hitting meetings, laying off the bottle, improving. I wasn't the same man. I was getting better. I could still be a pain in his ass, but the days of getting blamed for murder were behind me.

"Jay," Turley said, shaking my hand with the pretension he always adopted when we had cause to meet in an official capacity. That's what this felt like, me the investigator extended a courtesy, despite not having a license or officially working the job. In fact, acknowledging these things to myself, I had to wonder why Turley called me at all.

He led me past the pair of Chevreport squad cars, two patrolmen bunged up like the cops in *Fargo*. An ambulance backed to the edge of the ravine, which ran down forty feet of tortuous, rocky escarpment. I could see the med-vac guys tugging their wooly beards trying to determine the most efficient way to extract a dead body. Someone had already ventured down there and confirmed identity and mortality status. Which was dead. Very, very dead. You could see from the edge of the cliff that the girl was a goner, all twisted and contorted, legs bent ninety degrees this way, arms one-eighty that, head cocked at an extraterrestrial angle, neck elongated, belly engorged with gases. Necrotic tissue tinged that special shade of blue the dead invite. In this cold she appeared almost luminescent.

Turley and I stood shoulder to shoulder. A small stream of water rippled through ice cut into the cliffside, moving too fast to freeze, rushing in and out of forged channels.

"What happened?"

"Broken neck."

"No shit, Turley." Emily's body resembled a deer struck at a hundred on the highway. "Guessing it wasn't an accident. How'd anyone even find her?" She wasn't visible from the road, and this wasn't a stretch inviting much traffic.

"Plow driver spotted the body." Turley nodded into the mountain trees, where, in the distance, a gleaming glass house perched on a precipice. "Some hotshot banker lives up there. County comes out to plow this just for him. Must be nice." He flicked a finger in Emily's general direction. "One of the EMTs rappelled down there. Gonna have a heck of a time retrieving the body. Can't say for sure without a formal autopsy, but it looks like she was strangled first—ligature marks around her neck."

"How long she been down there?"

"Hard to say. A day at least. Maybe two. Looks like she's been dead longer than that."

"Killed first and transported?"

"Transported and tossed. Doubt the car even slowed down." He panned over, glance turning to glare. "I know you were at the CCC today."

"And?"

"And I thought I told you to stay away from the Lombardi brothers."

"Yeah. You did."

"Why do you have to cause me aggravation, Porter? Haven't I been good to you?"

"Good to me?" I had to think about that one. "You've been okay to me. Besides accusing me of attacking Tom Gable last year—"

"I told you: you were never a suspect—"

"Like I said. You've been okay."

"Then why'd you have to show up at that ceremony? When I specifically asked you not to? You knew I'd take the heat. Already fielded calls from both Adam *and* Michael. Then four more from various assistants, including a secretary, who chewed my ass out. Took up half my day. Now I have to deal with this mess. It's hard enough earning the respect—"

"Christ, what's your damage, man? Coos County is public property."

"No, it's not."

"The ceremony was open to the public. Press was there, townsfolk, regular Joes. Do Adam and Michael have a restraining order against me? No. Because I haven't done jack to warrant one. No grounds. I've left those two alone for five years, despite what I know about their fucked-up family; despite Adam hiring a thug to break into my apartment and pound me senseless; despite Michael ordering those dirty cops to drop me in the ice."

"We never could prove any of that."

"*We?* Is this why you called me up here? Because someone didn't like seeing my face? Maybe I shouldn't leave the apartment. What if I run into a Lombardi cousin at the Price Chopper or Gas 'n' Go?"

Turley gusted, belly inflating and bouncing over his belt. Sure, he'd dropped a few pounds, but he'd always be a big guy. He nodded toward the edge of the cliff where the med-vac crew lowered a basket. "You know the sister, Jay. Thought you might want to check in on her." Turley pawed at the back of his doughy neck, stuck between playing the heavy and being friendly. "I know you said she's in recovery. I remember how hard Chris' death was on you."

We stood in silence, watching while the crew tugged the rope, hand over hand.

I slapped his shoulder. "Thanks."

Turley turned to me, pleading. "Stay away from Adam and Michael, okay? As a favor. To me. I do you right. You do me right. Deal?"

I waited a second, before offering a reluctant nod.

"I'll check into Emily's time at the CCC," he said. "I'll share what I can. Despite you not being a licensed investigator. See? Another favor."

I flicked my burning ember, watching it die in the snow.

* * *

This was not a conversation I was looking forward to having. The police had already called and explained her baby sister was dead. Murdered. Brought up a lot of shit for me, too, and I did my best to push the whirling thoughts out of my maddening mind as I drove to Amy's place, the memories it conjured, the guttural response of when I'd been on the receiving end of such loss.

We'd had sex. And it had been good. Maybe it was ending a long dry spell, the first time getting laid since I stopped drinking, but the second I entered her, every nerve ending sparked, like I was coming back to life. The orgasm felt like it lasted half a minute. I didn't want to be that high school dweeb getting his first handjob and mistaking it for love, but I owed her this much. We weren't dating, and she was involved with another man, but Amy needed me right now. I wanted to be there for her. That sack-of-shit wasn't going to offer any comfort. I didn't think she'd run right out and piss away a year of hard work. I figured I had time.

I was wrong.

When I knocked on the door, Dan the Hooch answered, and I saw Amy splayed on the couch behind him, wasted, wrecked, high as shit. I could see the whites of her eyes rolled back in her skull, rubber tourniquet still clamped around biceps.

"Hey, it's the junkman," Dan said. "Come on in. Join the party."

"Party?"

"I mean, we're in mourning of course. You heard about her sister?" He let his head drop the requisite distance. "Fucked up, yo."

I brushed past him, rushing to her side, shaking her, calling her name to make sure she was still alive. She stirred from the torpor, moaning. The needle lay on the table beside the burnt spoon and cotton, the tools of the trade. A trickle of blood dried in the crook of her elbow.

"We're getting out of here," I said, reaching for her arm, which responded like an overcooked noodle. I tried to sling it around my neck as I picked her up, but she slipped off, flopping back to the cushions.

"Yo, bro," Dan said, coming up fast behind me. "What the fuck you think you're doing? You can't touch her. That's my girl."

I spun with my forearm locked in a tire-iron L, driving it into his neck, pushing him back with all my weight, across the living room, over the empties and used cartons, unwashed clothes and scattered shoes, pinning him against the wall, cutting off air supply. Dan wasn't a small guy, and he was relatively sober, far as I could tell, which meant the punch wasn't unexpected. He threw a decent one. Landed flush on my hard head. But he was pressed against the wall and didn't have much leverage, and I had that rage problem, which right now was a good problem to have. I was feeling no pain, running on adrenaline. I drove hook after hook into his ribs, rapid, clean shots that wedged up in his guts, sucked the breath from him. Throwing my arms over his shoulders, I grabbed him from behind his waist, flipping him upside down, letting my anger carry me. We spun one-eighty and I body-slammed him onto the table, remnants of dope, water, spoon, and syringe spring-boarding in the air. Dan landed flat on his back, smashing pieces of cheap plywood. He was down. But I didn't stop there. I knelt over him and clocked him in the mouth another three, four, five times. Full-on, wound-up, cold cocks. I didn't give a fuck if I broke his nose or jaw or fractured an eye socket, gave him a concussion, knocked him unconscious. In that moment, I didn't give a good goddamn if I killed him. When I was good and winded, I left him writhing on the floor, curled fetal, groaning, spitting blood.

Grabbing Amy under the arms, I lifted her up. When I passed the Hooch, I kicked him in the ribs one more time because I could.

Back at my place, I worried Amy had overdosed. During the drive, she wouldn't wake up no matter how much I shook her, no matter how much ice-cold air blasted through the vents or how loud I called her name. I didn't know enough about heroin to bring her back if she'd overdosed. A trip to the hospital meant a visit from the cops. Most of what I'd learned about dope came from pamphlets in rehab waiting rooms. Or the movies. And I wasn't stabbing anyone in the heart. So I waited. Checked to make sure she was still breathing, still had a pulse.

I made a pot of strong coffee, which is what you did for drunks, but I couldn't get Amy to drink any. She lay on my couch, where I'd carried her, propping her up so she wouldn't choke on her own vomit. She went in and out, semiconscious, eyelids fluttering, occasionally mumbling "Emily, Emily, Emily," which, of course, broke my heart.

Don't feel bad, baby brother. Wasn't nothin' you could've done.

Oh, shut the fuck up.

I was tired of conversations with the dead. I was sick of fighting with myself over mistakes I'd made and wrong turns I'd taken. I'd done the best I could. I had a family of my own at the time, was barely scraping by. How was I supposed to be my brother's keeper, too? The guy was ten years older than I was. Our folks dead, he should've been the one taking care of *me*. Charlie had the same fighting chance I did. When the hits started coming, I stayed on my feet. He went down for the count. Goddamn, I wanted a beer.

All I had was the lorazepam, and grappling with fears Amy might die, having to wrestle with whether to make the 911 call, I felt justified in chewing several until my heart rate subsided to a mere feverish gallop.

I'd also just beat the living shit out of a man. I'm not the toughest guy in the world; I'd put my win/loss record somewhere around Rocky's. Meaning I'd gotten my ass kicked plenty, winning percentage like taking the AFC North, a tick over .500. But that fight was as one-sided as they come. I'd kicked his ass. Years of pent-up fury and hostility fueled by righteous indignation guided my fists with pinpoint precision; we're talking Irish Micky Ward, Round Nine, sans Gatti comeback because he never got the chance. I'd broken his nose. Maybe cracked his jaw. The worst part? I didn't give a shit. I blamed Dan for Amy's condition. She'd been trying to stay straight and that asshole dangled relief right in front of her.

Time passed deep into the witching hour. At any moment Amy's heart could seize up or the police would arrive on my doorstep because I'd thrashed the hell out of a man before taking off with his woman, and of these charges I'd be guilty as fuck. Then again, as Amy pointed out that first night in my truck, people like us can't go to the cops. Would a stoner, junkie, drunken bum call the police because he'd gotten his ass kicked? Or would he show up himself, seeking redemption? I know what I would do. Then again, I was also of the firm belief that if you beat a man bad enough, he knows when to stay down.

Around one a.m., after I had chain-smoked an entire pack, Amy finally came to. I walked to the couch and kneeled close to her. I realized just how long I'd lived alone. Aiden came to visit, of course. But my son was always on loan. My fat cat had run away. Amy was here to stay now. We didn't have to talk about it.

She had nowhere else to go. I wasn't letting her return to that drug-abusing asshole. When her gaze settled on me, the expression carried the expected shame but also an ounce of gratitude. I'd cared enough to get her out of there. We were alike, she and I. Over the past few years, after my wife and I split up, there'd been two women in my life. But we didn't match. Nicki was too young, too edgy. Alison too put together. Amy and I matched. We both carried the same burden. In the rooms, they had a saying: water seeks its own level. We were the same level.

"How do you feel?"

"Like shit."

"Do you need water? Let me get you water." I stood and started to turn toward the kitchen, but she called me back, pulling me to the couch beside her, leaning her head on my shoulder. She didn't cry and she didn't cling. She put her head next to mine. We didn't speak for a long time. We sat there. And despite the tragic circumstances that brought us together, it somehow felt right.

"I couldn't save her." She gazed up with those wounded doe eyes, filling with tears. "Why couldn't I save her?"

"It doesn't work that way. We can only save ourselves." I was saying that as much for my benefit as I was hers.

Soon our hands were touching, and our arms entwined, and then we were lying down, body atop body, relieving the pain the only way we had left. We didn't move fast like the other day. It was a slow burn. The need to escape. I was happy to play my part. All too often my head was a thousand miles away. I didn't spend much time in the moment, too busy regretting yesterday, dreading tomorrow, never present. But right then I was locked in on her. The touch of her hands, the smoothness of her skin, the heat between her legs. We moved from the living room to the bedroom, and for hours we made love. Two bodies fused into one, two broken bodies housing wrecked hearts and battered souls, moving slowly toward redemption. I couldn't recall the last time I had sex that long. At thirty-six it had been a while. But when we were done, Amy fell asleep in the crook of my arm, on my chest, snuggling close, and for the first time in a long time, I didn't feel alone.

CHAPTER FIFTEEN

THE COUGH IN the kitchen woke me, reminding me that Jenny still had a key to the apartment, which hadn't been an issue before. Now that she was in Pittsfield, my schedule as unpredictable as ever, she would often arrive early with Aiden for our weekends together. I'd given her a key, happily. Didn't want her and my son stuck idling in the icy cold if I got hung up on the other side of town. I didn't entertain other women enough—or ever, for that matter—so, until now it hadn't been an issue.

The door to my bedroom was open. Amy was still asleep. Sheet off, half her naked body exposed, rump up. I didn't have a plausible excuse. Not that I needed one. Jenny was married to another man. I didn't need to explain a damn thing. Even if I felt the pressing need to. I covered Amy with the blankets, grabbing my boxers and tee off the floor, getting dressed, half hopping, half tiptoeing out of the room, gently shutting the door.

My wife, ex-wife, had her arms folded, muckling her mouth, her tell that I'd gotten under her skin.

"Company?" Jenny said.

I stood on the cold linoleum in my boxers and tee, no socks, freezing. I had this fancy heating system I almost never used because the gas companies, bloodsuckers that they are, jack up the cost of fuel in the winter, which is when you need the goddamn heat. I cranked the thermometer anyway.

"You want to put on pants, Jay?"

"Nothing you haven't seen before, Jenny." I lit a cigarette off the stove.

"Who's your new friend?"

"Why do you care?"

"I don't. But if my son is going to be spending time around a strange woman, I think I have the right to know, don't I?"

"*Your* son? Last I checked he was *our* son. Is Aiden with you?"

"No."

"Then what are you so worried about?"

"One-night stand?"

I had to laugh, dropping in the kitchen chair, draping an arm, smoking and savoring. Jenny was riled. She seethed envy. I shouldn't be getting off on the idea as much as I was. Her arms still folded, she cast narrowed sideways glances at my closed bedroom door. I could've made it easy for her. Explained the situation, like minds and bodies, heartache and hurt. But why should I? She'd broken my heart first.

"If you're not drinking—"

"I'm not."

"Then I'm guessing it's someone you met at a meeting."

"Why are you so concerned with who I'm sleeping with?"

"I'm not." Jenny nodded at the burning cigarette. "Good to see you've quit that, too."

"I don't smoke around Aiden. And where I meet women is none of your business. How's Steve doing?"

"*Stephen*," she said, emphasizing the name, "and I just got back from vacation."

"With Aiden?"

"No. He stayed with my mom."

"How is your mother? She still hate me? It'd be nice if you mentioned when you are going out of town. It's called being considerate."

"Impromptu. Sorry. Couple nights at a B&B. And Stephen didn't have to take the job down here. He did that, at my urging, so you could see your son more."

"I'm sorry. Did I miss a child support payment? Scheduled visitation? Why are you so upset I am dating someone?"

"Dating?"

I tried not to smile.

"Don't smirk, Jay. It makes you look smug, and that's not a good look on you. And stop flattering yourself. If you want to rebound with a dope fiend drunk you met at AA—"

"Wow."

"Don't wow me. You know the shit storm you caused with your little phone call?"

"Yeah, about that. Been meaning to call you back. Been busy."

"Obviously."

"Not just with Amy."

"Amy." She repeated the name as though it were a ludicrous stripper's stage name, like Sugar or Destiny or Bubbles. "I don't give a shit what you and *Amy* are doing. I hope the two of you are very happy together. Enjoy your rebound . . . whatever. But you can't call *my* house and leave a message sounding cracked out, rambling about how we're all in danger and need to get out of town and stay hidden. Jesus, I defend you all the time. Do you know how pissed Stephen is?"

"I appreciate your 'defending' me. I've only known you since we were kids. But I don't give a fuck how pissed Stephen is. If he has an issue with me, he can come and talk to me himself, in person, like a man, instead of sending his wife."

"You sounded like a lunatic on that message. Psycho hunters trying to kill you? Lure you in the woods to assassinate you? If you weren't drunk—"

"I'm not drinking."

"I know. I can tell—but do you have any idea how hard it was to convince Stephen of that? Now, do you want to tell me what the hell is going on?"

I gestured to keep her voice down. It was still early, and the last thing I wanted was Amy walking out of that bedroom in the morning light for a showdown with my ex. Eliciting a little jealousy? Sure. A guilty pleasure. Separating a catfight was further down my to-do list for today. "Please. Sit. Keep it down. You want coffee?"

"No."

I nodded at the closed door. "Her sister is missing. Was missing. She asked me to help find her."

"Missing?"

"Not anymore. Turley called yesterday. They found her body way up in Chevreport. Broken neck."

"Dead?"

"That's what happens when you break your neck. Although in this case it looks like she'd been strangled first."

"How do you keep getting messed up in this shit?"

"This shit? Someone's sister died."

"That's not what I mean. Ever since Chris, I swear you seek out trouble. You want this. You yearn for drama, pain, tragedy."

"Yeah, I'm a glutton for punishment. I guess that's why you still have a key to my apartment."

I heard stirring in the bedroom and hopped up, hoping Jenny didn't hear the same. I hurried to her side, trying my best to usher her out of my kitchen, out the door, back to her car. "Give me a call later. We'll talk about it."

No one can rush Jenny Price. She wasn't going anywhere.

"I overreacted," I said. "About the hunters. Might've been stress, y'know, the PTSD." I hated leaning on that one, hanging all my sins on that catchall hook. "I'd forgotten my meds that day." Which was a lie. "Won't happen again."

But Jenny wasn't listening. She was looking at the open bedroom door, where Amy stood sheepish in one of my tees, long legs showing underneath. Amy had been attractive enough when I met her, but standing in my doorway, the gray day backlighting her all-but-naked body, the tousled, just-been-fucked-good hair, she never looked better. And, sure, it was petty, but Jenny, who was as pretty as pretty comes, was bundled up like Randy in *A Christmas Story*, not her sexy best, and for the first time in a long time, I savored having the upper hand with my ex-wife.

Jenny was right. My call had been bat-shit crazy. I'd admitted that again, with Amy standing there, in between the awkward intro, nonconfrontational hello, and quicker goodbye. Amy asked where the towels were so she could take a shower. I told her. Then I walked Jenny to her car.

We stood outside her new Mazda, courtesy of Stephen the investment banker.

"Was that Amy Lupus? From high school?"

I nodded, and waited for more snark, low blows about my choice in women, but instead Jenny stuck her hands in the pockets of her winter coat, panning over the garage, out to the fields of white.

"I'm sorry, Jay. I don't have any right. I'm the one who's remarried."

"No, I get it. It was unexpected."

"You deserve to be happy. You shouldn't be alone." When she turned back around, I saw the tears fill. "I . . ."

"What?"

"It hurts, okay? I know it shouldn't, and you can date whoever you want, but sometimes I forget, too. Sometimes I forget the years that have passed, don't remember it's not Jenny and Jay forever, like it's carved in a stupid tree by Silver Lake."

"It's still there, y'know."

"I'm sure."

"No, it's true. I was in Coal Creek. Few weeks ago. Had to pick up a dresser. Took a detour, drove down to the lake."

"In this cold?"

"Went for a walk. Sat on the banks. Skipped stones off the ice. Saw the tree. It's still there. We carved that heart deep."

Jenny wiped her eyes. "It's been a bad day. Stephen and I had a fight on the way back into town. Nothing to do with you. Not directly. At the house, I played the messages. My mother was dropping off Aiden. She didn't help the situation." She caught my eye. "You know I don't let anyone say a bad word about you to our son? No matter how furious you can make me. And believe me, I was fired up about the phone call."

"You should be. I wasn't thinking when I made it. I worry about you and Aiden. I jumped the gun."

"So, what did happen in those woods?"

"Nothing. A couple hunters had an accident. I was driving by at the wrong time. It was dark. My mind got away from me."

"I don't under—"

"Adam and Michael are back in town."

"The Lombardis? Really? Still?"

The weight she placed on the word "still" could've sunk a freighter on Lake Ontario.

"I said I overreacted. But Amy was looking for her sister, who was supposed to have checked into the Coos County Center, then Adam and Michael Lombardi are in town, and I find myself in the woods, and—"

"And what?"

"What I thought were monsters ended up being trees." I lifted my shirt to show the bandage. "Swung a knife in the dark. Hit the only man out there. Me."

Then Jenny did something I didn't expect. She threw her arms around my neck and held on tight. I let her. I didn't return the gesture. It didn't feel like that kind of moment. This was her needing to hold onto me, for whatever reason. I got the sense she didn't dare let go for fear I'd disappear. Through all the years, the lanes and the miles, being near her, smelling her skin through the layers of padded protection and self-erected walls, her touch still soothed. Jenny would always feel like home.

"Be careful," she said, letting go.

I wasn't sure if she was talking about the murder, my psyche, or Amy. Maybe it was all three. I didn't get a chance to ask. She got in her car, and drove away, leaving me in the swirling, kicked-up snows.

"So that was the infamous Jenny," Amy said when I'd walked back in the kitchen. Amy knew damn well who Jenny Price was. She'd said so several times. Three weeks ago, I couldn't pay a truck stop hooker for a sympathy handjob. Now I had two women fighting over me. Or maybe I was assigning weight that wasn't there. I *had* left a whackjob message on Jenny's machine, and if she'd fought with her husband because of it, I could understand her anger, which I might've conflated with envy. And no woman is going to feel comfortable around an ex-wife. Plus, Jenny and I had a kid together.

Any competition was short lived, as Amy, now dressed, wet, dark locks finger-combed back, asked if I had any coffee, before planting a soft kiss on my cheek.

I didn't want to talk about elephants in the room, Emily or the relapse. There was also a third unpleasant subject: that I might have put her boyfriend in the hospital. Amy was high as a kite during the takedown, barely conscious. Had she been cognizant enough to know there was even a fight? *A coma patient would've had a tough time sleeping through that noise.* Furniture was broken. Blood was shed. I didn't have a scratch on me. Not from the fight, at least. And she was here with me, so there was little doubt as to who won. She didn't bring it up. So, neither did I.

I waited till the pot brewed. Amy sat at the kitchen table. She bummed one of my cigarettes without asking. I wondered which she'd broach first: her sister being murdered or her having blown her sobriety. Not that the two were mutually exclusive.

Amy had taken a lot of pride in her clean date—any addict would—and now, like Emily, that accomplishment was gone. I didn't want that slip to spiral into a full-fledged relapse. I didn't want to make the same mistakes I'd made with Chris and Charlie. I searched for the right words of encouragement. I didn't get around to giving any pep talk because Amy cut me off before I had the chance.

"I didn't know what to do," she said, pretending to laugh it away. "It's not like I had to go far. Dan had gone out and copped before I asked. I know that sounds terrible, but I needed it. That's why he did it. I would've asked anyway. I know you don't think much of Dan—"

"The guy is a flaming turd. You're telling me, this whole year you've been clean, he's been getting blasted, right there, in your apartment?"

"I know it looks bad."

"It *is* bad."

"Jay, we're not like you. We're not coming up."

I made a show of panning around my dumpy apartment.

"You choose to live this way," she said. "Don't get me wrong. I understand. I can't go the nine-to-five route either."

"You can't go back to him."

"And what else am I supposed to do? Stay here?"

"If you want to stay sober? Yes."

"I sorta blew that last night."

"You'd just found out your sister died. That scumbag had the shit on him. No one is that strong. Let me help you."

"How's your ex-wife going to feel about that?"

"Jenny? Jenny doesn't have a say. Besides, she's married to some hotshot investment banker. Or annuity planner, whatever the fuck he does now. Doesn't matter. She's gone. There is no more Jenny and Jay. I'm my own man. I can see whomever I want."

"You want to date me?"

"If that's what you want to call it, sure. I want you here."

Amy placed a hand over mine, and then patted it with the other. Though the gesture was meant to be reassuring, I didn't feel reassured about anything.

CHAPTER SIXTEEN

I MADE AMY promise she'd rest up. I didn't have much food in the fridge but said I'd fix that on the way back, hit Hank Miller's grocery mart downstairs and stock up. I didn't want Amy leaving the apartment. Spend the day in bed, recoup. Let your body, spirit heal. Whatever you do, don't go back to that asshole. I told her I had work to get done but would be back early. Today was the last day left to deliver a shipment. Down south to Lake Winnipe-saukee and that asshole Owen Eaton, former competitor of my ex-boss Tom Gable. I was too bush league for Owen to view as a threat, and I did my best not to do business with the dirtbag—he'd swindled a company that was rightfully mine—but we'd worked out a nice deal on a chest of drawers and Wepner stool, and I needed the cash.

I hadn't been at my storage space twenty minutes, when I saw Turley pull up. I was in the middle of loading the dresser onto the back of the truck, straining my lumbar, bracing for more ball busting. Stay cool, I told myself. This is payback. You've spent the last several years drinking too much, acting like a jerk, being a pain in everyone's behind. Suck it up, buttercup. It takes a while to earn back trust. They preached it in the AA rooms all the time. But there was that other part of me still in there, the one with the short wick and loose wires, and he wasn't good at things like calm and patient. Sober or not—how much longer till he snapped?

"Those hunters," Turley said, ambling over. He slapped his police hat off his pant leg, swatting away snow. "The other night."

"The ones you told me I made up?" I jumped down. "What about them?"

Outside my shop, stacked cracked pallets and scattered milk crates replicated a homeless encampment. Moving blankets I hadn't brought inside had frozen over barrels and boxes into unholy, crooked angles. Turley glanced around the snowy, windswept alley. I waited for him to try giving me a citation for being messy and unorganized.

"Man, I have to get rolling," I said. "Got a tight schedule. I have to go way down to Lake W—"

"Describe 'em to me again."

"The hunters? What for?"

"Do it."

"Thought you said I was cracker-jacked."

"I didn't say you made anything up. I thought you might've had one of your episodes." He puffed up, before dropping shoulders in a mea culpa. "Okay. You're right. I thought you overreacted, panicked, heard a moose call and let your mind get the best of you. Would it help if I apologized?"

"Don't bother." I didn't add to the conversation I'd wondered the same.

He nodded up the road, in the direction of the Desmond Turnpike. "Fry cook. In Chevreport. Not far from where we found Emily Lupus' body, the Black Bear Den. Young kid, Matt something. Said he served a couple guys. Not long after your experience in the woods. The way he described one of the men . . ."

"What about him?"

"He said one of them looked like . . . Ferris Bueller. I remembered you said that the other day. About the baby face." Turley lowered his voice as if looking that young was scurrilous. "He had to card him. Guy was forty-seven."

"Name on the ID?"

"He couldn't remember. And of course, they paid cash. How about the other guy?"

"Told you. Never saw him. It was dark out there. Couldn't see my hand in front of my face. The first Carl said he was fat."

"The fry cook did say the one fella was . . . on the heavy side." Turley kneaded his chins.

I lit a cigarette, cupping a match to block out the wind. "Not to play devil's advocate, but why would he describe a guy I never saw so accurately?"

What's it matter if they planned to kill you, baby brother?

"Who knows how some men think, Jay?"

"Now you believe me?"

"Struck me as odd, is all."

"I appreciate you coming down here to tell me I'm not nuts."

"I never said you were nuts. Fish and Game checked the gate on the road leading up to Gillette Gorge. Still locked. If it was the same men, looks like them boys were headed for the Canadian border anyway. Next logical move from Chevreport if you're on the run. So you should be safe."

"Wonderful. If these two are headed for Canada, why do you care?"

"Emily Lupus was a resident of this town. It's my job to care."

"Good luck with that."

"I checked with the Coos County Center. Emily didn't sign herself out. They never admitted her. Didn't test positive for any drug. According to staff, Emily showed no signs of being an addict."

I'd suspected as much but didn't feel like bonding with Turley, who a couple days ago was ready to have me committed.

"Makes this whole thing harder to understand," he said. "Kid mixed up in the drug scene dies . . ." He didn't need to finish the sentence.

"Run a rape kit?"

Turley shook his head. "No signs of sexual abuse."

He shut it down after that, back to town sheriff unwilling to discuss an ongoing investigation, which didn't make me want to volunteer my thoughts on the subject either.

Turley tugged his furred brown hat back on, wiggled the belt around his belly, making ready to go. "I need to fax Canada everything I can on these two. I get a sketch, you willing to take a look?"

"Sure."

Maybe my call to Jenny wasn't so neurotic after all.

* * *

Despite assurances that the Carls were in Canada by now, Turley's news didn't leave me feeling too confident. He said he'd have a patrol car cruise my block. Even if Turley didn't see it, I felt the noose tying me to Emily tightening. People without drug and alcohol problems don't check into rehab. What had Emily hoped to find in the CCC? I mulled possibilities and the best I could come up with was she wanted to speak with another patient there. Rehabs are safe havens for criminals. Maybe someone with a piece of information about this poison in the ground.

Walk me through it, little brother. She tries to get admitted, go old-school undercover. When I dealt with Alison Rodgers and the abducted Crowder boy last year, I'd considered the same play. *Two killers named Carl?* Whatever their real names, someone didn't want Emily poking around. *I don't like it.*

I didn't like it either, but it was all I had. Otherwise I didn't see how those two topics, dirt and drugs, had a goddamn thing to do with each other.

No matter how much I needed the money, I didn't have time for the lake or Owen Eaton. I called to reschedule. I needed to press Amy harder. She must know something she wasn't telling me. Why was she hung up on this idea of her sister as fuck-up when everyone else painted Emily the exact opposite, a grindstone overachiever and straightedge wunderkind?

When I got back to my apartment, Amy lay curled on the couch, burritoed in a blanket, awake but dead-eyed, staring at a television that hadn't been turned on. She looked so shell-shocked and helpless. I plunked down beside her, and she curled into me like a wet, dewy kitten rescued from the rain. I tried to extrapolate these thoughts from my brain, wrap my tongue around the words, find a tactful way to ask these questions I needed to ask. Before I could get a word out, her head slid from my shoulder to my lap, hands searching me out. She started giving me head, and then we were fucking.

We hadn't even said hello. The need urgent, like desert plants in need of water sucking up every drop of moisture. Every thrust took us further away from present worries and concerns, which neither one of us wanted to deal with. No matter how much I tried to convince myself otherwise, I yearned for the escape every bit as much as she. I couldn't drink her in fast enough. I wish I could say the pursuit of truth took priority over escape. That's what beer was for me. A break, a respite, a vacation. In a weird way, being sober felt like being buzzed because it was the new normal, my baseline, which left me nowhere to go. Sex with Amy got me drunk. But the good kind of drunk, that euphoric buzz that lifts you up before the sadness slogs you down; those early seventeen-year-old drunks when you don't get angry or depressed but look up at the stars, amazed at how big and bright this place can be, overwhelmed by all the good things waiting for you.

Collapsing in gasping heaps, we didn't rest five minutes before we were at it again. I couldn't remember the last time I'd had sex like that. Usually when I'm done, I pass out. This was like being sixteen again, when a stiff wind could get me hard. As we went at it, our bodies in lockstep, the sensation transcendent, I felt the sickness, too, like the sex was a salve for infection, a balm to mask the burn.

By the time we'd wrapped up round two, which had lasted a lot longer than round one, we ordered Chinese for lunch. The Great Taste. Best Chinese food on all of Lamentation. Also the only place that delivered. Wasn't until I tipped the driver and asked Amy to grab plates that I realized: it was the first full sentence we'd exchanged since I'd come home. Even when we were ordering the food, she pointed at the menu items she wanted, silent. I made the call. Naked and exposed, we were safe; clothed, we were vulnerable.

"I saw Turley this morning," I said, ripping open the cellophane-stapled egg rolls. "I know this isn't easy to talk about—"

"Then why are you talking about it?"

Someone, or someones, had killed her little sister. I understood her reluctance to revisit the subject. Me? I'd want to pay back the hurt, regardless of who I hurt in the process, including myself. I wasn't going to lie and say my approach was healthier.

I twirled pork lo mein around my fork. Amy's face coiled in anger. I braced for her to lash out, which would've been fine. I'd take her outrage, be her crying shoulder, carry that stone. Let it out. Let it go. I was tough enough. Instead, she said nothing.

We both returned to poking at food neither of us wanted.

I didn't know if I was sitting next to my new roommate, girlfriend, or the sister of a murder victim in a crime I was trying to solve. Outside of the sex, which was very, very good—the best I'd ever had—there wasn't a lot of connection going on between us. I felt the distance growing. How could two bodies join in such harmony, two becoming one, not like mittens but like gloves, but we couldn't have a simple conversation when we were done? Getting her to talk about what was going on inside her, like excavating frozen tree roots from the tundra. For a second, I appreciated how hard it must've been for Jenny to deal with me.

Amy split a wonton, then dropped her utensils, making to get up from the table.

"Amy," I said, grabbing her wrist, easing her back down, using as much tact and sensitivity as I could, "we need to talk about your sister."

Amy shoved aside the dumplings she'd barely made a dent in. "No, Jay, we don't."

"I know it's hard—"

"I'm tired. I don't have the capacity right now. They found my sister with her neck broken. At the bottom of a cliff. They killed her."

"I know they did. I'm trying to find out who *they* are. I need your help."

"Why?"

"What do you mean *why*?"

"It's not your job. Let the cops figure it out."

"The cops up here don't solve shit."

"I can't help, okay? I didn't know my sister. Like, at all."

I could see the tears building, the fragile emotional dam I'd insisted on kicking about to burst, and I wished I could go back five minutes and keep my mouth shut. I didn't want to be anyone's sounding board. That's what a good man would do. Maybe I wasn't a good man.

"When she called to ask me to bring her to the CCC," Amy said, "it was the first time we'd spoken in ages. We don't have parents. For a long time, it was just her and me. Emily and Amy. But I fucked up. Started using. My baby sister followed my lousy example."

"She wasn't an addict."

"You don't know that."

"I do. Turley told me this morning. That's why Emily left the CCC. She didn't sign out against medical advice. They kicked her out. Because there were no drugs in her system."

"I've talked to the cops, too. What do you want me to say?"

I tried to stroke her hand, but she snatched it back.

"Finding out who did this isn't impossible," I said.

"You just said the police won't do anything."

"They won't. I will. I have a lead. There were two men seen at a restaurant the same night Emily . . . had her accident. Remember when you asked about my ribs the other day? I thought I'd had an episode. I have PTSD. From when my brother died."

"I know that," Amy said, bored with the obvious. "You've mentioned it. Several times. What's that got to do with Emily?"

I ached to explain the situation. How I'd found a knife at a house I was clearing. How I'd doubted my sanity for a moment, convinced myself I'd seen monsters in the forest and stabbed myself by mistake. I now knew I wasn't crazy. A fry cook had seen the two men, too—proof I didn't imagine the whole thing; I just had lousy aim. I'd been able to talk to Jenny. But I couldn't tell Amy any of this, even if the news directly related to her. It certainly concerned her more than it did my ex-wife.

"You don't think I know my sister was murdered?" she finally said. "If Emily wasn't using, who'd want her dead? If she was strung out, I could understand. Dealers and junkies, scumbags owing money, bad people doing bad things. This wasn't random. This wasn't rape. How do you expect to solve this? You clear junk for a living. How does that work? What does any of this have to do with you? Maybe everyone is right about you and you are crazy."

She's hurting, little brother. She's hurting . . .

"I'm looking into this, asking questions . . ."

"And what good is that going to do?"

"That's what I'm trying to find out. But I need your help, need you to think. Did she mention anything about dirt?"

"Dirt? On who? I told you! We hadn't spoken in years! I tried to make amends after straightening out. She wanted nothing to do with me! Then one day she calls out of the blue, says she has the same problem I do, wants me to bring her to rehab. How many ways can I tell you the same story?"

Amy stood, snatching my smokes, lighting one with a jittery hand. "I have to go."

"Where?"

"Back to my place."

"Dan? That asshole?"

"We live together. All my shit is there."

"Do you want to stay clean?"

"What difference does it make? I already fucked up."

"You go back there and all your hard work is gone. You think Emily would want that? Stay here. With me."

"You want me to move in with you?" She blurted a laugh. "Just like that?"

"What else are you going to do? You need to build yourself back up. How long you think your resolve will last with that temptation? I know it's not much, but . . . we can help each other."

"And how is your wife going to feel about your new living arrangement?"

"Jenny is not my wife." I came closer, took her hands, held firm. "If you need something from your apartment, let me go get it."

"I'm sure Hooch will love that."

"I can handle Dan."

"Oh, he's itching for the chance."

We hadn't talked about the fight. She'd been so dazed and confused I wasn't sure what she'd seen.

"I was half passed out," she admitted. "I didn't know how bad you fucked him up. Until we talked this morning."

"You talked to him?" This was the first time she'd mentioned they'd spoken.

"Of course we talked. He's my boyfriend. You got lucky last time. Hooch has a vicious temper. I've seen him break a man's arm over a pack of cigarettes."

"I can hold my own." I grabbed a red-letter bill off the table. "Write down what you need on the back of that envelope. I will get it for you."

"You don't have to do that."

"Yes. I do. Clothes, toothbrush, makeup, whatever. Give me a list. Let me worry about Dan."

Amy gnawed on her knuckle before relenting. I told her to dead-bolt the door and keep the lights low. She looked at me like I had two heads. As I clomped down the rickety well to my Chevy, I wondered if she were right.

I called Fisher from the road.

"Emily Lupus is dead."

"Tell me something I don't know. Read about it online. Fucked up. Where's her sister?"

"At my place. Been staying with me."

There was a long pause. "Dude, if you are hitting that, please tell me you're wrapped up."

"It's none of your business." I wasn't answering if I was "hitting that." But, yeah, intravenous drug use and communicable disease. I wasn't a fucking moron. "Your professor friend."

"Ostrowski."

"I talked to him. Drove up to White Mountain the other day."

"And?"

"And Emily got a job at the *Berlin Patch*. Must've made a helluva impression during her internship."

"Why are you so concerned about Emily Lupus? Little late, no?"

"I think the paper hired her based on her findings."

"What findings?"

"She was working on a piece about toxic soil in New Hampshire. A bunch of construction workers got sick, died. Emily didn't leave AMA. She didn't test positive for any drug. They tossed her out. I'm wondering—"

"I'll call you later," Fisher said, slamming down the phone.

Sorry to inconvenience you. Asshole. Why was I so concerned about Emily Lupus? Because she was dead. Murdered. And I didn't want to join her.

CHAPTER SEVENTEEN

DAN ACTED LIKE he was expecting me, beer in hand, smirk smeared on face, which was swollen from where I'd cracked it against the table. He looked like Frazier after Manila, eye puffy, bruised and battered. I'd handed his ass to him. Why so smug? I stalled a second in the hallway, wondering if he'd called over a bunch of buddies who waited in the shadows.

There was no one inside but Dan the Hooch. An untouched six-pack of beer, just taken out of the fridge, sat in the middle of the table, cans perspiring. Did this asshole think this was payback? Like I'd see a beer and fall to pieces? This was why I wasn't an addict. This was why I didn't have a problem.

"Good to see you again, Jay."

"You, too, Dan."

"It's Hooch. Remember?"

"Yeah. I do. Dan." I looked around the hovel. The place hadn't been neat the other day, but there was a woman living here. Without her presence, the apartment had dissolved into little more than a crack den. Dan's wares spread across the table, a surgeon with his self-anesthesia tools. Maybe that was the reason for his smarmy demeanor. He was lit up. Syringes and blackened glass stems. I understood now. Dan was a junkie, too, but while Amy was getting her shit together, he'd switched to pot and beer. With Emily dead, he had license to get them both back on smack. A momentary suspicion flashed, exiting as quick. Dan the Hooch wasn't driving to Chevreport to commit murder. I wasn't putting it past him. Morally, he'd be up for it. But dude was too incompetent to get away with it.

"Bitch's shit is over there." Dan pointed at a corner with a couple trash bags and a Tupperware container filled with makeup.

"That's a nice way to talk about your girlfriend."

"Hey, she's your problem now." He laughed. "I'll send you the bill."

I thought about coldcocking the sonofabitch again, he was begging me to, but by then I'd already started toward Amy's stuff. And what was the point? I didn't feel the ire I did the other day when I found her slumped in that ratty couch after her sister died. Dan was just another sad, pathetic loser. I felt sorry for him. Let him bang away at his scarred-over veins until he scored a bad batch and the State could dump his ass with the rest of the vagrants nobody claimed.

At the door, I reached for the knob and started to open it, when he came around and kicked it shut.

I dropped the bags. If he wanted to do this again, fine by me. I'd taken him down once. I'd do it again. He stood there, eyeing me.

"If you want to give me a kiss goodbye," I said. "Make it quick. I have places to be."

"You think you're the first, huh? You're something special? Gonna save her, eh, Jay the Junkman? That it? Rescue her from her big, bad boyfriend?"

"I don't think you're all that big, or that bad. I don't give a shit what you think, period."

"She'll be back."

"Let me make this clear. You go near Amy, and I'll stomp on your head till your eyes pop out or your skull caves in. Whichever comes first."

There was that smirk again. "I won't have to go to her, Jay the Junkman. She'll come to me." He looked over his shoulder, at the table littered with party favors. "I can offer things you can't, bro."

I nodded at his sink. "Go wash your dishes. Your place smells like shit." I motioned at the bathroom. "And take a shower. You smell like shit, too."

Sitting in my idling Chevy, I shook, rattled and furious. He hadn't gotten to me when I was inside, but now, alone, I had a tougher time. I toppled a couple pills and lit a cigarette, staring up at that dickwad's window, wondering why I hadn't kicked his ass a second time. There was a truck in the lot parked beside mine. Another Chevy. Same year, make, model, color. I knew it was his. How did a fuckwad like Dan the Hooch score a truck like that? Dealing. No other explanation. I was in the wrong business.

My cell buzzed. I was surprised to see Fisher's name after his abrupt hang-up.

"You got a pen and paper?"

"Why?"

"Get something to write with."

Up above, I caught Dan Hooch close the curtain.

"I found a pen. Now what?"

"Take down this name and number. Dude's name is Paul Grogan. The reporter Emily was working with at the *Berlin Patch*. Call him."

"Glad you care." I scribbled down the contact.

"I care, Porter. I want to help you. I just don't want to see you lose your mind over a dead end. And it doesn't get much deader than Emily Lupus. Sorry. That was a shit thing to say. Call Grogan. He's the one you need to talk to."

"How'd you find this out?"

"Don't worry about it. I have my sources."

"The last time I trusted a reporter, I got fucked over." During that kids-for-cash scandal, I'd trusted a journalist down in Concord, this turncoat weasel named Jim Case, who, along with my partner, Nicki, sold me out.

"You're the one who wants to pursue this. I'm giving you the reporter's name. I don't know if you're on to something or what, but Ostrowski was scared."

"Ostrowski? That's your source? I already talked to him. He didn't know anything. He was laid back, chill as fuck."

"He wasn't today. He was skittish. Something's spooked him good."

"Emily Lupus being murdered?"

"Maybe. Took me a good fifteen minutes for him to give up a name."

Ostrowski had sworn he didn't have this information. Why lie to me? "Anything else?"

"Yeah. Ostrowski said not to call him again. He was taking a sabbatical. Effective immediately."

* * *

Between dropped calls and no one answering, I decided the shortest distance between two points and my sanity was to pay Paul Grogan a visit in person. The drive to Berlin sludged along the cluttered Turnpike. An accident had diverted all northbound traffic into one lane, bogged down by the wintry slush that only grew worse the farther north you drove and closer to the border you got. I started to call Amy, then tried to send a text, but I couldn't think of what to say. Even a simple "Thinking of you" or "It's gonna be okay" rang false, and waiting in the bumper-to-bumper grind found me spending way too much time deliberating over which emoji to include.

By the time I made it up to Berlin, snow fell steady along the quiet Main Street. Parked in front of the *Patch* offices, I peered through the glass storefront counting three desks, two filing cabinets, and a coffeepot. On the opposite end, I could make out a closed door with a teeny window. The claustrophobic setup prompted flashbacks to one of the worst years of my life working corporate at NorthEastern Insurance, the terrible weekly jokes about "hump day" that never got funnier.

I'd spent a good chunk of time on the drive up thinking about the questions I wanted to ask Paul Grogan, how best to represent myself, which angle to take. Friend? Investigator? Concerned citizen? When I got to the front desk, I asked if I could speak with the reporter.

The old woman manning reception said nothing, shuffling back to the office. A moment later a man returned, grim-faced with languid eyes and a PBS telethon haircut.

"Paul Grogan?" I said.

"No," the man replied. "Mr. Grogan is no longer with the *Patch*."

I waited for a "What's this pertaining to?" Or "How may I help you?" But the man didn't say anything else, staring at me, though glowering was more like it.

"I was hoping to talk to him about a friend of mine. A former student interning—"

"Paul Grogan doesn't work here. We don't have any students interning." He pointed over my shoulder. "I think you should go."

"It was about a story—"

"We are a small paper. Under a tight deadline. We don't hire students. For the last time, Paul doesn't work here. Please leave before I call the police."

"Sorry?"

"Don't apologize. Go. You are trespassing. Leave." And when I didn't move fast enough, he spoke over his shoulder. "Sandy, can you get Bill Briggs on the horn?"

"Can you at least tell me how I can find him?"

He kept eyeballing me while barking at his secretary. "Sandy. Sheriff Briggs. Now."

What could I do? I wasn't hanging around for the cops to show up even if I hadn't done anything wrong. I hadn't had the best experience with local cops in shit-kicker towns.

Snow silhouetted beneath the daytime streetlamps, an odd contrast, sodium yellow carving slate gray, peppered with flecks of pure white. The passenger seat carried Amy's life, plastic bags stuffed with clothes, plastic bin full of eyeliner, nail files, and ChapStick. I sat far down the block, watching plumes of breath crystalize in the frigid cab. Up and down Berlin's tiny Main Street, no couples walked holding hands, no strays rummaged, the scene eerie as a ghost town.

When I first got sober, someone told me that stopping wasn't the hard part. It was that idle day at three p.m., somewhere down the line, when you had nothing better to do. You needed an answer to the question "why not?" Why not call the man? Why not stop off for just one beer?

There was a bar past the trestles. The neon sign read Berlin Station. Happy Hour 3–6. Maybe that's where everyone was in this godforsaken town.

I wasn't ready to go home. I needed answers. I tried calling Fisher to tell him about what happened at the *Patch* offices, but he didn't pick up. I got the impression he was ducking my calls. If I couldn't count on anyone else's help, I was on my own.

I hit the Desmond Turnpike, in search of Chevreport and the Black Bear Den.

Once Turley told me about the fry cook, I knew I'd be making this trip. Whatever happened in those woods, I hadn't invented the Carls, and this fry cook might've been the only other person to see them. At least who was still breathing.

The Black Bear Den, like the Olympic, never closed. Despite running through tiny mountain towns, the Desmond Turnpike enjoyed enough long-haul trucker traffic that keeping a restaurant open for twenty-four hours made sense.

By the time I got there it was almost dinnertime, the lot all but deserted. Didn't take long to locate the fry cook. The tiny tin car was about half the size of the Olympic. There were only two people in the place.

The fry cook, Matt Matusi, wasn't much older than Curtis G-Money the Grocery Bagger. Wasn't any bigger either. He looked ready to drop dead from another long shift, eyes rimmed raccoon black. Unlike Curtis, the sleeplessness stemmed from pulling double duty as cook and server, and not from taking the easy way out.

Matt shouted to the other guy at the end of the counter that he was going outside for a smoke. I didn't know if the other man worked there or was just a customer Matt trusted not to rob the till. Or maybe there was nothing to rob.

When we got outside, Matt fired up a cigarette. Under the restaurant lights, I saw he might be even younger than Curtis G., barely out of high school. And this was his fate.

"I ain't had a day off in two weeks," the kid said. "Only way I make rent." He nodded up the road. "Work part-time at one of the dealerships, detailing cars."

I could see why guys like Curtis Michaels and the Hooch opted to deal dope. At least there was a chance to get ahead.

"So, you want to talk about that girl who got killed?" He knew right away why I was there. Which shouldn't have been surprising. Not every day someone gets murdered in a small town like Chevreport. We used to be able to say the same thing about Ashton.

"You served a couple men just before—"

He looked over my work coat and big black boots. "You a cop?"

I didn't know why people kept asking me that. There was nothing about me that implied I was. Matt didn't wait for me to answer before he dropped his butt and pulled another kind of cigarette from his grease-splattered apron.

"Yeah," Matt continued, ducking past an old-fashioned payphone booth, around the corner, leaning against the big blue trash bin. "Weird dudes. You seen that old movie *Ferris Bueller's Day Off*?"

I held up a hand. I wasn't in the mood to talk about movies, especially with a kid who considered *Ferris Bueller* old. Besides, I knew it was the same guy. "Did they say anything—did you overhear anything? I'm trying to find where they might've gone."

Matt reached in his jeans pocket and passed along a matchbook.

"I'm good," I said.

He nodded down at the cover, unable to speak because he was holding his breath with a hearty toke. Then he exhaled, caught his wind. "The cover."

"Double Spruce Motel," I read.

"I think the fat one left that matchbook behind."

A snowplow lumbered up the Turnpike, pushing more accumulation into a bank.

"Why didn't you tell Turley?"

He looked confused.

"The cop you talked to?"

"Oh, yeah. That guy." Matt rolled his eyes. "Because I found it wedged in the booth after I talked to him, for one."

"How do you know another customer didn't leave it?"

Matt laughed. "Man, you seen inside. No one stops by here. Only reason I even carded the dude was because the fucking owner stopped by. Not that he helped do shit." He thumbed back. "This place'll be boarded up by spring, and I'll have to find another job. No, man, that matchbook belonged to them."

"You didn't think to let the cops know?"

"Know what?" Matt inhaled the rest of his roach, then dropped what was left into a bucket overflowing with snow.

"Nothing, Matt. Thanks for your time."

* * *

I knew where the Double Spruce was. It wasn't far down the Turnpike, about halfway back to Ashton. If Turley were right and the Carls were in Canada, I could cruise by, reassure myself everything was fine, go home. After Emily's murder, there'd be no reason for them to stick around. Then again, there hadn't been much reason to any of this.

Soon as I pulled in the lot, I saw the truck.

CHAPTER EIGHTEEN

Driving home, I called the station to tell Turley to send someone up to the Double Spruce, stat. That was their truck. I was certain. Well, pretty sure. It was at least worth the trip to check it out. Turley wasn't in the office. I left a message and marked it urgent.

When I got back to my place, Amy seemed in a better mood, stirring leftover hot and sour soup on the stovetop. I dropped her stuff by the door. She ladled out dinner. We were back to normal. Or whatever normal was for people like us. We even talked like regular people as we ate.

She told me I'd gotten a call on the landline. She hadn't meant to eavesdrop. I checked the message. My ex-wife was verifying what time she should drop off Aiden next weekend and if he'd be spending the night. It was a polite message, but I read between the lines. Aiden *always* stayed the night when it was my weekend. Jenny was hinting, none-too-subtle, that we might want to discuss who'd be around my son. Meaning Amy. No big deal. I'd call her later and we'd hash it out.

Amy and I hit the meeting at St. Paul's Church. I told Amy to head in, that I needed a moment alone. The snow had stopped, skies clear but bitter and cold, my eyes watering with each icy gust. The funny thing is, I wasn't *that* nervous. Just jumpy, tightly wound. My usual resting state. Jenny's call. The truck. I didn't even know for sure if that was the Carls' truck. Not like I'd memorized the license plate. I honestly couldn't even remember the make, model, or color from that night in the woods. No distinguishing characteristics other than the blue tarp. I didn't get close enough this time to see if the tarp was in the bed. Instead I'd done the right thing, headed home, called the cops. Didn't play hero. Didn't poke around the room. Let the authorities handle it. I was taking care of myself, hitting a meeting, still on the righteous path.

I went back to my truck and slipped a couple lorazepam, which performed as advertised, calming me down.

It was an okay meeting. Like the other night when I accepted my nine-month chip, I spoke. I'd probably done that half a dozen times, total, since I started coming to these meetings. Tonight, I talked in more general terms, about how life still got hard but it was easier without drinking. Which was sugarcoating but also true. I am not the world's greatest public speaker. Still, I stood up and shared, and I felt good about myself for doing that.

After the meeting ended, Amy milled. I courtesy-swilled coffee that tasted like ball sweat filtered through a gym sock.

This old guy came up to me, pinched face, sour expression, like he'd gotten a strong, unexpected whiff of a urinal cake while taking a piss. Most of the people who came to these meetings were older, the hard-core lifers. They didn't smile much, grumpy bastards. Who could blame them? A lot of them hadn't had a drink in fifty years. I'd be grumpy, too. I winced a smile. Surviving to sixty years old on this mountain earned a lifetime achievement award in my book. I thought he was coming over to say congratulations because I recognized him from the other night when I accepted my nine-month chip. Couldn't be sure. At a certain age, everyone up here adopts a similar visage, like split acorns found in the spring, cracked, hard surfaces decaying in soft, unexpected places.

He said, "I saw you in the parking lot."

"Cool." I didn't know what he was getting at.

"What was in the bottle?"

"Excuse me?"

"Before the meeting," he said, "I saw you go back to your truck."

"And?"

"And you were taking pills."

"So?"

"You know how many years I've been sober?"

"No." I spotted Amy across the room, waving me over. "However long it's been, good for you, man." I gave him a phony thumbs-up and started to walk away. The creepy acorn dude grabbed my arm.

"I was here last week when you accepted your birthday chip."

I pulled my arm away.

"What was in the bottle?"

Who did this dude think he was? The sobriety police? "Not that it's any of your business, but I have an anxiety disorder. I get panic attacks. My doctor wrote me a prescription. Happy?"

"Then you're not sober."

"What?"

"If you're taking pills, you're not sober, and you shouldn't say you are. It undermines the hard work of everyone who comes here to live a clean and sober life. You are still on drugs. You are not sober, and you shouldn't say you are clean." He waited. "Because you're not."

"Okay. Thanks." Appreciate the unsolicited advice. Now go fuck yourself.

I left with Amy.

When we got in the truck, she asked what was wrong. I said nothing.

* * *

Agitated was an emotion I was used to, my baseline. Wake up. Agitated. Pump gas behind the idiot who can't figure out which side of his car his tank is on. Agitated. The inconsiderate prick with twenty-eight items in the express lane. Pissed off. You get used to it. But over the last nine months, I had experienced a change. Not like I was suddenly happy-go-lucky, all sunshine and puppies and shit, but I'd begun feeling more positivity, or rather like I'd opened the door to the possibility of positivity. And a little light had begun creeping in. I owed a huge part of that to not crutching my emotions on beer. This morning my agitation was back, stronger than ever, returned with a vengeance, tenfold; I'm talking teeth-grinding, wanting-to-punch-a-hole-in-the-wall, enraged. And I knew why. That decayed acorn asshole at last night's meeting trying to undermine all *my* hard work. I hadn't been nice to him. But I didn't tell him to fuck off like I should have. The old Jay would've. The new Jay? Grinned, bent over, took it like a punk. What he said burrowed beneath my skin, feasting off me like a parasite.

The phone rang and I snatched it, not wanting to wake Amy.

"Jay. Turley."

"I know." Even without the caller ID, Turley had one of those voices, where it sounded like he was always battling a cold. I figured he was returning my call from last night, and was anxious to learn what he'd discovered. Best-case scenario, they'd caught the guys and he'd ask me to come down to the jailhouse for an ID. But that wasn't why he was calling.

"Can you account for your whereabouts last night? Around three a.m.?"

"Can I what? Account . . . for my whereabouts?"

"Yes. What were you doing?"

"Um, sleeping?"

I'd left the message to check out the Double Spruce last night before eight o'clock. By three a.m., I was long in bed. I expected a little blowback that I'd been up to the Black Bear asking questions. But that would be a minor transgression compared to what I'd discovered: the possible whereabouts of the two men who killed Emily Lupus, and who may've tried to do the same to me.

"Tomassi," Turley said. "The construction company." No question. Statement of fact.

"Bought Lombardi Construction. So what?"

"Security guard spotted a truck late last night. Around three a.m. Hanging outside the offices. The truck matched *your* description."

"Did you get my message about the Double Spruce?"

"Yes, Jay. I did. Don't even get me started on you playing investigator again, poking around the Black Bear."

"Nice way to thank me for doing your job."

"One, that kid fry cook's a pothead. I wouldn't trust his memory."

"It was good enough to ask for my help with a police sketch."

"I didn't ask for your help. I asked your opinion. A mistake I won't make again. And I sent a squad car to the Double Spruce. Not the same truck. Belonged to a seventy-year-old guy from Manitoba, down here ice fishing. I should send you the bill for wasting county resources and my men's time. But I won't. It's my own damn fault for listening to you. Now. I'll repeat. Three a.m. Can you account for your whereabouts?"

"Who the fuck can account for their whereabouts at three a.m. except meth addicts? This? This is why you are calling me, Turley?"

I rubbed a hard hand over my face. I needed to shave. I didn't mind the scruff but I was growing the same beard everyone up here had, wannabe lumberjacks who buy small-batch IPAs but can't change a tire. "Maybe it's early. Maybe I fucked too long last night and didn't get enough sleep. Dumb it down for me. Why on Earth would I want to break into Tomassi?"

"Because you know the Lombardis're in town. Because you know they partnered with Tomassi to build the CCC. Because you know Emily was researching Tomassi construction workers who got sick."

"How do you know that?" It was true but I didn't recall sharing that last bit with him.

"I'm the town sheriff. I'm not the dumb hick you think I am. I'd like you to come down to the station so we can talk about this. In person."

"I'm going to drop some knowledge on you. Fuck the Lombardis. Fuck Tomassi. Fuck you, too. I have to go to work. If you want to arrest me for something, I'll be at 612 Four Rod Road." I hung up the phone.

* * *

When someone dies and you move in to clear the house, there's no power. First thing relatives do is cut the power, water, too. Why pay utility bills for someone six feet under? I was operating by lantern, hauling chairs and headboards from the top floor to the U-Haul, and just my luck, this old house had one of those winding, wraparound, narrow staircases, adding an extra layer of pain in the ass to the situation. I often brought a portable radio with me because it can get quiet, leaving you with nothing but your thoughts, and this wasn't a day I wanted to be left with my thoughts. But I hadn't picked up new batteries for the radio. The only background noise: my own labored breathing and Ashton's wilderness wailing.

Despite his tough talk, Turley never showed up. Not only had I chased down a prospective lead, I'd done the right thing by calling the police with what I'd found. I didn't take matters into my own hands. Didn't play vigilante. And what had it gotten me? A breaking-and-entering charge. I wasn't canvassing construction offices or hopping fences into job sites. That was my brother. That was the old me. I wasn't drinking anymore. How about a little credit? The accusation was sobering all the same. I had to accept that, from now on, any time a crime was committed in these parts, authorities would round me up with the usual suspects. I was a Porter.

After the anger subsided and I started thinking with my head and not my heart, I began to view Turley's early-morning wake-up call from a different point of view. Inconsideration and short-changing aside, his reproach was actually good news. At least in terms of my investigation.

He said *Tomassi* workers had gotten sick. Up until then, I'd been operating under the auspices of the generic, nameless, all-inclusive "construction workers." Tomassi, along with Lombardi before them, built half the state. Not a big surprise. But Turley's comment sparked a chain reaction, brought me back to something Bowman, Lombardi's old head of security, said to me one night, long ago.

Bowman and I had a complicated relationship. Aside from him beating the shit out of me when we'd first met, clubbing me unconscious in my own apartment, we'd developed a rapport. At least I think that's what it was. After he fell out of favor with the brothers, he tried to do the right thing. Last year, he'd sent Joanne Crowder, Ethan's abused ex, my way because he knew I'd help her.

What I was thinking about now, though, went back further, to the kids-for-cash scandal four years ago.

Bowman had called me that night, asking to meet. We both knew the Lombardis were using Judge Roberts, jacking up bullshit possession charges on teenagers to justify building the Coos County Center. Like with the molestation accusation against their father, there wasn't enough evidence to go to the cops. There never would be. Adam and Michael were too well insulated.

The night I met with Bowman to talk about Judge Roberts, I'd still been hung up on the hard drive Chris found, how I'd let Gerry Lombardi walk. This was in the immediate aftermath, the raw cut of cowardice gouging deep. I now recalled Bowman's response.

"I don't know what the old man did or didn't do. But that wasn't what had Adam and Michael so worried. That hard drive your brother got his hands on contained something far worse."

"Far worse." His words. When I asked what he meant by that—what exactly was on that hard drive—he said he didn't know. I dropped it. Now I couldn't stop thinking about it. Adam had pulled out all the stops to get that hard drive back. I always assumed it was because of those pictures. A family as prominent as the Lombardis couldn't allow charges of pedophilia to reach the press. Except there wasn't anything conclusive. Any decent attorney would have the case tossed in preliminary. Still, people died. Not just Chris, but also his buddy Pete, too. If the photos weren't worth murdering for, what was?

Bowman's words haunted me, as chilling as a Lamentation nor'easter.

That wasn't what had Adam and Michael so worried. That hard drive your brother got his hands on contained something far worse.

Despite the dude being a 'roided-out gangbanger, in and out of prison, a legitimate sociopath, Bowman had a strange trustworthy quality about him. Call it honor among thieves. Bowman was a killer, and didn't bother denying it or expressing remorse; but it was a source of pride that he wouldn't cop to crimes he didn't commit. And despite his murderous tendencies, I wished I could talk to him right now. I felt like he was the missing link in all of this.

What had the brothers so worried? Surely the original hard drive had been destroyed by now. Hadn't it? What if Bowman was right? What if this feud between Adam and Michael and me was never about any kiddie porn pictures? What if that hard drive contained "something far worse"? What if Emily found out what that something was and it got her killed? I'd been fixated on this toxic soil business because it was the one part that didn't fit. That was because it *didn't* fit. One had nothing to do with the other. Like the name of Fisher's conspiracy rag, *Occam's Razor*, we were back to the most logical solution being the correct solution: that rehab. Whatever was on that hard drive had to relate to the CCC. Emily had gotten herself admitted to explore that lead. And it got her killed.

And if the men who strangled her were still hanging around, how long till I was next? An old man ice fishing, my ass. I didn't believe for one second Turley took my message seriously. He was all hung up on Adam, Michael, Tomassi, protecting their interests, their money. I doubted he sent anyone. His attitude toward me this morning left no doubt: drinking or not, my credibility with the guy was shot. If Turley wasn't going to do anything about it, I would.

I didn't see the truck this time, didn't see any cars in the Double Spruce lot. There was a little strip mall with a liquor store and fabric outlet next door, a few cars, enough that I could park my truck there and be less conspicuous. I climbed up the snowbank, over the metal railing dented by drivers who thought they were in control, walking across the lot to the Double Spruce motor court, to the same room where I'd seen the Carls' truck parked. The motel, like so many on the Turnpike, was one level, a handful of rooms, cheap, nothing fancy. Lingering by an icemaker in the subzero, day ending fast, I watched for motel guests, the owner, the Carls' truck pulling in. No one came or went.

I waited a while, then walked along the landing, peeking in the window to their room. The curtains were parted, room empty. I backtracked and knocked anyway, watching for movement. Nothing. I spotted a maid's cart outside a broom closet, by the soda machine, other side of the court. I casually made my way over, saw the big key ring dangling, and took the liberty. I returned it before anyone noticed it was gone.

Inside, the bed was made, floor vacuumed, no signs of guests. Maybe I had the wrong room? I pulled chest drawers, slid open end tables. Nothing beyond Gideon. Bathroom clean. No toothbrushes. Maybe Turley was telling the truth and I had the wrong truck. An old man from Manitoba had been ice fishing and was already headed home. Just as I was about to leave, I spotted a slip of paper under the chair.

Brittle, yellowed sheet, a scrap cribbed from a legal pad. Couple lines of text scribbled. It wasn't English. I didn't know what the hell it said. Looked Indian, all boxed letters, with big curly Qs and sharp square Ns. Made sense. A lot of these motels were owned by Indians. I heard the key fit the tumbler, and jammed the slip in my back pocket. There was nowhere for me to run or hide. I couldn't dive under the bed or get to the bathroom in time. The door pushed open.

A short, dark-skinned woman stood there, holding a stack of towels.

We stared at each other a moment.

"I'm looking for a friend of mine," I said. "Two friends of mine, actually. I was supposed to meet them here." It was the best I could come up with under the circumstances.

"Checked out," she said in broken English. "This morning."

"Two of them?"

The housekeeper gawked like she didn't understand. Before I could find a way to rephrase, she nodded. But I wasn't sure if she was confirming it had been two men, or she didn't know what else to do with a strange man standing in a room he had no business being in.

"Must've gotten the time wrong," I said, brushing past. "Sorry to bother you."

I hopped the railing to the strip mall next door, lost my balance, sliding down the dirty, icy embankment on my ass. I swiped away the snow and filth, and climbed in my truck. I'd chewed up a good chunk of day, accomplishing nothing. Between the house clearing, fending off charges of a B&E, and my fruitless trip to the Double Spruce, I never even got around to calling Jenny. I'd call when I got back to my place. It was petty of me, but I wanted Amy in the room when I did it. Present a unified front. If Amy was part of my life now, she'd be part of Aiden's, too.

I stopped for takeout. I'd written a note that morning saying not to bother making dinner. I'd take care of it. I ordered from Portofino's, which was the nicest restaurant in all of Ashton, splurging on eggplant parm and gnocchi in butter sauce, with a loaf of fresh, hot Italian bread. We had a lot to talk about.

It didn't strike me as peculiar that the lights were off. If she didn't have to make dinner, Amy was probably kicking it in the living room watching one of the thousand DVDs I owned or taking a nap. Didn't hit me when I opened the door and called her name and she didn't answer. Wasn't until I turned on the light and saw the note on the table in the bowl of fake fruit.

Felt like I'd read a version of this letter my entire life.

Dear Jay,

I've gone back to my boyfriend. Please don't come for me.

Amy

PS Thanks for everything you tried to do.

CHAPTER NINETEEN

CIGARETTE CLAMPED IN teeth, I raced the slick country roads into the center of Ashton fast as my Chevy could handle without flipping over. Why? Why go back to that piece of shit? He was a loser, a bum, a junkie. Amy had kicked her habit. She was doing well. *We* were doing well. Together. Her. Me. By going back to that scumbag, she was pissing away all the hard work she'd put in. She had to know that. One misstep didn't have to mean a head-first dive into ruin. She could come back from a slip; she wouldn't come back from this.

I bottom-fisted the apartment door, and Dan answered, greasy satisfaction smeared across his face. There was no surprise. He knew I'd come. Like he knew she'd return. And he was right about the reason why. At the time, I thought he was betting on him over me. I win that wager every hand. I wasn't a world-beating success but I bested that chump on my worst day. Her choice had nothing to do with either one of us.

Amy was sitting on the couch, like she'd been the other day, trainspotting into the cushions, slacked off but still awake. "Jay," she slurred. "I told you not to come."

I went after him, caught him like a linebacker on a blindside blitz, driving him back in to the sink, but he was ready this time, matadoring to the side, and flinging me into the fridge. We fought in the kitchen. I wish I could say I did as well as the other day. I didn't lose. But I didn't win either. We threw a couple punches but no one connected solid. We wrestled at close range, grappled, dropping to the floor, rolling on the grimy linoleum, using the limited space we had to hook each other's ribs, try to knee one other's balls, but there wasn't enough room to do any real damage, until Amy, suddenly coherent and alert, ran in the kitchen and split us up.

"Dan," she said, admonishing with a stern maternal tone. "Let me talk to him." The way she said "to him" laid out the new dynamic, the restored pecking order. I was the odd man out, the one who didn't belong, back on the bottom and out in the cold.

She guided us into the apartment hallway, the most privacy we could get, a musty common area clogged with cat dander and things that smelled cheap. She shut the door.

We stood in the hallway outside her place. The sound of a blender, a kid laughed, cat meowed. Maybe it was on the television. For a long time I stared at her. I searched for guilt, a sense of hesitation, apprehension, goddamn second-guessing, a hint of shame, but she couldn't even give me that.

"This is what I do, Jay," she said, matter-of-fact, like a marathon swimmer explaining how she dives into the frigid Atlantic every morning before dawn. "This is who I am." Predisposed to fate, destiny, no matter how bizarre it appeared to the outside world.

"You had a year. You were clean." I clenched my fists. "Don't do this!"

Amy shook her head, sad, slow, pathetic. "You don't understand heroin."

"I don't understand heroin? My brother was a junkie."

"No," she said in that same calm, measured tone. "Your brother did meth."

"He did anything you loaded in a needle."

"But not you. You drank. Beer. You can stop those things. Heroin? No one stops heroin. Once that shit gets its hooks in you, it's over. You might get a year. Maybe three. Heard rumors of guys stopping for five, ten. Never lasts. No one stops the opiates. Anyone who tells you otherwise is a goddamn liar."

"Bullshit. You had a year. You got your chip."

"You know where that chip is now?" She laughed. "When you get a year chip, you can trade it in to your local dealer for a free welcome-back bag."

I scoured that musty hallway, with its poor lighting and frayed carpet, searching out hope trapped between the threadbare and trampled. "We . . . we had something."

"We had sex, Jay. What did we ever talk about? Nothing. We filled the space in between fucking with eating and sleeping."

"It was more than that." I looked up and down the hall, the walls closing in on me, lowering my voice for no reason. "The best sex I ever had."

"Yeah, it was." This, too, she tossed off with all the enthusiasm of winning honorable mention in a third-grade science fair. Not that she was lying. She seemed to mean it. But it also didn't seem to mean all that much.

"Is this even about me?" she said.

How could I answer that? What kind of question was that? Was it about her? I was trying to do something good. Help. I was doing the right thing. We were getting better. Together.

Amy reached out and touched my face. "You're a sweet guy, Jay. And I like you. Hell, maybe I could've loved you." She nodded back through the closed door. "But I love something more."

"Dan the Hooch? You're shitting me, right?"

"I'm not talking about Dan."

It took a moment.

She leaned over and kissed me.

"And no matter how good the sex was? You're still in love with your wife."

"Ex-wife."

"Can I give you some advice about women?"

What do you say when a person asks you a question like that?

"I haven't been in love with my boyfriend for a long time." She held up a hand. "Don't look at me like that is the saddest thing you've ever heard. Most relationships are like that. The fire burns out. You stay together because you don't want to be alone. It's not tragic. Dan has his good qualities, too."

"I'll take your word for it."

"That's not my point."

"What is?"

"I saw the look in Jenny's eyes when she was near you. I don't care who she's married to. I don't care how much money he makes. That woman is still in love with you."

She grabbed my hand and gave it a tight squeeze, before pushing off to get rid of the unwanted solicitor. "It's too late for me. But it's not for you."

She dropped my hand, opened the door to her apartment, and returned inside, shutting me out.

* * *

My friend Charlie and I used to like watching movies together. Old movies because most of the new ones suck. *Rocky* was a favorite. That was the film he had on loop when I found him dead in his chair, clutching a glass of vomit. But it was another movie we both loved that I was thinking about now, *Casablanca*, the scene where Ilsa comes back to Rick after the missing years, and tries to tell him a story, but he says he's heard it before; it's the one about a guy left standing on a station platform in the rain with a comical look on his face because his insides have been kicked out. That's how I felt. Only instead of standing on a rainy platform station on the brink of war, I was sitting in my truck, looking up at the dirty lights of a junkie's apartment. I didn't lose out to Victor Laszlo, leader of the resistance, a hero trying to liberate the world from an oppressive Nazi regime. I lost out to a piece of shit who made up his own nickname. I lost out to dope smuggled up somebody's ass, a syringe, a wad of torn cigarette filter. And unlike Rick, I didn't have the bottle to numb my pain.

A pair of high beams flashed at me from the street and I heard a truck engine rev. My heart seized, gripped in anticipation. The motor roared, tires squealing, lights locked on me. Pinned between a big trash compactor and the Hooch's truck, I was gripped by fear, unable to react . . .

Then the headlights fanned up the road, and whoever it was drove off in the other direction. I searched the center console for my pills. Empty. Padded down my coat. Nothing. I jammed it into gear, reversed, K-turned, spinning onto the wintry roadway, chasing after the truck.

Where are you going, little brother? You're tweaking . . .

Wasn't on the road a minute before the blues and reds flashed.

The squad car rolled up behind me, and out came Turley, hitching up his giddy, furry brown cap cradling apple cheeks, strutting along with his new slimmed-down figure, which still cast a wide shadow. Didn't matter if Turley dropped another forty pounds, he'd still be a fat fuck. I'd known the guy forever, but still he felt the need to pull the flashlight, holding it sideways in that special way cops do, like inner-city gangstas and a Glock. I shielded my face from the light. Using his other pudgy fist, he gestured for me to roll down my window.

I waited for him to read whatever riot was on tonight's docket so I could tell him to fuck off. But his irritation waned to empathetic. "You okay, Jay?"

"I'm fine."

"Have you been crying? Your eyes are all red."

"I haven't been crying. It's cold as shit out here. The wind makes your eyes water. What do you want? You following me now?"

"I thought I told you to come down to the station."

"Yeah. Like ten hours ago. And I told you no."

"We can do this the easy way—"

"Or the hard way? Seriously? How about we play good cop and fat cop first?"

"Jesus, Jay. Follow me to the station, okay? I'm gonna drive on ahead, and you're going to follow me back to the precinct. It's cold as a witch's tit out here. We have to talk." He looked out over his town, sporadic houselights flicking on and off through the blustering snows. "I'm getting in my car. I expect to see you on my tail. If you want, I can flip around and chase you down, follow you back to your place, wake up poor ol' Hank Miller. You want to do that to the old guy? What's the point?"

I flicked him off, whatever. I waited for him to pull ahead and followed him to the police station. Not like I had anywhere else to be.

*　*　*

We sat in the interrogation room. Turley brought out his little tape recorder and hit the big red button. And I can admit what I did next was childish and immature, but I don't regret for one second backhanding the thing and smashing it against the wall. Nor do I deny the joy elicited in watching the cheap, plastic, made-in-China piece-of-shit shatter into a million little pieces. I might've laughed.

Which would've been funnier if I got Turley's goat, but I didn't elicit the slightest rise out of him. He shook his head. Which made me feel worse. Because nothing I did surprised him anymore. My antics commonplace, juvenile behavior expected, I'd succumbed to a horrible fate: I was predictable.

Brother, it hits you hard when there's no one left to let down because no one believes in you anymore.

I longed for confrontation. Let me rail against something, seethe against injustice. To rebel you need opposition. No one was fighting back. I wasn't worth the effort.

"Fine, we can do it your way." Turley pulled his notepad from his breast pocket. "So, you don't have an alibi for last night between the hours of three and four a.m.?"

"Nope. Not anymore."

He didn't pick up on the "not anymore," the implication of my newly single status. Although I realized by this point I had never been more than a momentary distraction for Amy, dick substituted for drugs.

"Are you still investigating the disappearance and murder of Emily Lupus?"

"No." I had no interest in sharing my latest theory, not now, not with Turley or anyone else. "And I'm not sleeping with her sister either. She just broke up with me."

Turley winced as though he prepared to say something sympathetic, but I glared through a narrow-eyed stare. Getting dumped by a junkie was enough humiliation for one night.

"A truck matching yours was spotted leaving the Tomassi headquarters last night."

"Yeah. You told me that already. Truck matching my description? Like everyone in this hillbilly town doesn't drive a truck." I nodded backwards. "That apartment, with that scumbag junkie, Dan? He drives the same truck as me. Remember those two hunters? Geez, they had a truck. And weren't you looking at them for murder?"

"I never said they were suspects. I'm looking for people of interest—"

"But you couldn't be bothered to check out a lead I gave you? I told you I spotted their truck at the Double Spruce. Did you even send anyone to the motel?"

"I'll do my job, you stick to clearing out garbage, and we'll be fine."

"You know what your problem is, Turley?"

"Yeah. I do. I keep giving you a break. Keep giving you the benefit of the doubt. I keep thinking that the old Jay is going to bounce back, that it's been a streak of bad luck, bad breaks, a bad run, misfortunes, and just when it looks like you might prove me right, you go and screw the pooch."

"Why would I break into a fucking construction office?"

"Why do you do anything you do? I've given up trying to guess. But I can tell you this. When something goes wrong in this town, whenever there's a problem, some messed-up, nutted pain in my behind, it always leads back to you."

"Eat shit, Turley. I told you. I was sleeping. I don't have a time-stamped photograph to prove it. I'm glad I'm your go-to guy when shit goes wrong, but if all you have is 'someone saw a truck,' I think I'm free to go. It's been a rotten day. I'd like to sleep."

"I'm not done."

"Are you arresting me?"

"I want to talk."

"I watch a lot of cop shows. If you are not arresting me, I'm free to go."

"I am asking you as an informal request."

"And I am telling you to take your informal request and shove it up your fat, flabby, pasty-white ass. I am not investigating jack. I clear estates, full-time. All I do, man. It's who I am. It's what I do. I'm a junkman, a scavenger."

Turley slapped closed his little pad. "Good. Now, next time someone asks you to find something—I don't care if it's a missing dog or a pack of bubble gum—I want you to tell them the same thing."

I gave him a thumbs-up and flashed a phony grin, then got to my feet, kicked aside the chair, and stalked out the precinct door.

The drive back to my empty apartment along deserted, iced-over streets delivered me to a colder, emptier apartment.

I never much liked my cat. We didn't get along. She ran away last year. For the first time, I missed that fat fluffball. I longed to touch something warm and alive inside, something with a beating heart. Instead I lit a cigarette, watching my wrath frost in front of me because I couldn't afford to keep my apartment heated.

CHAPTER TWENTY

"OH FOR FUCK'S sake! Like last night wasn't bad enough. Jesus Christ, Turley, what?! What now? What horseshit jackoff rancher's shack got broken into this time? Did someone set a hobo on fire? Kick a cat? Hurt a kid's feelings? What? What could be so goddamn important that the first thing I have to see when I wake up is your ugly mug?"

I was worked up, unsettled by the lack of sleep, furious at the harassment. But the second I finished my harangue and saw the expression on Turley's face, I knew what was coming next, a feeling in my gut, déjà vu replayed a tick too quick, a glitch in the Matrix.

"Can I come in?" Turley's tone cemented the bad news.

"Sorry, Turley. I didn't mean . . . yeah, sure. I didn't sleep much."

Turley walked in, sheriff's hat folded over chest in memoriam.

"You want coffee or something?" I didn't want him to say it. If I could hold him off, he couldn't say it, and if he couldn't say it, then it wasn't real. Until he said it, it wasn't real. "How are things down at the station? Sorry for yelling at you. I don't sleep so good and, man, I've had a lot—"

"Jay, Amy Lupus overdosed last night. She's dead. So is her boyfriend. Thought you should hear it from me."

I stopped short of the coffeemaker and dropped in the chair. I turned over my shoulder, at my unmade bed, where Amy lay less than twenty-four hours earlier. I hadn't known her that long.

There was no deeper, spiritual connection between us. Like she said, it was sex. It was never about her or what she could offer. It was all about me, what was lacking inside, the holes she filled. I could still smell her scent on the sheets when I went to bed last night. I cradled my head, swept back my long hair—long for me—and forced a laugh.

"That must be a record, Turley. Going from dumped to dead in less than twelve hours."

Turley glanced at the front door, which was open. He'd closed it but not all the way. Now the harsh winds breaching the seals had swung the door wide. I could tell he wanted out of my depressing little one-bedroom above a gas station. *When you hit rock bottom, keep digging.* No one wants to watch a man till his own grave. But he sat at the table with me. "There's nothing you could've done."

Outside the window in the stairwell, the tips of Lamentation loomed, glacial peaks teetering on the shelf, bordering on avalanche. I got up, slammed the door shut, lit a smoke off the stove.

"I know I've been rough on you," he said. "Shit, I don't know how to act around you anymore. I try to be your friend. I try to be an authority. Ride you hard, give you a break, play it tough, take it easy. I want to help. Nothing I do seems to work. Nothing I do seems to lighten your load."

"It's not your job to 'lighten my load.'"

"I feel bad for you."

"Don't."

"Don't what?"

"Pity me. I hate that shit. Insult me, accuse me, bust my balls. But don't say anything nice to me right now, okay? Please. I'm serious. I don't want to hear anything nice or kind or decent or sympathetic."

Turley stared, perplexed, which was the response any sane person would have to such a bizarre request. It's human nature to want to soothe others in times of tragedy. I couldn't explain that, for me, in such moments kindness was cruel. Moments like this I longed to be kicked, punched, ridiculed, rejected. When I hurt, I wanted to hurt worse. I could deal with the pain and sorrow. Ankle deep in the cesspool, I braced to battle an enemy. But once another human being showed me an ounce of compassion, I'd lose it. I didn't want to lose it now. No man should ever cry in front of another man. I turned away, got it together, changed the focus fast as I could.

"What happened?" I asked.

"She just started back up, right? My guess? She injected what she was used to. Was too much."

"Who called it in?" I asked. "Found the body?"

"Neighbor."

"Which neighbor?"

"Not sure. Claire answered the phone. Whoever it was didn't leave a name. Maybe another junkie pal had been there and didn't want to stick around?"

I was at their place late. They were already getting high, alone. That wasn't a complex where neighbors come knocking on doors to borrow butter.

I'd spoken with Amy, and she'd perked right up for our conversation. Dan the Hooch and I fought, and he'd held his own. I remembered the truck in the road and the high beams, the sensation that it aimed to drive straight into me. Out of time, place, the scene wrong.

I hung my head, thanked Turley for coming by, reassured him I'd be okay. I said I was going to hit a meeting. I created the sketch of a grieving ex-boyfriend who'd just found out his girlfriend died. I sprinkled in the requisite amount of sorrow, worked through the five stages of grief in under sixty. I might've glossed over anger. I had enough of that particular emotion on tap to last a lifetime.

Worked as fast as I could to get Turley feeling good about himself and out the door.

Once I heard Turley hoofing down the steps, I grabbed my landline. Fisher picked up after several rings.

"Stopped by the *Patch* last night. Paul Grogan is no longer with the paper."

"People quit jobs, Porter."

"Didn't sound like a harmonious split. I basically got tossed on my ass and threatened with the cops."

"So?"

"You want to take a ride with me?"

"Not really."

"You still at your mom's house?"

"Yeah. I am. But you're not listening. I'm busy."

"Fine. But can you do me a favor? Find out where Paul Grogan lives. I've checked the Internet. Looks like he had a house in Berlin but he sold that before he got canned. Or quit. Or whatever the hell happened. Can you do that for me? Or is that too much to ask?"

"Give me twenty."

I'd have a tough time remembering where Fisher's mom lived anyway. It had been fifteen years since I'd been there, a one-off with Charlie, picking up the runt for a party by the lake. If Charlie were alive, he'd be making this trip with me. But most of my friends were dying or already dead, so I had to work with what I had.

Twenty minutes later, Fisher rang back. He gave me an address, which wasn't in Berlin, already a trek from Ashton, but west, over state lines into Vermont and the tiny outpost of Fish Creek Hollow. I'd fetched an armoire there once, long time ago. The Hollow, as it was called, had a filling station that closed at noon and a lot of small, cheap houses dotting a dark basin.

"How did you find him?"

"That's why you called me," Fisher said. "I have access to information you don't."

"Meaning?"

"Meaning I can use the Internet. The address is for his aunt. She died years ago. House never changed hands. I found a forwarding contact through Social Security. Couple other resources. Mail, credit cards. Grogan had an apartment in Berlin, too. But that's already listed as vacant."

"Why have a house and an apartment?"

"Maybe he was boning the secretary on the side. How the fuck should I know? Looks like he's been at Fish Creek the past couple weeks. Can't guarantee it, but I'm banking you'll find him there if he's on the down low."

"You found all that out in the twenty minutes?"

"I'm good with computers."

"What else do you know about Paul Grogan?"

"Not much. Been with the *Patch* for ages, small-time reporter, small-time paper. And that Emily Lupus had been assigned to him."

"To head an investigative piece on contaminated soil. How does dirt get someone murdered?"

"Beats me. Maybe someone built a mall on an ancient Indian burial ground. You keep asking me questions, man . . ."

But I wasn't asking the questions for his benefit. I was working out the puzzle in my head, answers coming to me faster than I anticipated, quicker than I could reassemble.

"I told you," Fisher said. "I was in the middle of something. I don't have time—"

"What? That crazy newspaper of yours?" Before he could answer, I cut him off. "You know what? I don't care what you're doing for work. I'm driving out to talk to Grogan. It'd be nice if you could be bothered to come along." At 5'1", Fisher would be useless in a fight, but for once I wouldn't mind his company; I didn't want to be alone.

"No offense, man. I don't feel like getting sucked into another Jay Porter mystery. Especially when it's not for you; it's for your girlfriend."

"One, she's not my girlfriend. And, two, she's dead."

"What?"

"Overdosed. Last night. After she left me and went back to her scumbag boyfriend. Turley just left."

"When?"

"I told you. This morning. Right before I called you."

"Kinda burying the lede, Porter."

"I don't think the overdose was an accident."

"Suicide?"

I let my silence answer that one.

"Murder? Why would someone want to kill a junkie? I know you were sleeping with her—"

"Nothing about this adds up." I said it aloud, but by this point, I was done with the give-and-take portion of the conversation. "Emily's working on a story about tainted soil. Then checks into rehab with a drug problem she doesn't have—"

"Doesn't matter. It's not like Amy was in on it. You told me yourself the sisters didn't speak much."

"It's called covering your tracks."

"Then why are you still here?"

"Good question. That's what I'm going to find out."

Fisher stammered, stumbling over what he wanted to say next. "What?"

"I don't know, man, but that was your girlfriend. The way you're acting—"

"How am I acting?"

"Like her death isn't affecting you."

"Don't worry about how I grieve. Thanks for the info. Have a nice day." I jammed receiver and cradle together.

Given the circumstances, Amy's and Emily's deaths, the heightened alert of Dr. Ostrowski, the Carls hanging around, Grogan vacating his own house for the secret confines of Fish Creek Hollow, I didn't know how happy the reporter would be to see me. I was guessing not very. Could've been he'd grown weary of the newspaper game. Or perhaps a heavier hand forced him out.

* * *

Fish Creek Hollow sat at the bottom of the holler. Rusting farm equipment and bucolic wasteland, copse and countryside, felled electric fences and abandoned barns whose roofs had collapsed under the weight of too much snow. When I left my apartment, the skies almost threatened to break through with a hint of silver sunlight. At the bottom of the basin, everything was darker. Towering evergreens cast shadows from taller mountaintops. Even when it was out, the sun didn't shine here, the valley bottom permanently shrouded in fog. I pulled up the long gravel drive but didn't get out right away.

What are you waiting for?

There were no lights on in the house, blinds and curtain drawn, buckshot holes in the mailbox.

Someone peeked out the edge of a drape.

CHAPTER TWENTY-ONE

I WAITED LONG enough for whoever was inside to grab a shotgun, kick open the door, and start blasting. You never could be too careful. Folks up here treated the whole "Live Free or Die" license plate mantra as gospel.

The curtain fell closed.

Baby brother?

"Let's go," I said under my breath. "Keep it slow and steady. Hands out and up."

Dude, what are you worried about? You are getting more and more sketched . . .

Grogan looked well beyond retirement age. He didn't kick open anything. He turned the handle like a kindly grandpa, letting the door fall inward, standing statue still, aiming a thirty ought six Springfield at my head.

"That," I whispered, "is what I'm worried about."

Leaving the *Berlin Patch* meant one of two things. Either longtime, well-respected reporter Paul Grogan had fallen from grace with the paper, or he'd seen the handwriting on the wall and decided to get the fuck out of Dodge. Neither of those options made me feel good.

"Mr. Grogan?" I said, showing my hands, walking forward cautiously. "I'm a friend of Emily Lupus. I was hoping for a minute of your time."

Maybe his willingness to take a flyer on a stranger owed to journalistic intuition, a successful career mined from trusting his gut and an innate ability to differentiate between a threat and whom you could trust. More than likely, as anyone with at least 20/40 vision could attest, Grogan saw a backwater country boy in over his head.

A grizzled Eastwood-type, Grogan waved me into his little cottage, which resembled a safe house in its minimalism. Not much furniture, and what remained was dust-covered and ancient. Tiny desk. A laptop. For files, I assumed, since the World Wide Web didn't include Fish Creek Hollow. Closet without a door. Some bread and peanut butter on the counter. The essentials.

"What can I do for you, son?" he asked, setting aside the rifle but keeping it within arm's reach. He knew why I was here, and calling me son felt like a slight.

He didn't offer me a place to sit because there wasn't one. But his eyes betrayed him.

Far from hostility, I saw gratitude. This wasn't a frontier cowboy looking to shoot an intruder or even a lonely old man relieved to get company; this was a tired soldier dying to be freed of the burden.

"I'd like to speak to you about Emily Lupus."

"So you say."

"You know her?"

Grogan nodded. "Emily had been sent to me on an internship from White Mountain Community. The newspaper takes on exceptional students, puts them to work on special projects."

"Can you tell me what this 'special project' was?"

Paul Grogan, seasoned, retired vet of the *Berlin Patch*, scratched his three-day white stubble. Sources and confidentiality. Maybe I pegged him wrong and he was going to pretend the *Patch* mattered, as if prematurely revealing the Queen of the Winter Bazaar violated professional ethics.

"Why are you here?" he said.

"Emily's missing. I'm trying to find her."

"You don't look like a cop. And you don't look like a leg breaker."

I tried not to take that personal. I'm not a small dude.

"And I already know Emily's gone. Gone, as in dead, not misplaced. So don't yank my chain, son."

"You heard about what happened to her?"

Grogan nodded. "She was a good kid, a sweet kid. She didn't deserve this." He tapped a miniature pyramid paperweight on his little desk that read "Reporter of the Year, 2004," before scanning his cramped office, still unsure whether more men waited for the cue to burst in. "How'd you find me?"

"Are you trying not to be found?"

Grogan stared but did not answer.

"My name's Jay Porter. I'm a friend of Emily's sister, Amy. I mean, I *was* friends with her sister. Amy is dead, too. Last night. Overdose. Emily's death wasn't an accident. I don't think Amy's was either. Someone slipped her a hotshot to shut her up. Cops don't suspect foul play. Amy was a junkie. The police know Emily was murdered, but I don't expect them to solve jack. The cops on Lamentation Mountain are a joke. They'll chalk up her death to the local drug scene because of her sister. They are too lazy to put in the legwork to uncover the truth. I think both sisters died because of what Emily was working on. With you. And since I'm now involved, I've put my own life at risk. And that of my family." I didn't add the more complicated parts about divorce and visitation rights. I pegged Paul Grogan as a straight shooter, a man's man. Just the facts.

I thought I'd done a good job laying out what was what. Direct, to the point. I'd enunciated, didn't rush or mumble. I spoke in a calm, measured voice. Clearly, what I heard in my head wasn't what he heard. Grogan's eyes cast suspicion, caution, confusion. I patted my pockets for the pills, coming up empty.

"Dirt," I said, pressing the issue, adding the key detail I'd omitted. "The rehab? The Coos County Center. Tomassi. Lombardi. Why was she there? Emily. Professors are running scared. Something's not right, man."

Grogan pulled back, forehead furrowed in response to my increasing mania, which filled me with escalating urgency. I felt another panic attack overtaking me as they so often did, blindsiding me at the worst possible times. I fought to stay clear-headed. This guy had what I needed, I was sure of it.

Pull it together, little brother.

"What I can't understand, Mr. Grogan," I continued without prompt, "is why Emily would check herself into rehab if she didn't have a drug problem. What does the Coos County Center have to do with toxic soil?"

He didn't get the chance to answer.

"The TC Truck Stop," I whispered.

Grogan knitted together his thick, bristled, old-man brows. "Entire site is poisoned."

How many years had that massive travel center been in operation? Giant tankers, rumbling off the Turnpike, on tight schedules to pump thousands of gallons a day. You get one hose not sealed properly, one thread not lined up, the fuel is going to leak, spill, gush, saturate the earth. Then there's the rust, cracks in the storage tanks, corrosion, defective equipment, eruptions in pipelines. We're talking decades of gasoline and diesel and God-knows-what-else seeping deep beneath the tarmac, festering underground, burbling out of the bedrock.

Grogan spun around to his mini filing chest, one of those portable black ones you can pick up at superstores or the Salvation

Army. He brought back a folder. "Emily was researching fast-acting cancers and pulmonary disease. I believe the property was contaminated from the get-go and that, furthermore, Tomassi knew about it."

I remembered that nice nurse, Ann, from the night I swung at a phantom in the forest, knifing my own gut. Maybe I didn't have such lousy aim after all. The answer had been there the entire time, right in front of my face. Or under my feet.

"Twelve documented cases of cancers, tumors, myelofibrosis." Grogan relaxed his posture, guard coming down. "Those fossil fuels are more toxic than lighter fluid. The Coos County Center was built atop a mound of noxious chemicals."

"You're saying Emily got herself admitted to go undercover?"

Paul Grogan looked about the room, still uneasy, before consenting, validating the recklessness. "It was her idea. I should've stopped her. I didn't think anything would come of it. I grew up in the era of gonzo journalism, the '60s, Woodward and Bernstein, Hunter S. I thought the experience alone would be worthwhile. At the time, I didn't understand how far this conspiracy reached. I didn't think anyone inside the rehab would be the wiser. Emily was a smart girl. I didn't fully appreciate the stakes. I never expected her to be hunted down."

"Hunted down?"

"Few weeks ago, I get a panicked call from Emily. Late. I couldn't understand what she was saying. The connection was bad. Wind. Static. I caught every other word. She wasn't in the hospital anymore. They threw her out in the middle of the night and didn't give her back her cell. She was using a pay phone at some restaurant. She'd hitched a ride far up the Turnpike. She was scared, running. I said I'd come get her. She said her sister was closer and that she would call me right back. But they got her first."

"Who's they?"

"That's the million-dollar question." Grogan threw up his hands. "I never heard from her again. I didn't spearhead this. This was Emily's baby. I'm an old man. A couple years left, I was mailing it in. Until she got assigned to me. I liked seeing her passion, reminded me of being young again. After she went missing, I started taking her claims more seriously, did some hard research of my own."

He passed me a file. I peeled the cover. Financial statements, portfolios, insurance documents. I recognized them from my brief stint at NE Insurance. Structured settlements. Annuities.

"That's when I started seeing things," Grogan said. "Cars outside my work, my apartment, watching me. Part of why I accepted this forced retirement without a fight, came out here, where I thought I couldn't be found." He eyeballed me.

"Emily never called her sister that night either," I said. "Whoever *they* were"—and I had a good idea who that was by now—"must've gotten to her first."

When the authorities found Emily's body, she'd been dead for a few days. She was MIA for three weeks. What had they done with her in between? She'd been kept alive for a while. The coroner ruled out sexual assault. Had they tortured her first? Was that why they dropped her from forty feet? Add new bruises to cover the old ones? I nodded at his little desk, this outpost Paul Grogan had been exiled to. "When did you move out here?"

"After someone broke into my apartment."

"You had a house in Berlin, too?"

"Sold that years ago. I was renting an apartment in town, little one bedroom, closer to work. I'm divorced, no kids. Didn't need a house that big. After Emily's call, might've been three, four days, I can't remember, I came back to my apartment, place had been ransacked, my desktop missing. Got a call that night from Jaren Havell, the paper's editor, said I was being let go. When I asked why, he said 'gross misconduct.' He made it clear the decision was made for him, that there were bigger forces at play. He suggested I take a permanent vacation. Out of state."

"Bigger forces?"

"If Tomassi Construction knew about it, Lombardi did, too. You know who they are, right? They couldn't take any chances with Michael Lombardi down in the senate." Paul Grogan leaned in. "Rumor has him eyeing a run at governor. He and his brother have business dealings all over the globe. A project that size has lots of moving parts. Outside contractors. Buckets of money to be made. Even more to be lost." Grogan pointed to a page in his folder. "No one is paying millions for a hunk of land without having teams of experts do an inspection first. Before deeds pass hands or a single shovel breaks ground, they want to know what they are buying."

"Why would Tomassi buy Lombardi Construction and assume financial liability for a contaminated job site?"

"Mutually beneficial deal for both parties. That real estate is a prime location. You think they are going to let a little tainted dirt hold up a sale of that magnitude? Lombardi had been after that land for years. Perfect spot to build that rehabilitation mill of theirs. Easy access via the Turnpike, far enough from the big city that parents feel safe. This had been in the works a while. Couldn't stop now. With the Century Cures Act passing in DC, New Hampshire is in line for a billion dollars, maybe more, to combat the state's opioid problem. Lombardi wants that money. They halt the project before it gets off the ground, forget about it. It's going to someone else. You have to understand, deals like this get set in motion years before the public sees any progress. Michael Lombardi's campaign runs on the promise to clean up the drug problem. Success at the CCC translates to more centers—more *for-profit* centers. State money. Private insurance. Subsidized. Take all comers, corner the market. It's all profit. Tomassi is the biggest outfit in New England. They can absorb the blow, write it off, bury it, divvy up losses among various policies. Lombardi hands are clean. Win-win."

"If Tomassi knew the ground was toxic, they had to know these workers would die."

"Of course they did. But it's a simple matter of mathematics, son. Bean counters at corporate did a cost analysis, determined it'd be cheaper to pay out the eventual wrongful death suits than halt the construction of a multi-billion-dollar project for a time-consuming cleanup. At that point, you have to call in state agencies, follow protocol, contend with the bureaucracy. Once that information's made public, doesn't matter your last name. There's no choice but to follow the rules to the letter of the law. OSHA, EPA, a bunch of other organizations with intimidating initials. We're talking years of costly excavation, years of taxes paid on a property generating zero revenue. That Federal Century Cures money? Lining someone else's pocket. I'm sure that was factored into the sale price. Insurance companies have insurance, everyone protected, everyone profiting. Except the little guy. It's the price of doing business. One big shell game."

"And you have proof of this?"

Grogan nodded but not in a way that made me feel confident.

"How?"

"Sources."

"Come on. You got to do better than that."

"Let's say there's a hard drive. An old computer. Belonged to Lombardi Construction. Got in the wrong hands. Several years back. Proves everything."

My heart sped up. "You don't have this hard drive by any chance?" Far as I knew, assumed, the original must've been destroyed.

"No," Grogan drawled. "But I know it exists. How do you think I got those copies?"

"Sources."

"Sources."

"But you're certain there is an actual hard drive? An original?"

He nodded, pointing at the copies. "Came from that hard drive two months ago."

"Give me a name."

"It doesn't work like that."

"Fuck confidentiality."

"I'm not worried about protecting identities. *I* don't know these people. The people I know don't know these people. We're talking middlemen of middlemen of middlemen, a drawn-out game of telephone. That's how journalism works, son. The *Patch*? Small potatoes. I'm low man on the totem pole. You have to work your way to the top."

"Why not go to the cops?"

"Cops? You might be able to convince a yokel town sheriff to hear you out, but by the time you get down to the cities, those boys own the courts and prosecutors, palms greasier than an extra-large Bronx pie." Grogan looked down at his wrinkled, liver-spotted hands. "I wasn't going to be at the paper much longer anyway. I don't have the fight in me anymore. I have printout sheets. Xeroxes. Wouldn't get past preliminary."

"After what they did to Emily?"

"It's not what you know, son; it's what you can prove. Lombardi and his cronies run this state." He caught my eye. "You're certain the sister's death wasn't an accident?"

"Yes."

"I'm a good reporter, did my due diligence. I put in my time. I'm not spending my golden years dodging bullets." He sifted through the documents until he found what he was after, and tapped a sheet of paper with a long list of names.

I read the names, glancing up.

"Tomassi construction workers. All dead or damn near. The families I contacted weren't happy to hear from me."

"Why wouldn't these families want the truth to get out?"

"Because they'd been paid off. Don't you listen? Tomassi, Lombardi, they settled with these people. Threw millions to keep mouths shut. Got out in front of the problem to make it a non-issue. Non-disclosure agreements signed. These aren't stupid men you're dealing with, Tomassi, Lombardi, their associates. Best lawyers money can buy."

"How do you know they've been paid off?"

"Construction worker widows aren't living in three-story mansions with brand-new Lexus hybrid SUVs in the driveway." He shook his head. "This is how the game is played, son. Enormous settlements split up and channeled into annuities, paid out by the insurance companies of the insurance companies for insurance companies. Without corroboration, it's all totally inadmissible, a spook story. Look on the web. Try to find *any* information about these settlements. Scrubbed clean. Entire histories wiped away, like it never happened. Not a trace. You know how hard it is to remove something from the Internet?" He pointed at the printouts. "That's all the 'evidence' that exists. At least all I got my hands on. You need to find the original hard drive. Wish I could tell you where to look."

"But there *is* a hard drive?"

"Yes. From what I understand, a disgruntled former employee got his hands on it, squirreled it away. And, no, I don't have a name. In lieu of that, you'll need either a family member to violate an NDA or someone in the know to call in a favor, get the ball rolling. *The Patch* won't touch this now. Forget a bigger newspaper. Not with a ten-foot pole. Everything Emily compiled? Not worth the ink it's printed with. I only wish I'd taken her claims to heart sooner."

"This is huge."

"It will be. If you can prove it."

First I'd been fixated on the rehab itself. The drugs. Every mess I'd gotten myself into over the past few years revolved around drugs. Drugs, rehab, junkies. Then it was the soil. And I was relieved. At last, a story dealing with different subject matter. But it was all mixed up together. This was the unifying theory I'd been chasing. I had my answer to what was really on that hard drive my brother stole, what got him killed five years ago. This wasn't a bunch of separate installments. This was one long story. I had my ending.

Except like before, without the actual hard drive, we were back to a case of he said/he said. And their side carried a fucklot more weight.

"Can I get a copy of these names? The sick workers? The ones who died."

"You can take that entire damned file. If you found me, means they can, too. Soon as you drive away, I'm going somewhere sunny and warm, where the drinks are cold and I don't know the names of the players." Paul Grogan stabbed a bony finger at the intel. "You asked for it. You got it."

"Thanks."

"Don't thank me yet, boy."

It sounded funny to be called a boy at my age. With a bum leg that worked some days and didn't most others, I didn't feel like a boy. I was thirty-six, divorced, on a bumpy ride with a busted heater. But I liked the idea I was still young enough to make a difference, and in that moment, I felt fire, however faint the flicker, return to my heart.

CHAPTER TWENTY-TWO

ACCORDING TO PAUL Grogan's list, there was one construction worker from that entire batch still kicking it. And he was not long for this world. Bill Ogden had been a Tomassi foreman for twenty-plus years. Sold his soul to the company store in exchange for home hospice and an adult diaper. Grogan had already begun packing his meager belongings as he filled me in on the rest. Ogden was instrumental in getting settlements for the other workers, the men under his charge. His supervisors kept him in the dark, too. Ogden didn't know excavating that ground would be lethal, this wasn't his cross to bear, but it said a lot about a condemned man that he was willing to spend what little time he had left fighting for others. Part of me wondered why he didn't blow the whole thing up, go to the press, television and radio stations, newspapers, offer an exclusive. Who knows how you're going to respond when you learn you are dying? Is it worth making grand stands? Or do true heroes fight for the ones they love? Which is justice? Which is empty vengeance? I knew the correct answer, and, sadly, what I'd do if presented with the same choice.

All the information Grogan handed over came from unnamed, unverifiable sources. Did I believe him when he said he'd told me everything he knew? Yeah, I did. At that point, I felt Grogan would've ratted himself out to settle the score, my arrival a godsend. Watching him stuff his suitcase, I saw a man unshackled, the onus transferred to me. Grogan hadn't been able to convince a single Tomassi employee to talk to him. This was a seasoned vet who'd spent a career pulling words from people who didn't want to talk. What chance did I stand?

My life had been cursed since I let Gerry Lombardi walk for his crimes. In doing so, I created bigger monsters out of his already heinous sons. Here I was again, presented once more with a chance to do the right thing. I could bring down the Lombardis. I saw the finish line, crossing it my sole focus. Five years ago, I had a team of people looking out for me. Charlie, Jenny, Fisher, even Chris. I'd pushed them all away, or they'd died. It was just me now. And I wasn't at my best. Like Batman having to fight as Bruce Wayne, sans a single gadget, not even a can of shark repellent. But, goddammit, I had the sonsofbitches in my sights. Lombardi's old head of security, Erik "Bowman" Fingaard, had told the truth. This was never about pedophilia. This wasn't about sons covering for the crimes of the father. This wasn't about protecting family name or legacy. That stolen hard drive was about serving a far more precious god: Cold, hard cash.

Snow started to pile up as I crossed state lines. Grinding in low gears, I scaled the other side of the mountain, up to Danport, another shit outpost in the rarified air. Without a heater in my truck, my teeth chattered so violently I feared chewing off a chunk of tongue. Iced-over evergreens brushed the escarpment. This side of the mountain, you had a couple tiny towns. And then a whole lot of nothing on snaking route roads with odd number and letter combos like 31R-L and 79S North. You had to check the tank early and often because if you didn't have enough gas to finish the journey, fuel would freeze, abandoning you to the elements; you wouldn't survive the night.

A trip that should've taken thirty minutes ended up taking closer to ninety because I couldn't go faster than twenty miles an hour. By the time I found the address, the snow blustered heavier and harder, the perpetual daily forecast this high up on the western front.

Grogan had tipped me off about what to expect, but I was still surprised. Foreman or not, unskilled laborers didn't score homes like this. As I steered up the drive, I grew less impressed, not by the size, which was colossal, but by the design, a McMansion, one of those monstrosities you find down south in the suburbs. The house was brand spanking new. Except unlike most McMansions sardined between other cookie-cutter copies, this one occupied its own solo plot, boundless grounds uninterrupted by property markers.

Houses on the mountain take a while to build. Can't drill through frozen earth. For one this size to reach completion meant these payoffs had started a long time ago, further lending credence to Grogan's findings. They'd known the soil was tainted from the start. Backroom deal brokered, paid for with the blood of the common man. They wouldn't get away with it this time.

A woman answered the door, and as soon as she did, I knew that I wouldn't be talking to Bill Ogden. And neither would anyone else.

"Is Bill home?" I asked anyway.

"My husband passed away last week. What's this about?" She didn't say it mean, more like any woman would ask if a stranger showed up on a bitter, snowy night, high in the sky, asking about her dead husband.

"He worked for Tomassi, yes?"

Now she got defensive, annoyance mixed with disdain, masked by a veil of secrecy. I glanced over my shoulder at the sparkling new sports utility vehicle hogging the drive. The woman peered over her shoulder at a kitchen table, where two young boys sat eating the dinner I'd interrupted.

The interior was banquet hall huge, immaculate, pristine as a staged home hitting the market. The woman stepped onto the porch, shutting the door behind her. She hadn't grabbed a coat, wrapping her arms around herself, rubbing for warmth. "Why are you asking about Bill?"

I didn't know how to explain the impetus behind my visit. If I was asking about his job, she had to suspect what I was getting at. But I didn't have an elaborate excuse that would satiate her question. All I had was the truth.

"This might sound weird . . . but do you know Emily Lupus? Did she ever stop by before your husband, y'know? How about a reporter named Paul Grogan?"

Grogan told me he hadn't been granted a private interview, but he must've attempted more than a phone call.

"No," Mrs. Ogden said, flat. "I don't know any Emily. Or Saul."

"Paul."

"Him either. I am in the middle of dinner with my family . . ." She trailed off, studying me, looking me in the eyes, which always creeps me out, like she had a question she wanted to ask before deciding not to bother.

"Sorry for stopping by like this," I said. "Emily's . . . my friend. She went missing. Someone told me she was acquainted with your family."

The statement didn't elicit a response. I wasn't asking anything. I could see her desire to be rid of me. But I saw another part, too. Like Grogan, she longed to lighten her load. Maybe because in both instances I was begging for the opportunity to carry it.

"I can't help with your friend," she said. "I never met anyone by that name. I am sorry to hear she's missing."

"Mrs. Ogden—"

"Cass."

"Cass, I'm an investigator." What else could I say? She wasn't inviting me inside anytime soon and my face hurt each time the wind blew. I'd already tried to offer her my coat, but she'd shaken me off.

"Where's your badge?" she said.

"Private."

"Don't you still have a badge?"

"Yeah. I left it in my truck. See, here's the thing. Emily's sister hired me to find her. Through my . . . investigations . . . I've learned that your husband and several other workers at Tomassi Construction contracted cancer . . ."

"Yes. Bill died of myelofibrosis. What's this have to do with your friend?"

I could lie, try to come up with a suitable cover story on the spot, but I was so cold my balls had retreated inside my abdomen; without a coat, Cass had to be near hypothermia. I heard the minute hand ticking down. So, I threw everything I had at the wall and hoped something stuck. I reiterated how Emily was looking into the rash of Tomassi workers who contracted terminal illnesses while building the CCC, her work with Grogan, her death under suspicious circumstances, my brother, Amy, Lombardi, auto-dumping for a good five minutes straight.

"What's this got to do with me?"

"I want to help."

"Help?" she said, stifling a laugh. Or maybe it was to hide the tears. "You want to help, Mr. . . . ?"

"Porter. Jay Porter."

"Mr. Porter, even if I wanted to talk to you, and I don't, I couldn't tell you anything. You've been investigating, you say? Then you already know what happened. Before my husband died, when we learned he was sick, we sat down as a family. I can't say who said what, or who advocated to take one road instead of the other. But a decision was made. Bill wanted us to have this house. He wanted our credit card debt erased. Our children to go to college." She turned back toward the house and the two sons Bill Ogden left behind. "First ones in the family." Cass dried the tears from her eyes. "My husband spent his whole life working in those infernal pits. He showed up fifteen minutes early, left fifteen minutes late. He gave everything he had to his job. And they sent him out there to die, and in exchange . . ." Cass swept an arm over the grand estate. "We get this. Because that is how much money is worth, isn't it? You can cut out one of your own kidneys and sell it for thirty thousand dollars on the black market. I'm sure the day will come soon where the poor can auction off their very bodies for the rich to do as they please. Set them loose in a field to use as target practice. Who cares? We are not poor anymore. Isn't *my* problem anymore. *That* was my husband's sacrifice."

"If you can just—"

"I can't 'just' anything. We never had this conversation, Mr. Porter." She hugged herself tighter and a weak smile breached her lips. "Maybe I haven't talked to anyone but my boys for so long on this godforsaken mountain, I felt extra chatty tonight. Maybe it was the extra cup of coffee I drank after six p.m. Maybe I like your eyes and your face because they remind me of someone I knew when I was young. Or maybe you just look as sad as I feel. I don't know. But you are on your own. I can't give you anything." She backed up into her house. "Good luck finding your friend."

Then she closed the door.

I walked through the snow, out of ideas where to go. Bill Ogden had been the last man standing. I was out of leads. Grogan and Ostrowski were on the run. Curtis G. locked up. Amy, Emily, even the fucking Hooch, dead. Who would I turn to now? Looking back at the house, where Cass Ogden returned to her boys, the three of them together, in that lovely well-lit home with all the luxuries one could desire, I saw a life paid for with blood and deception—but it was a life paid for all the same. Would I make that same trade for my son? In a heartbeat.

Climbing back up in my cab, I pulled out the list of names from my back pocket to see if there was one I recognized, one that instilled confidence, invited hope, evoked another angle to explore. Stubborn as I was, I couldn't let this go. My family wasn't safe. Except instead of the list of names, I picked the wrong pocket.

I stared down at the yellowed sheet of paper I'd found under a chair at the Double Spruce Motor Inn where two murderers had been renting a room. They were sitting right there, and I'd driven away, called Turley, expecting him to handle the mess. Just like with Gerry Lombardi, I let my inability to act become someone else's problem. I read the two lines, or rather stared at them, because they were written in pencil, in a foreign language, and I had no idea what it said. I'd automatically assumed the writing was Indian because Indians ran most of these Turnpike motels. But I didn't know that for sure. In fact, the longer I stared at that slip of paper, the more I realized it could've said anything.

CHAPTER TWENTY-THREE

"SHUT UP AND pay attention," I said, barging past, sheaf of print-outs clenched in my fist. The early dawn light broke the high mountain sky, shifting planes of silver, granting glints of gold. It had taken me damn near an hour to remember where Fisher's mom lived, this dismissible subdivision on the east side flats. Every street was named after a tree—Sycamore, Maple, Oak—rotating random suffixes—Circle, Drive, Court. I wasn't calling first and giving him a chance to duck me. My temples throbbed, pulsed to the beat of tires rolling over uneven road. I hadn't slept, pulling an all-nighter, running through every Google translation until I deciphered the code. And I didn't stop there. I took everything Grogan had given me, compared it to what I knew, reconfigured zero sum games to beat house odds. No, there was nothing on the web about the contaminated soil. Like Grogan said, the 'net had been scrubbed clean. But that didn't mean there wasn't evidence. You just had to dig deep enough.

"Dude, do you know what time it is?" Fisher said, gesturing to keep it down. "My mother is sleeping. What the fuck are you doing here?"

"Trust me. You want to hear this."

Fisher brought a finger to his lips, waving me deeper into the old lady's house, which smelled of malt and fish chips, interior design culled from a *Home and Garden* advertisement, circa 1971.

Wood paneled slats floor to ceiling, striped wallpaper and vinyl seats, predominant color scheme: mustard, orange, and brown.

After I got back from Cass Ogden's late last night, I was running on all cylinders, like "Eye of the Tiger" were playing on perpetual loop. Even if the third installment of *Rocky* sucked, that soundtrack still kicked ass. A pot of coffee, two packs of cigarettes, three Red Bulls later, I had what I needed. Soon as I deciphered that note, or at least the part I needed, I knew where to go.

Fisher brought me to a back basement room that looked like it was being used for storage, folding chairs and tables, Christmas decorations in paper bags. "Sit down, Porter. You look awful. When was the last time you slept?"

"I'm fine. Listen. The CCC and that soil. They knew, Fisher. They knew!"

"Slow down. Who's they?"

"Who the fuck do you think? Lombardi. Adam and Michael!"

Fisher walked across the room, peeping out the accordion partition into the family room, sliding it shut. He grabbed a chair, whispering it across the shag carpet.

"Jay," he said, calm, measured. "You're acting manic, okay?"

"Manic? Fuck you. I found something. Evidence, bro. What we started. Me, you, Charlie, Chris. All those years ago. We can finish it now."

"What evidence? What are you talking about?"

I pulled the piece of yellowed paper with the boxy, penciled letters I'd found in the Carls' room at the Double Spruce, pressing it in his palm.

Fisher stared at the paper and then at me, then back to the paper. He shrugged.

"I spotted their truck, snuck into the room. Found that."

"Whose room?"

"The hunters'!"

"Hunters? You mean . . . the Carls?"

"I told you I don't know their real names, man. That's the names they gave me." I didn't remember telling Fisher about the Carls.

You told Turley. Which means they've been talking about you, little brother . . .

I pointed at the two scrawled lines. "I thought it was Indian or Sanskrit or some shit at first. It's not. It's Russian."

"Russian," Fisher repeated.

"Russian." I pointed at the part I'd deciphered on the web last night. "Can you read Russian?"

"No, Porter. I can't."

I beamed, leaning over, tapping the word in the middle, glad to be the one enlightening for a change. "Fingaard. That's what that word says. Fingaard."

I waited. He had no reply other than the confused look in his eye.

"That's Bowman's real name," I said, stabbing down. "I found that slip of paper where they were staying. Bowman. Lombardi's old head of security. Why would they have his name written on a piece of paper?"

"Jay, I can't read what this says, period."

"Because it's in Russian!"

"No, because it's in light pencil and all chicken scratch. There's no discernible letters. From any language. Looks like a six-year-old wrote it."

"Where's your computer? I'll show you *right* now. *That* is Russian, and it says Fingaard. And why do you think they want to talk to Bowman?" I bobbed fervently. "Chris told me he had a secret that would rock this town. I didn't listen. This is, like, international conspiracy shit." I hopped up, running fingers through my hair, scratching my scalp. The more I scratched, the more it itched. I sat back down.

Fisher remained motionless. How could he not understand?

"Because of what he told me at Dunkin' Donuts," I said, the answer so obvious. "How there was something far more incriminating on that hard drive. I've got to find him before they do."

"Jay, first of all, that writing isn't Russian. It's not even writing. It's a bunch of squiggles. A doodle. You are seeing things that aren't there, forcing connections that don't exist."

"Fine. Whatever. Don't believe me. You'll believe this." I waved the bunched-up papers and shook them in his face. Fisher couldn't rationalize this away. Grogan and Emily's research. Hard, fast numbers. I'd also included WebMD summaries of pulmonary illnesses, cause, effect, myelofibrosis, fast-growing tumors, a whole sheaf of incontrovertible evidence linked to fossil fuels. How annuities worked. Dates of purchase. Dates of construction. Dates when illnesses were contracted. Dates when new property broke ground. I even uncovered when survivors' families started sending their kids to private schools, bought new cars. Fucking Facebook had pictures of half this shit. Iron-fucking-clad. But I couldn't release my grip on the papers, hand them over. I couldn't think how to present my findings in an order Fisher would understand, and when you don't sleep, thoughts get scrambled. I hadn't taken my medicine in a few days. Not since that old man at the meeting. No, I'd taken it after that. When did I stop?

You ran out and didn't get a refill.

I got a fucking refill.

No, man, you didn't.

Yes, I fucking did.

"Who are you talking to?" Fisher said. "Porter, I think you need to rest, okay?" He pointed at the accordion doors. "Lie down on the couch in the living room. Whatever you need to tell me will still be there in a couple hours."

"I don't have time. They're—they're still out there."

"Who? The hunters? No one has seen these guys. Except you."

"Bullshit. There's this fry cook . . . They killed Emily. Then they killed Amy."

"Why not you?"

"Huh?"

"If they, the Carls, are going around killing everyone investigating this, why not you?"

"They did try! In the woods! I'd been inside Emily's apartment. They must've been watching the place, figured I was her boyfriend. He got stabbed in the neck with a screwdriver. Maybe they mistook me for Dan, Amy's boyfriend. We were about the same size." I resisted adding the joke from *Fletch*, "from the waist up at least." I wasn't sure why that line popped in my head, now of all times, but it made me laugh, which made me look nuts. I steadied my breath, slowed my speech. "I don't know, man. But they know who I am by now. Which means I'm not safe. Neither is Jenny or my son, or you, or—"

"How do you always land in the middle of this shit?"

"That's the rub, Fisher. There is no *all*. It's just the one. Ha! It's *all* connected. Last year when we were looking for Ethan Crowder's kid, remember?"

"That was right before Charlie died. Of course, I remember."

"It traced back to the Lombardis. Crowder Steel built the CCC. Lombardi. Bowman worked for Crowder. Lombardi. Tomassi bought the business from . . . Lombardi. It's all the same. And it all goes back to my brother and that hard drive."

"The . . . hard drive." Fisher poked his fingers in his eyes, dragging his hands down his face, letting go a long, exaggerated, condescending sigh.

"The one with Gerry Lombardi and those young boys!"

"Jay, that was five, six years ago."

"No shit! Don't you think I know that! That's what I'm trying to tell you. What Bowman tried telling me. It was never about kiddie porn." I hopped up again, ecstatic escalating to erratic. I lit a cigarette without asking, sweeping the hair from my eyes. Fuck, I hadn't showered for a couple days. I sniffed my shirt. I stank.

Fisher opened a window. Cold wind blew in. "Sit back down."

"Bowman told me something."

"Bowman, the psychopath locked up in Mass Correctional. That Bowman?"

"He said—and I remember this clear as day—we were at the Dunkin' Donuts on the Merrick Parkway—and this was in the middle of the Judge Roberts' kids-for-cash scandal—"

"Another mess you happened to fall into. That also traced back to the Lombardis."

"Don't patronize me. You know it did!"

"Peripherally."

"Peripheral, my ass."

"Porter, the Lombardis, Tomassi, Crowder, man, they are all in the same line of work. Construction. It's like discovering an E. coli outbreak at a fast food chain. Everyone's getting ill because they all get their shitty beef from the same contaminated slaughterhouse. This is all in your head."

"Of course, it's in my head! Where else would it be? In my ass? And it's nothing like that. That's a terrible analogy. People aren't cattle. Bowman told me—"

"Bowman, the career criminal—"

"Will you shut up and listen for a second? We've already established Erik Bowman, Fingaard, whatever his real name is, is a bad guy. Doesn't mean everything he said was a lie. Bad people can still tell the truth. You don't want to believe that's his name in

Russian on that paper? No problem. Fine. But it doesn't change what he told me that night at Dunkin' Donuts. That isn't open to interpretation."

"Okay," Fisher said, dropping his shoulders, worn down and resigned, my specialty. "What did the murderous sociopath say?"

"He said that Adam and Michael didn't pull out all the stops to get back that hard drive because of their father and child pornography. He said that hard drive, and I quote, 'contained something far worse.' End quote. This, this, this—toxic soil, sick workers, payoffs—*this* is what they cared about."

"So, you're saying Michael, state senator with huge political aspirations, didn't care there were pictures implicating his father in child pornography?"

"Why won't you pay attention to what I'm saying? Does anyone listen when I talk? Those pictures, fuck, man, we didn't know if that was their dad. That's why we didn't take it to the cops. Inconclusive, mutherfucker!" I jammed my hands to my temples, he was giving me such a headache, frustrating me deliberately, but I had that stack of papers in my hand and when I went to rub my head I gave myself a thousand little paper cuts.

I had no choice but to thrust my stack of printouts at him, which he didn't accept, and they scattered to the floor, swirling with the frigid stream blowing through the opened window, forcing me to my knees to gather them together, a sheaf of mixed-up, messed-up papers, the ramblings of a madman, collecting them to my chest, a freshman with too many textbooks bullied on the first day of class. I held out my offering.

I was out of breath. I couldn't talk. He didn't accept my offering.

You need to sleep, little brother.

Fisher brought me to the chair, sat me down, and collected the strewn documents. When I tried to move, he motioned to stay seated. After he'd collected all the evidence, he began sifting through, settling on the WebMD one. "Myelofibrosis," he read.

"Contracted via contaminated soil. All twelve of those names, cancer, tumors, blood and autoimmune diseases, conditions directly linked to gasoline and lighter fluid in the ground."

Fisher pinched the bridge of his nose.

"All those names Paul Grogan gave me?" I said. "Dead. Families paid off. I saw a house last night. Man, just like the Judge Roberts case. Except this's bigger. This is government money. To the state. Billions to fight addiction. That project couldn't be halted. These payouts, man, we're talking hundreds of thousands, millions. To each family. All those workers died, Fisher. *After* building that treatment center. Don't you see? It all makes sense now. Why Adam sold the company. How much money they must be banking if they can afford to pay out so much in wrongful death suits." My laughter came unhinged. "This is the kind of money you die for, the secrets you kill for. They can't let me live. I need to talk to Bowman. I need you to find out if he's been released from prison yet. Where he's living. Or if he's still locked up, arrange a visit, man. I can't make heads or tails of the Mass Correctional website. There's all this paperwork you need to file and—"

"Where are your pills? Are you out?" He checked his cell for the time. "The pharmacy opens in a few. I can head over there—"

"Lombardi knew, they all knew," I said, weakly. "The hard drive will prove it."

"Jay. It's been five years. There is no hard drive."

"Fuck you. You don't want to help? I'll do it myself. I snatched back my evidence, feeling dizzy from sleeplessness, Gollum jonesing for the ring. It was all jumbled now, all my hard work scrambled.

Fisher backed away from me like I was a wounded, wild animal, most dangerous when cornered in his unpredictable state. Cautious, toward the handle, both eyes on me, feeling for the way out, opening it wide, never letting his gaze falter.

I ran from the room, sheets flying from my hands. I knew that the second I left, Fisher was calling Turley. That bullshit about being a danger to yourself or others. I'd had my brother involuntary committed more than a few times over the years. But I wasn't drunk. I wasn't crazy. I'd never been thinking more clearly. And I had an ace in the hole.

Last person I ever thought I'd turn to for help. But fuck it. Desperate times and measures. The enemy of my enemy is my friend. Or something like that. Even if he was fucking my wife.

CHAPTER TWENTY-FOUR

In hindsight, I should've showered. At least combed my hair, changed my shirt, picked a different cap. The current white one I was wearing had taken on serious hobo stains. But I didn't have that luxury. I had a reputation for this PTSD shit, breaks with reality, fugue states, whatever anyone wanted to call it, and Fisher, who'd never been my friend, was going to rat me out to the local cops. I wasn't able to articulate what I wanted to tell him, but I *wasn't* paranoid. All Fisher had to do was hint I'd threatened Ashton's golden boys, the Brothers Lombardi, and I was staring at a seventy-two-hour court hold.

"Jay," Jenny said. "What are you doing here? We agreed, remember? You have to call first. You can't just show up. Besides, Aiden's on a school field trip."

"Is Stephen home?" Not that I didn't want to see my boy. Jesus, I wanted to see his face right then more than I wanted to breathe. But it was best Aiden didn't see his father like this.

Jenny's eyes widened as she shushed and pushed me onto their porch, which was bigger than my entire apartment. She shut the door behind her. She was still dressed in her bathrobe, which she cinched tighter. My wife was as beautiful as the day we met.

"Are you out of your fucking mind?" She sniffed. "Are you drunk?"

"No! I haven't had a drink in nine months. You know that." I blew hot breath in her face. "You smell alcohol?"

Jenny backed up. "I can't smell anything over that ashtray you call a mouth." She peered through the atrium. "Stephen is upstairs, getting ready for work. If he catches you here—"

"What's he going to do? Take a swing?"

"Grown-ups don't throw punches," my ex-wife said in that pedantic tone of hers. "They call the authorities."

"I'm not violating any restraining orders."

"Is that what you want? Because he can get one. Last time you had any close contact with my husband, you tried to break his jaw."

"That's when you were my wife. Were you sleeping with him then?" I didn't mean to sound so melancholic. I'd been wondering for a long time.

I'd gotten incredulous looks from Jenny over the years. I'd said stupid, outrageous things, my timing not always on spot, putting foot in mouth a talent. The shell-shocked configuration contorting her face—horror, contempt, disgust—the way she cinched her bathrobe tighter to her throat—damn thing was already broaching asphyxiation—told me I'd achieved a new personal best in terms of all-time low.

"I have a right to know."

"You want to know if I was fucking Stephen? You mean when you were fucking that college girl?"

"I never slept with Nicki." Which was true. We'd messed around for a few. That was it.

"This conversation is over, Jay. Go home. Sleep. We will talk about visitation *next* weekend. Or the weekend after that."

"Honey?" I heard the voice call from inside. "Are you on the porch? Who are you talking to?"

Jenny's eyes were already as wide as they could go. Any bigger and they'd pop out of her head.

Stephen opened the door. And the three of us stood there. The fancy banker man in his fancy banker man suit, the woman who was—and who should still be—my wife, and me, Jay the Junkman, crazy Chris Porter's equally crazy brother. I figured the day would come where the three of us would get together in a social setting. Hadn't pictured it quite like this, but, fuck it. Life on life's terms.

"What are you doing here, Jay?"

Jesus, they even talked alike. Probably had fucking matching His and Her bathrobes, too. I found myself wishing I'd at least hit the pharmacy and refilled my 'script. I needed to stay calm. Lashing out wasn't going to help anyone.

I held up my hands, the universal sign for I don't want any trouble. At least in the Old West. Or movies about the Old West.

"Hear me out, okay?" I said. "This isn't about any of . . . this." I waved a hand over my wife, my ex-wife—she wasn't my wife anymore—like she was an untouchable commodity. "I need your help with something. It's legit. Call it a favor."

"You want me to do you . . . a favor?"

I can't tell you how hard I bit my tongue not to scream. That was the least the jerkoff could do after he stole my family.

Instead I nodded.

He looked to Jenny, Jenny to him, both at me, then back at each other. Until all that was left to do was open the door and let me in.

In the foyer, nothing changed. Jenny and Stephen stood staring at me, the ragamuffin gypsy who'd arrived via caravan, bartering rubies in exchange for a fortnight's lodging. In the long mirror, my worst fears were confirmed. I looked like a Tom Waits character camping out in the ironweeds. I needed a haircut, shower, a shave would've helped, at least a clean goddamn tee, and, yeah, I should've taken a power nap. Regret would get me nowhere now.

"You want coffee, Jay?" Stephen asked me, turning to Jenny, guiding the party into their expansive Crate and Barrel kitchen. "We have coffee made?"

"Yes, we have coffee made."

"Let's get Jay coffee. Would you like coffee, Jay?" Stephen pointed to a chair at their cherry wood kitchen table. "Why don't you have a seat, Jay?"

I remembered reading a while ago that when people use your name in conversation over and over they're trying to manipulate you. In normal conversation, we don't use each other's name. We don't say, "How are you doing, Sam? Nice day, isn't it, Sam?" I didn't appreciate being manipulated. I kept my eye on both of them. I wasn't letting either leave the room to call the fucking cops. I needed them to hear me out. They were both acting as skittish as Fisher had been. If Stephen wanted to treat me like a scary monster, fine, let him. I expected the benefit of the doubt from Jenny.

My ex set the coffee in front of me, no attempt to hide her hostility. I returned the contempt with beady-eyed glare and tight-lipped grin.

"So, what can I do for you?" Stephen asked.

I reached for my back pocket and both of them flinched like I was pulling a weapon. I shook my head and slapped down the printed-out, rolled-up papers. They'd gotten crinkled. Took a moment to smooth them out. I'd lost the Double Spruce note with Bowman's name and some other pieces at Fisher's. Probably for the best. In my truck, I'd tried to rearrange, highlight the essential. Toxins in the soil, myelofibrosis, tumors. Payouts, annuities. That's what I needed. Stick to the cold, hard facts.

I pointed for Stephen to take the papers, have a look. He took them. One finger at a time, dragging them away, me to him, like extracting a bone from a pit bull.

Stephen took his time reading the pages, pulling that pretentious move of licking his thumb before turning a sheet over. Jenny watched his expression, every so often casting sideways glances at me. The hate and anger had dissipated. And it wasn't pity or confusion that had taken its place. For the life of me, I couldn't name the emotion. I thought about what Amy said, about that time Jenny stopped by unannounced and found us in bed, how Amy saw love in my ex-wife's eyes. Is that what I saw? What did I know about that particular emotion anymore? I'd known Jenny Price since we were eight years old. Our first date was the Berlin Fair, back when my mom and dad were still alive. Chris didn't come, already a lost cause. There was a running joke about the Berlin Fair because it always took place in early October before the snows, and it always rained. Without fail. Could set your clock by it. Organizers switched weekends. Didn't matter. Rain followed the event no matter the date. I'd spent all my money that day. It had taken me months to save up twenty dollars, which, for a boy that age, was a lot back then. Jenny wanted to cover a red circle with these metal discs. She was so determined to erase that damn spot. I spent every penny I had trying to make her dream come true. She never did win. Wasn't her fault; it was a con game.

"What is it?" Jenny asked him.

Stephen half sighed, half exhaled, half held his breath. I'd never been great at math. "Lawsuits. Payouts to avoid lawsuits. Allegations of EPA violations. Collusion. You know that new treatment center they built in Ashton? The Coos County Center? Many of the construction workers involved—all it seems—got sick. Contaminated soil. Terminal."

They did that panning back and forth thing again. I waited for it to play out and his attention to return to me.

"What is it you want me to do with this, Jay?"

"First off, stop using my fucking first name, okay?" I held up my hands. "Sorry. Please, stop repeating my name every time you address me. It's annoying. These payouts. They are all annuities. Which means that investment houses, insurance providers, purchased the debt, doling out monthly installments to the widows, children left behind." I could feel Jenny's stare at the back of my head. I turned to include her in the conversation. "This way the insurance companies can invest the money, appreciate interest, so they aren't paying out on the principle, only the earnings." I turned back to Stephen, who, for the first time since I met him, looked almost impressed. "I'm not a fucking idiot, man, okay?"

"I didn't say you were, Jay."

"You work with annuities, right? That's your new job? Setting them up? Can you get the names of these insurance providers handling the payouts? Maybe open the door for me, vouch for me? So I can talk to someone."

He stared down at the table, pretending to ponder.

I grabbed the sheets, restacked them in a neater pile. Make it easy for him. "Here's what I think happened. Adam Lombardi—" And at the mention of the name, given personal histories, I hastened my pitch— "I think Adam Lombardi knew that the soil was contaminated. It was on top of a truck stop." I had to laugh. "A truck stop! Him and his sleazeball brother had already sunk millions into the project. They weren't going to let a few expendable manual laborers stand in their way."

Stephen and Jenny waited for the rest.

"I think when Adam tested the soil and found out they couldn't build that rehab of theirs, not without serious excavation and delays and added costs"—I stabbed a hard finger at the papers—"I think he struck a deal with Tomassi, who could take the punch. They worked out the particulars, factoring in the eventual wrongful death settlements, signed on the dotted line, and then sent those men to die."

"But what do you want *me* to do about it?"

I stared at Jenny. This. *This* was the man she chose over me.

"I want you to do the right thing," I said to him. "You work in the industry. You know all these goddamn companies. I want you to find out who holds the annuities. What are the terms? Did families have to sign an NDA?" I turned over my shoulder at Jenny. "Yes, I know what a non-disclosure agreement is." Then back to Stephen. "I want names. I can't talk to any of the workers; they are all dead. Spouses and remaining family have been paid off, silence bought. There has to be language in there, something, a loophole—a technicality. If I can prove that Tomassi knew the soil was contaminated, then I can prove Lombardi did, too."

"Jay," Stephen said. "It doesn't work like that. My position at Alliance Life doesn't fast track me to a membership card, like a secret club. There are countless insurance companies that handle annuities. Why don't you call your friends at NorthEastern?"

He knew damn well I was on the outs with NE. And they were strictly home, life, and auto.

"If this is what happened—"

"It happened!"

He showed his palms. He had tiny hands. Like a girl's. "Fine. It happened. But you'd have to talk to a lawyer—and something of this magnitude? Records are going to be sealed."

Once you notice a man has tiny hands, you can't stop noticing them. Dainty, delicate, thin fingers, like bite-sized, spongy cakes.

"You'd need court orders to unseal them. No one is going to talk to you." He stared down at the research. "I'm surprised you were able to uncover this much."

"Listen, my brother found a hard drive that came from a Lombardi Construction office. Jenny will back me up. At the time, I thought there were only dirty pictures of their father diddling little boys. They sent people after us to get that computer back. It's how my brother died. That hard drive is still out there."

Now his expression washed empathetic, but it wasn't because of Chris or me or any other personal loss on my end. He was going to dumb down what I already understood, his concession to my sorrows, didactic and insulting.

"This is the cost of business," he said. "Companies do it all the time. It's lousy, I agree. You're probably right. If someone tested that soil and they found out it contained dangerous levels of harmful chemicals, they have someone crunch the numbers. If A and B add up to more than C, they opt to pay out any wrongful death suit because it's cheaper. You see it in the automobile industry with recalls all the time. It's terrible, what happened to these men." He paused to make sure he had my attention. "I believe you, okay? I do. But there is no recourse. If settlements have been reached and signed off on, and according to this paperwork that appears to be the case, it's a done deal; you'd need an act of God to get a court to open them up."

I fumed with righteous indignation, fists balled, ready to grab my papers and storm out, take my chances with . . . I didn't know where else to go.

But when I moved to get up, Stephen hoisted a tiny hand, gestured for me to sit down. He asked for the papers back and read through them again. I turned over my shoulder to look up at Jenny, who seemed as confused as I.

Stephen held up a finger. "Wait a second." He tapped the table three times, staring at the papers for-fucking-ever, with lots of "hmms" and "umms," which irritated the fuck out of me. "You might be on to something here, Jay," he said, pointing down at the findings. "The date of this first payout. When was the CCC built?"

I'd heard Jenny storm out of the room by now. The one person I thought I could count on left me to twist in the wind. The other, a guy whose guts I hated, remained, at least willing to hear me out.

"Tomassi started construction," I said, "as soon as Lombardi bought the old TC Truck Stop and Maple Motor Inn."

"That was, what, three, four years ago?"

"Closer to five. They were in negotiations long before that, I'm sure."

"That still wouldn't have left time to extract poisons from the soil." Stephen was finally coming around. "How long had the truck stop been there?"

"Long as I can remember. Thirty years?"

"So, we're talking hundreds of thousands of gallons of leaking fossil fuels. Seeping into the ground. Year after year. Never cleaned up, never counteracted. Allowed to fester." Stephen massaged his baby-smooth chin. "And you think Adam Lombardi was aware of this?"

"Hell yeah he was! I already told you that. I don't think Lombardi kept anything secret. Tomassi would sue the shit out of Adam if he tried to pull a fast one. Tomassi Construction is doing its homework. This is big, man. Insurance companies have insurance companies, right?"

"That's right, Jay."

"The Lombardis—and don't kid yourself Michael was in on this, too—sell the company but stay in the game." I'd always wondered the impetus behind Adam's sudden bailing on the family business. And right after a major real estate score like this? Why not build the thing as well? "Tomassi moves ahead with the project, assumes legal responsibility. I'm sure Lombardi bankrolled that, because let's face it, they can afford to. What they can't afford is Michael's name mixed up in the mess. Especially if he wants to capitalize on recently allocated government money. That Century Cures Act or whatever it's called."

"I think you're right, Jay."

"Can you help me?"

"Yes," he said, "I think I can. But, listen, I'm going to need to hear the whole story, from the start. Every detail, however mundane. Go back to the hard drive and your brother. I need to know all the facts. Take your time. Go slow."

I reiterated the last five years of my life, starting with the night I got the call that Chris had been picked up by the Ashton police, how he'd been prattling on to Turley about a town-wide conspiracy, gacked out of his gourd, how when I bailed his mangy ass out, yet again, he tried to tell me what he and a buddy found on a hard drive they'd gotten their hands on. The computer, he said, belonged to Lombardi Construction. Chris hated that family, stemming from a high school wrestling snub. I told my brother I didn't want to hear it. Next morning, he was gone. Then they found his junkie pal, Pete, beaten to death behind the old Peachtree Restaurant. When I finally found Chris, or rather he found me, it was at Jenny's ex-boyfriend Brody's place, and my brother kicked his ass. It was about the pictures, I told Stephen. Except it was never about the pictures, see? It was like Bowman said: There was something far more incriminating on that hard drive. Whatever's on that hard drive was enough for Adam and Michael to murder. Or rather hire others to do it for them. But make no mistake about it; they have blood on their hands. And when they're done with me, they'd come for Stephen, Jenny, and Aiden next. They'd come for us all. They had to be stopped. None of us were safe with this information. I told Stephen, like I told Jenny, that once he called the people he needed to call, they should take cover, find shelter, hole up in one of his summer homes until this all blew over because this was going to be big. This was going to rock the entire town, the entire state. Maybe the country. And when I said that, I realized I'd been at it for three quarters of an hour, maybe longer; and it brought me back to sitting in my truck on the edge of Echo Lake with my brother, five years previous, as he passed along a partial copy of that hard drive, thinking I was going to help him, because I encouraged him to keep talking. Because I'd been killing time. Listening to his story, placating him, waiting for the police I'd already called to arrive . . .

The universe strives for balance, and karma has a way of coming back around to bite you on the ass. A smile cracked my lips when I heard the sirens, saw the swirling squad car lights strobing snow. I watched Stephen ease out of his chair, back away, then practically sprint to the door. I didn't move. I sat in the chair and gazed out their big bay windows, at the resplendent view of Lamentation Mountain. It was neat seeing it from the other side.

I might've already been standing when Turley and the others came in; already had my hands clasped behind my back. I can't remember the exact order of events. By then Jenny had returned downstairs. I caught her eye. I don't know what I looked like to her. But I know what she looked like to me. As they slapped on the cuffs, I kept my gaze locked, watching her expression twist up, let the guilt sink in. She knew what she'd done. I savored the blade of betrayal slipping ever deeper into skin.

CHAPTER TWENTY-FIVE

"You know why you're here?" the nurse's aide asked.

I didn't bother answering.

"Because you look like shit," he said.

I'd gone through the Involuntary Emergency Admission process before with my brother. I was familiar with the protocol, which began with the laughably named "Complaint and Prayer Form." Jenny did the honors. Though as suspected, Fisher had also called Turley, citing me not taking my meds, being manic. Baring my soul to Stephen, that Judas jerkoff, only added fuel to the fire, or in this case cause for a judge to issue a mandatory hold at the New Hampshire Hospital.

Such procedures were a dog-and-pony show. And like any circus, I knew I wasn't going anywhere without jumping through some hoops. A doctor at the Community Mental Health Center conducted the evaluation. At this point, my best option was to keep my fucking mouth shut. I'd done enough damage. Sharing theories on contaminated soils and conspiracies involving the rich and powerful wasn't helping me any.

Another long, sleepless stretch, going from nurse to doctor, from doctor to psychiatrist—and since I didn't have one of my own anymore, relying on my old shrink to phone in refills, that last conversation took a while. Mental health workers, social workers, residents, interns, they all wanted their turn to poke and prod. And take more vitals. For whatever reason hospitals really care about your blood pressure.

With the coming of night, I was officially committed. Plastic bracelet popped around my wrist, looney gown draped over my head, bare ass exposed. I'd been deemed "a danger to myself," meaning the door to my room had to remain open all night. An orderly came by every half hour shining a flashlight in my face. I was ready to pass out. But my racing thoughts weren't cooperating. And that flashlight in my face wasn't helping.

I'd be the first to admit, I cracked after my brother died. When I found myself holed up in the same skid row motel rooms he called home, the parallel was indisputable. If ever there were a time I should've been committed, it was then.

Evidence existed. I could try and make my case. But Turley had confiscated my data. Fisher, the little shit, had turned on me. There was Matt Matusi, the fry cook in Chevreport who'd served two men matching the Carls' description, but Turley wasn't going to corroborate that. Pinning my hopes on a stoned fry cook seemed misplaced. My word was flimsy at best, and my history of violence worked against me. If he were alive, Charlie would've vouched for me. But Charlie, like Chris, like my mom and dad, was gone.

That left Jenny. My wife. My ex-wife. My soul mate, love of my life, mother of my child. I didn't see her at the hospital when she signed the commitment forms. The last I saw of her was inside her marble halls as the police led me into the gusting snows and stuffed me in the back of a squad car.

The doctors blamed my mania on me not taking my meds. You'd think they'd give me something to help quell my nerves, help me relax, rest. No one gave me shit. Not for the panic. Not for the sleep. Not so much as a Tylenol PM. They let me squirm.

They let me suffer under the hot white light. I swear they reveled in it. But it was okay. I knew how to play this game, too.

They are legally allowed to hold you for three days, not including weekends. But the joke was on them. Because by the time of my mandatory hearing, I'd had the chance to sleep, they'd given me my meds. I was allowed to shave, supervised of course. They even washed my clothes for me, gave me a comb, and I cleaned up nice. When I arrived at court for the hearing to determine my competency, the judge had a hard time knowing whom they were talking about. I looked better than my public defender! Looked better than fat-ass Turley or that ugly elf Fisher, that was for sure. My favorite part was that they'd forced Stephen to show up, along with Jenny, of course. Thankfully, they left my son with his grandmother, my ex-mother-in-law, Lynne, who must've been relishing the possibility they might lock me up once and for all.

Except they couldn't. I hadn't done anything. I'd gotten amped up, over-excited, lost out on sleep, forgot to take my pills, lost my cool. But three days in a psych ward? Where you're the only sane guy there? No work. No bills. Free meals. A goddamn vacation compared to the past couple weeks. I made friends with the orderlies. They brought me books. I read and vegged by the communal television. When it came time to present my side of things, I was well rested and raring to go.

Their side had to prove I was incompetent. I didn't have to do anything but act normal, which I had no problem doing, because after one good night's sleep and employing a few meditative practices I learned in AA—I mean, that's what they called it, to me it was common fucking sense, push out the negativity, be grateful, that kind of shit—I was right as mutherfucking rain.

The proceeding didn't last ten minutes, and it was hilarious. Listening to that fat fuck Turley try to talk about why I needed to be held against my will—I had my faults, sure, but secondhand stories of one bad day at the Kenilworth Motel four years ago didn't hold water, and my recent "episode" didn't warrant long-term, forced inpatient hospitalization. Turley stammered and stumbled. He couldn't bring up the two hunters or the fry cook because it would undermine his argument that I was delusional. Stephen wasn't repeating my charges against the Lombardis and Tomassi. Forget construction collusion; hinting at slanderous allegations where his investment buddies were concerned was a career ender. He offered nothing to the proceedings but clipped yeses and nos and head shakes. He couldn't get out of there fast enough.

I knew Jenny regretted ratting me out, and her answers reflected that. Her testimony made me sound like a good guy who'd had a bad day. She went out of her way to talk about how I was a great dad, citing never missing a child support payment despite her financial privilege and my hardships. She talked about how difficult it was for me losing my parents, my brother Chris, my best friend Charlie. That didn't bother me much. When she mentioned Amy, I got pissed. Jenny hadn't hidden her reservations about my new friend. But I didn't show the judge that. I hung my head with the requisite amount of grace, contrition, and humility.

In the end, the evidence they used to bunge me up for three days was like spitting in the wind, former strengths now weaknesses, and vice versa for me. When the state's psychiatrist tacked onto what Jenny said about the recent "accidental" overdose of my "girlfriend," the testimony only served to reinforce me as a sympathetic figure.

When Charlie was alive, he used to say how I could've been an author. He'd bring up these stories I wrote in high school. I always brushed him off. It was embarrassing reliving the glory days of a has-been that never was. Long time ago, different life. I was a junkman, not an author. But I could use my words effectively when called upon. And I was so fucking geared up when the time came for me to speak, I wished they archived proceedings, because I'd love to hear that performance played back in Dolby stereo. I opined and proffered and waxed like a mutherfucking champ. Fear of public speaking cast aside, I admitted fault where appropriate, drew upon the tragedies in my life, hinting at deep-seated sorrows lying underneath the surface, while never using them as an excuse. The end product amounted to nothing short of masterful.

I could already see the judge was perturbed having to deal with this bullshit. I was far from perfect, but here was a man, nine months sober, attending meetings, self-employed, keeping up on his child support despite a paltry income. Shit, the way the judge made it sound *I* was the victim. She all but apologized on behalf of the state before saying I was free to go.

I shook hands with my public defender, who'd just earned the easiest payday of his life.

There was one moment though. I hadn't left yet, glad-handing my defense team, slipping off the loaner necktie. I looked across the aisle, and there they all stood, Turley, Fisher, Jenny, all on the other side, and I realized just how alone I was. I'd been on my own since my dad drove the family car into Echo Lake. Chris was more burden than brother. For a long time, I had Charlie, but he abandoned me, too, off the deep end in his own tormented, alcoholic's world. Tom Gable, my former boss and surrogate dad, moved to Florida. I had my son Aiden, who I could visit once every couple of weeks, but after this, who knew when I'd see him again. I guess the difference was, before, I embraced my lone wolf status; it was by choice. This time I'd been exiled from the pack.

I wasn't halfway down the courthouse steps when I heard Jenny's voice calling after me. I'm sure she expected me to be angry with her. I wasn't. For a guy who could hold onto grudges—and I'd been supplied with powerful ammo this time—I felt strangely serene. She approached, biting her lip, timid, apprehensive. I knew she felt guilty about calling Turley and helping get me locked up. I could've made it easier, risen to meet her, but I let her take each step down, descending to my level, one by one.

Stiff winds blew recycled snow off the cement statues of justice. The low winter sun threatened to crack the clouds but couldn't quite pull off the feat; the skies forged uneven shades of aluminum, gunmetal blue, titanium, hints of gold but never wholly lighted.

"I'm sorry," Jenny said. "I didn't know what else to do. You were all geared up, cracked out, talking crazy. I was . . . worried."

"It's okay," I said. I almost meant it. "I hadn't slept, forgot to take my meds. I've given you cause in the past."

My ex-wife waited because she didn't believe that could be it. That was the response of a grown-up, mature adult, words seldom used to describe me.

"I know you, Jay."

"Yeah, you do. I know you, too."

I kissed her. Not a peck on the cheek either, not a kiss shared by parents with a child together. We weren't former lovers meeting in the frozen food section of the grocery store on Christmas Eve. I kissed her full on the mouth, right there on the courthouse steps, in plain view. I didn't care who was watching. She didn't stop me. Maybe she'd tell a different story if Stephen saw us, say I caught her off guard, but she kissed me back. Not all the way. But enough for me to know that part of us wasn't dead. Then again, maybe she knew this was goodbye.

When I pulled back, Jenny looked up at me like she used to, like I was the strongest man in the world, mining to bring something out of me. After my unexpected display of affection, she expected more, but that was all I was giving. When I decide to shut it down, the Jaws of Life can't pry me open.

"Tell Aiden I love him."

"Don't say it like that."

"Like what?"

"Like you're never going to see him again. If you want to be angry with me, be angry with me. Don't go do something stupid." Jenny turned around, checking up the steps, where no one waited. "I know what you did in there. You've always been able to turn on the charm when you want to. I'm not saying you deserve to be locked up. I said as much. You heard me tell the judge that, right?"

"Sure."

"You don't let anything go. Never have. You harbor resentment harder than any man I've ever met, Jay Porter. No one comes as stubborn. When you get something in that head of yours, there's no stopping you. I don't know what you plan to do, but whatever it is, please, please, please think long and hard. Aiden needs his father. What you were saying about the Lombardis—"

"It's like I said. Didn't get enough sleep, forgot to take my meds. All good now."

My ex-wife descended one more step so we were on level footing. "Don't do this to me. Don't shut me out. I didn't abandon you."

"You moved on. It's okay." I tried to laugh. "It's funny. You know the last thing Amy said to me? Before she died? She said you loved me."

"I do. And I always will."

"No, she meant you were *in* love with me. That we were still *in* love with each other. She's right. At least on my end. I am still in love with you. Always have been, and I always will be, Jenny."

"Jay—"

"Don't worry. I had my shot. I blew it. I have to live with that. I can't tell you how many nights I sit in my apartment, staring at pictures of you, the three of us, our family, wishing I'd done better. I tried. But I couldn't let . . . this . . . go." I opened my arms wide. I didn't need to explain what "this" was. "I'm going away for a while."

"Where?"

"Somewhere you won't be able to find me. But that message I left the other day? Remember?"

"That's what started all this—"

"I'm not wrong. If you've ever believed in me, Jenny, please, trust me on this."

"We have the best security money can buy. You're scaring me."

"I'm not trying to."

Jenny reached for my hand, but I was too far away by now. "How are you getting home?" she said.

"Bus."

She turned back up the steps. I saw her trying to figure out how to ask Stephen if I could catch a ride with them. She must've known there was no way I'd accept.

"It's okay," I said. "Bus station is a block away."

Jenny kept glancing around, unfocused, like she didn't know whether to stay or go. "This isn't the right time. But I don't want you walking away without knowing—"

"Whatever you have to say, say it. You're not getting another chance for a while."

"I'm pregnant. Stephen and I are having a baby. We haven't told anyone. It's very early. I wanted to tell you. Not like this but—"

I clasped her hands. "That's great, Jenny. Aiden always wanted a little brother or sister."

She didn't believe my congratulations were sincere, but I was telling the truth. I was happy for them.

I was also happy for me. That was the final piece I needed to break free. The chain had been unshackled. I could move forward now. We were over. We had been for a long, long time. But the heart wants what the heart wants, and my heart was a slow learner. Somewhere in there, I'd clung to the impossible, the belief that, someday, I'd win her back; someday I'd have my family again. It was a pipe dream, lofty, foolish, childish. The look on Jenny's face said telling me now was cruel, but Elvis was right: sometimes you got to be cruel to be kind.

I gave her hand a last, tight squeeze and headed down the stairs to catch the bus to the impound yard where they were storing my truck. I felt her watching me, willing me to turn around for one last wave goodbye. But I kept walking, eyes locked on the road ahead.

CHAPTER TWENTY-SIX

I PARKED A couple streets over, watching my place. Regardless of the song and dance I'd performed for the judge, I knew I was right about the CCC, and I wasn't pulling into Hank Miller's parking lot, waiting to get ambushed. They'd be coming for me. At first they might've confused me for Amy's or Emily's boyfriend, attributed my questions and research to one of those clowns. But by now they knew who I was. In my apartment, I'd be deader than a wooden duck in the flotsam of Paper Goods Pond.

After I paid the impound yard, my balance dipped below twenty-five bucks, the bank's version of the Mendoza Line. I closed the damn thing out. The skies had lowered, darkened, threatening blizzard. I hadn't heard of a storm approaching, but you live up here long enough you get to feel it in your bones, the raw, electric charge in the atmosphere. Like an old farmer with a lazy, sleeping dog. Or a man with severe nerve damage and circulation problems in his left leg because the main vein had been severed.

Despite cleaning out my bank account, I wasn't without resources. I had two pills the hospital sent me home with, and a 'script for more antianxiety meds, but I didn't need them. I was calm and cool as a cucumber. I thought about that old timer at the AA meeting, the one who told me I couldn't be sober if I was taking medication; that if I needed pills to stay alive, I was better off dead because then at least I'd die sober. And I decided he was right. Not about what he said—it was a dick thing to say—but the idea that I didn't need any drugs to calm me. I also had my shoebox stashed in the hall closet with close to two grand in emergency cash.

I sat in my truck, waiting till nightfall. I turned on house lights remotely with an app on my smart phone, the one technological advantage I enjoyed, a gift from my old boss, Tom. If someone prepared to ambush me, the lights would either scare them off or spur them on. When neither happened, I grabbed a claw hammer from my toolbox and crept through neighboring backyards, scaling the chain-link of the automotive graveyard behind the filing station. Back to the wall, I slinked along to my second-floor apartment.

Once there, I didn't waste time. I stuffed a canvas sack with essentials—tees, boxers, socks, toothbrush, my black knit cap, granola bars, half a tin of stale nuts, photos that meant something to me, the ones of me and my boy, me and my brother, me and my parents, Jenny, my family. I kept all these in a small photo book on the half bookshelf. Then I grabbed the shoebox full of cash.

Knowing I wasn't coming back for a while, I tried to summon a goodbye. I had lived above Hank Miller's filling station most of my life. I was leaving it all behind, flat screen I'd scored at auction, movies Charlie and I bought in our teens, my computer and a search history I'd rather not have made public. Me and every other man in America. I'd scrawled out a quick note, which I planned on slipping under Hank's door. Then I crumpled the note and two-pointed it into the bin. Hank wouldn't toss all my shit on the curb. But if he did, so what? There was nothing that couldn't be replaced. My life fit in that one canvas knapsack.

I stood in the doorway for a good five, ten seconds, willing closure. Unable to get it, I double-checked I had my contact book, turned off the lights, and shut the door.

Driving on the Turnpike, I followed the Lamentation Mountain range, heading toward Lake Winnipesaukee. When I found a nice, quiet, out of the way motel, in between towns, not too cheap or rundown, I got a room for the night. Night clerk at the hotel didn't ask for an ID. And I didn't use my real name.

I had one asset to sell: my company. Being in the position I was in, I'd be taking pennies on the dollar. If I had the time, I could go item by item—the inventory in that storage unit was worth at least forty grand—but I didn't have the luxury. I knew one guy who'd bite, and he'd lowball me, because he was a dirtbag. But he'd pay in cold, hard cash. And he'd pay fast.

Owen Eaton ran the largest clearing house in New Hampshire, which was called, unoriginally, the Clearing House. It was way down by the Lake. I made the call, gave him a rundown of what I had. Didn't explain my circumstances, only that I had to move all my merchandise, and I had to move it now. Fifty grand worth. I'd let it go for twenty.

"Aw shucks," Owen said, doing his huckster routine. "I'd love to help, Jay, but business is business. I can go as high as three thousand."

I didn't lose it or call him a chintzing, dirtbag SOB. I pushed back hard as I could, calm and levelheaded, talked up the high-end inventory. The Serapi carpet alone was worth at least eight grand.

In the end, I got him up to three five, final offer, firm. Fifty might've been overselling it; three five was an insult. I had no choice. We agreed to meet first thing in the morning, crack of dawn, before anyone else arrived, before I could be seen. Owen grew squirrelly about that. But I insisted. Said I had a tight schedule, had to hit the road, and he wasn't risking losing out on the bargain of a lifetime so he had to agree to the terms.

I didn't sleep much that night, preoccupied with what I had to do. Three days in lockup, I had my plan, simple and elegant: I was ending the Lombardis, however I had to do it. Whatever it took, however long it took. If it killed me. I'd let Gerry Lombardi's crime go unpunished, and it ate away at me like cancer chewing organ and bone. I'd gotten pushed around by Adam and Michael for too long. They killed my brother. Maybe they didn't pull the trigger. But they put that gun in my brother's hand all the same, made sure the cops were in the right spot at the wrong time, built the perfect bomb, lit the fuse, stood back and laughed in the flickering flame. And I knew, as certain as I was breathing, which might not be for much longer, they were behind these construction workers getting sick and dying.

I hadn't been able to prove the pedophile stuff. Judge Roberts had fallen on the kids-for-cash grenade. Crowder, like any man of power, got off paying far less than he owed. But this, this I could make stick.

The contaminated soil left a paper trail, witnesses; it was courts and documents and settlements and annuity payments deposited monthly in traceable bank accounts. This was permanent record, routing numbers. This was tangible. With enough time, money to hold me over, I could—and would—hold them accountable.

It was still dark when I started out driving down to Lake Winnipesaukee. Two hours of restless, agitated slumber hadn't done much to recharge batteries, or help quell panicked thoughts, these plans of dark pursuits taunting, tormenting, plaguing me with self-doubt and insecurity.

The weather was shit, that slushy, mushy slop where the gods can't decide between cold rain and wet snow, so they clobber you with both. Ice accumulated fast and heavy on my windshield; my wipers couldn't clear a path, quitting halfway into the job. I computed figures best I could in my head. My profit margin wasn't great but my cost of living would be cheap. I'd give Owen the key, get the cash, and be on my way. I'd rent boarding rooms, motels where they didn't require ID, stay on the run. Talk to the players I needed to talk to. Grogan, Ostrowski. If I couldn't track down the reporter or professor, I'd try the *Patch* or White Mountain. If the paper and school shot me down, I'd try another avenue, maybe Jim Case at the *Monitor*, get him to remember journalistic integrity. Like a shark, I'd never stop swimming. I just needed one person to talk, one family to take a stand, a widow to violate an NDA, a son or daughter, aunt or uncle willing to go on record. I'd coerce signed confessions, affidavits, whatever it took. Then I'd hand-deliver the story to the press, television stations, news outlets, any and all media, fucking bloggers, I didn't care, but I'd lock in someone, anyone to testify that Lombardi knew that dirt was poisoned. I'd run their legacy into the ground.

Didn't think any further than that. Just had to see as far as my headlights and keep driving till I got where I was going.

Heading down from the motel, I was smoking, trying to dial in the radio. Nothing in the sticks. Heater busted, freezing balls. It was storming bad, heavy goop splattering the glass, sleet and snow and freezing rain sloshing the roadway. At least I had my new stereo with CD player. Popped in Springsteen.

By the time I made it to the Clearing House, the sun still wasn't up but morning had broken. As I pulled alongside Owen Eaton's truck, hallmarked by the obnoxious LQUID8 license plate, the only vehicle in the massive lot, the last thing the Boss sang: *I pick up my money and head back into town . . .*

The biggest reason I accepted the lowball offer: Owen had the cash on hand. I'd been in his office before. Giant ol' Schwab safe, impossible to crack, lots of room to stack. If I got hold of another wholesaler, he might offer me more money. But it would take more time. I'd have to deal with walking into a bank, waiting for the check to clear. The less time I spent in the public eye the better. The thirty-five hundred plus the two grand at the motel gave me little over five large. I could live a long time on that much money. I'd lived a lot longer on less.

The front door of the Clearing House was unlocked, and I saw Owen's office light on. Good. Punctual. I could count on him for that much. People think you pay for product, but that's not true; you pay for product *and* convenience.

I rapped on the door, which creaked open, ajar. The first thing that told me something was wrong: the open safe. Owen wouldn't leave a safe open. I stepped around the desk and saw the pair of polished cowboy boots poking out. He lay face down in a pool of his own blood. Couldn't see the entry wound, there was so much gore. Gun. Hatchet. Brain bashed in with a brick. No idea.

Like a rat baited, I'd walked right into the trap. The punch to my kidneys and roundhouse to my jaw were overkill. I'd gotten the message by now.

Sack over my head, they shoved me in the backseat of the truck, right behind the driver's seat, which wasn't as much a backseat as extra storage for groceries, two-by-fours when it rained, maybe stash a body in a pinch. Didn't leave much room to move. Of course, they'd relieved me of all my earthly possessions. Cell, wallet, keys, hope.

The Carls talked, but not to me, and not about anything important. I listened for an accent but didn't detect one save maybe a slight southern drawl. Maybe Fisher was right and that letter I found at the Double Spruce wasn't in Russian, it didn't reveal Bowman's real name, was another figment of a desperate, overactive imagination. I didn't plead my case. I had nothing to add to the conversation, and I didn't require a recap to understand what was happening.

About an hour later, I could tell we were headed back up the mountain. That's the thing about mountain living. The higher the altitude, the thinner your blood, the thinner your blood, the less oxygen pumps to your brain. Gets you all fucked up in the head. Go high enough, you can't think at all. But I knew this mountain. Lived on it my whole life. I was used to diminished capacity; I had tools and skills they didn't. Unable to see, I relied on my internal sense of direction. We weren't too far from Ashton. I'd cleared houses all over the state, could tell you the names of half the streets based on the bumps and potholes. Didn't take long to deduce where we were headed: Gillette Gorge.

I had to hope the Carls picked up my scent at the Clearing House and not my motel room. If I wriggled out of this, and it wasn't looking good, I'd need that cash in the shoebox more than ever. I sure as shit wasn't getting any of Owen's money. All I was getting from Owen Eaton was a murder rap.

I was now a wanted man.

CHAPTER TWENTY-SEVEN

GILLETTE GORGE EARNED its name from the mile-deep gully carved in the Lamentation Mountain Range, a sheared-off shelf of granite that dropped straight into the black fog where screams never end. A mile was a guesstimation; no one had taken accurate measurements. One thing's for sure: you fall into the Gorge, no one's retrieving your remains. I imagined countless corpses, single men no one would miss, who'd gone hunting alone, over-enthusiastic adventurers from out of state, unfamiliar with the terrain, thinking they'd bag a buck or bear, only to lose sight in the thick mountain mist and go flying over the edge, never to be heard from again.

The Gorge was its own summit. We were high up, way higher than Danport and the Ogden McMansion. I was lightheaded. I'd lost blood. Takes a while to acclimate to the thin air, oxygen in short supply. They still hadn't taken the sack off my head as they led me inside. The lighting made me think hospital. We weren't in a hospital, of course, and not just because of the arctic temps outside. I could tell by the swoosh and swish of the winds, which subtracted from already negative numbers. The walk from truck to front door took about six seconds, and in that time, despite the bag over my head, my face went numb.

They pulled the canvas sack off my head, planted my ass in a hard, wood chair, and cut me free. In the truck my hands were zip-tied behind my back, the tortuous route and cramped space cutting off circulation. I rubbed my wrists until the blood flow returned.

Maybe that hadn't been their truck at the Double Spruce. This was their hideout, and they'd been here a while. I smelled the smoldering ash, saw the carcass remains of dead animals gnawed on for lunch. Bits of dried meat, caramelized as jerky, clung defiantly to the bone.

One of the Carls, the bigger of the two, built a fire. When he dropped to hoist the logs, his long john sleeve rode up. A bandage covered his right forearm, deep, dark crimson seeping through the gauze, like he'd recently been sliced with a sharp hunting knife. According to Turley, Fish and Game verified no one had broken through the gate. There was just the one road in. Nice police work, Turley. You had one job. *They must've cut the lock, replacing it with one of their own.* Or Turley never called Fish and Game.

"If we're going to be here a while," I said, "you mind telling me your real names? It'll make conversing easier if I don't have to call you both Carl."

"Yeah. Mine's none of your fucking business—"

"Relax." The heavier of the two held up a hand. "I'm Andre. That's—"

"Shut the fuck up."

Andre caught my eye. "Keep calling him Carl." He winked. "No worries. Some people need to speak with you. That's all."

"Can I ask you about the night in the woods?"

"Keep talking," Carl said. "See what that gets you."

"A misunderstanding." Andre reached into a sack and tossed me a Ziploc baggie. "Eat. Is all going to be okay." A sandwich. That they bothered to bring me a sandwich was nice of them. It also confirmed we were waiting on someone. Unless this was the last meal before an execution. There were worse spots to die, I supposed. I ate the sandwich. Egg salad on white bread. I fucking hated egg salad as much as I did Wonder Bread. But I was famished and in no position to refuse. I finished my sandwich with an exaggerated lip smack. "Tasty."

"Can you shut up?"

With a spattering of spread-out cabins and blinds, the Gorge was remote, but not so remote that I couldn't be found. If someone were looking for me. In this regard, being wanted for murder should work in my favor. Then again, how long would it take for Owen Eaton's body to be discovered? For Ashton PD to be called? After which I was relying on Turley and Co. to make the connection and round up a posse. I wasn't sure I had the time for that dim bulb to spark. It might be hours until an APB was issued, and even longer until someone made it up to the Gorge.

I couldn't overpower both men, not in my compromised condition. They'd hammered me hard before hauling me to their truck like a rolled-up rug scored at auction. My leg didn't work too well in the cold. There were two of them and only one of me, and one of them, Andre, was like two of me, and the other held a shotgun.

"How long do I have to wait before Adam and Michael get here to kill me?"

"Shut up."

"Can you answer a question for me?"

I was talking to Andre but Carl answered. "I can crack your eye sockets open. How you like that?"

In the brighter cabin light, I could see his crazy eyes. I hadn't noticed them when we first met in the forest, transfixed by his baby face. It had been dark, and I didn't know then that a psychopath was accosting me.

"Nobody is killing anyone." Andre had a similar unnaturally youthful face, less obvious with the extra weight. "Just want to talk, that's all," he repeated.

The more I panned between them, the more certain I became they were closely related. Something not right with the space between eyes, length of chin, asymmetry of features.

"Like you talked with Owen Eaton?"

"Will you shut up?"

I'd seen a show on the History Channel a while back, about royal families and incest. There were signs of inbreeding. Besides the ones I noted, stuff like blood diseases and clubbed feet. I couldn't be sure about that last one since they both wore big, black boots. But I changed my assessment from cousins to brothers, or maybe they were both.

"Eaton is going to be fine," Andre said.

"Didn't look fine to me."

"He'll be waking up any minute now. Gonna have a bad headache, that's all."

"What about Emily? She have a bad headache, too?"

"Will both of you shut the fuck up?"

"You got this all wrong, Jay," Andre said. "Don't worry. We're gonna clear this up real soon. In the meantime, relax. Is all okay."

Baby-faced Carl was hotheaded, angry, mean. Predictable. Andre was so calm, measured. Confident. Like he believed every reassurance. I'd seen Owen Eaton's skull split open with my own two eyes, head bashed in, oozing cerebral fluids. I wasn't sure which one scared me more.

"You know your problem?" baby-faced Carl said to his brother/cousin. "You talk too fucking much."

"Way I see it," Andre said, panning between us both. "We're here for a few, no trouble, we get along. Make time go quicker, yes?" Andre nodded at my hands. "Took off restraints, yes? Bag too. Stay calm. This will all be over soon."

"The annuities," I said.

"Shut up—"

"That night in the forest, why did you let me live?"

Carl made to stand.

"Jay," Andre said pleadingly, gesturing his partner to stay put. "Please. I'm trying to make you as comfortable as possible. Don't piss him off by asking questions about Emily Lupus or Alliance Life or anything that's happened over the past few weeks. The night in the forest? Like I said, a misunderstanding."

"Had to move my truck? Plant something? Get your ducks in a row, what?"

Carl jumped up to slug me in the side of the head, but Andre blocked his path, motioned to sit back down.

Andre leaned down eye-level with me. "You've been a real pain in everyone's ass. Now is not time to talk. Please. Sit tight." He nodded at the fire. "Getting warm, yes?"

I wasn't up for getting punched in the mouth by his inbred relative so I nodded.

The two men returned to their stations, and I took Carl's advice and shut up, my time better served looking forward than trying to untangle yesterday.

Out the dingy window, I glimpsed a snowmobile. Hunters often left them up here. I doubted there would be keys dangling in the ignition. I didn't want to stare too long, but my first impression? The snowmobile appeared to be an older model Yamaha. I saw plenty of them at swap shops. This was good and bad news. Older models, you didn't need to hotwire. You rip out the ignition, starts right up. *You make it outside, don't get shot, get to the snowmobile and it does start?* No way that hunk of junk outruns a truck.

"I gotta take a piss."

Andre pointed across the room to a door on the left. "Shitter's in there."

"Don't get any ideas."

Walking the three and a half feet across the room, I dragged my left leg behind me. My head throbbed like I'd spent the last two hours under the bass speaker at a rave.

"Leave the door open."

I left the door open. Didn't matter. There were no windows to crawl through. An attached outhouse yielded a giant hole in the floor, piss and shit so frozen it didn't even stink. No counter, no shelf, nothing to slip in my pocket like a nail file or even pair of goddamn tweezers.

When I finished the world's longest piss, relieved not to see any blood in my urine—my kidneys felt like they'd been used as a football—I slinked back, drawing out my limp. "So what happened to Emily Lupus?" I asked, sitting in my little chair.

"Shut up," baby-faced Carl said, the two words that made up the bulk of his vocabulary.

They had to have a plan for me; they hadn't shot me yet. Would Adam and Michael risk being spotted for the opportunity to gloat in person? How big were their egos? No telephone wires ran up here, forget tower service, so unless an order was coming via SOS, I had to believe someone was delivering my fate in person. I studied each man, watching for signals, tics; like poker games and buyers at flea markets, everyone has a tell. They stuck by the door, split by the fireplace and small cot, and didn't pay attention to me. The big one rocked, the other read a skin magazine, gun on lap.

It was a pleasant cabin. Tiny but intimate. Cozy bearskin tacked to the walls, homey knick-knacks and artifacts. Time ebbed. Right now, time was as much an ally as it was an enemy.

Gave me opportunity to think, play back everything I'd heard.

He said Alliance Life. That's Stephen's company. He didn't need to look into who managed the annuities. *His company handled the payouts.* He'd known all along.

It started getting cold, fire dying out. The smell of my own breath made me sick. Halitosis and egg salad, stale nicotine gumming up the works, that filmy white paste in your mouth that needs to be scrubbed away.

Baby-faced Carl remained by the window, peering up from his magazine periodically, waiting for headlights to appear, drumming fingers off barrel.

This high on the mountain, the strong jet stream pummeled the little hut, bowing planks, hurling icy daggers, hail the size of golf balls. The fire started to die. Andre huffed to his feet to stoke the flame. He added kindling, crinkled old, brittle newspaper, dropped a couple more big fat logs, struck a match. Then he picked up one of the two big bottles of lighter fluid on the mantle, squirted a stream, and soon a fire roared back to life, the cabin nice and toasty.

I hated Billy Joel, but he was right about one thing: *Closer you get to the fire, the more you get burned.*

"I'm cold, man."

"Wrap this around you." Andre ripped the thick wool blanket off the cot and threw it at me. "Give the fire a minute. It'll warm up again soon."

I slipped the blanket around my shoulders. "I really could use a smoke."

When Carl made to stand, furious that I kept talking, ready to crack my skull open with the butt of his gun, I added, "Please?"

"Please" was an old trick I learned from my junkie brother. Yeah, it's manners and common sense and one might wonder why being polite would matter in times such as these. But there's something disarming about that particular word, a meek subservience that brings out innate desires in others to help, no matter how selfish or wicked. Chris used to tell me that when he was bumming smokes on the street, the difference between getting a free cigarette and not getting one, nine times out of ten came down to that one simple word. Please.

Carl sat back down. Andre tossed me my own pack they'd confiscated, plopping down in the rocking chair. I gestured at the matches on the mantle, standing up, reaching out. "Mind if I light it?" The gun was on the other side of the cabin, out of reach. It was a harmless request.

Now if Andre said sit tight, he'd get it, I'd have to sit tight, savor my smoke, which might well be my last. But he didn't move or say a word.

When I got to the mantle, I lit the cigarette, took a deep inhale.

Then I grabbed both bottles of lighter fluid and threw them into the fireplace.

CHAPTER TWENTY-EIGHT

THE EXPLOSION WASN'T that big, but in the tight space and freeze-dried confines, it was big enough to cause a distraction; big enough to confuse baby-faced Carl and Andre; big enough to throw flames out of the fireplace and lick the drapes and old bedding, set the dehydrated tinder ablaze. Most important, it was big enough to get me out the door.

On the shelf of Gillette Gorge, this time of year, the storm was perpetual, like the snow chimneys in Antarctica or the Door to Hell, an open pit of swirling, frostbiting winds diving deep inside the Earth, gathering fury, hurling icy shards like drunken darts aiming for the soft tissue.

I smelt the burning plastic and wood of the old cabin going up in smoke. I didn't make for the snowmobile, which I couldn't see through the thick haze anyway. Hoping to jerry rig the thing fast enough before they started shooting? No way. And I couldn't outrace their truck, regardless. Common sense dictated I run down the mountain, so I ran up it, my only play. I made for the safest place: the bottomless crevice of the Gorge itself. I prayed with the limited visibility, I could get to the edge, find a shelf, a cave, an alcove, a big fucking rock, somewhere to shield my-self from the worst of the winds. I still had the blanket wrapped around me. I wouldn't last long without it. I'd last even shorter with a bullet in my brain.

Behind me, the men were screaming, but not from the agony of being on fire. They'd screwed up and needed to get my ass back there before their bosses arrived.

Thousands of feet in the sky, with the snow and ice and thin air of the mountaintop, I couldn't see three feet in front of my face. The impenetrable black smoke drifted, seared with the wind. Strangled by the altitude, I had a tough timing breathing, the pressure like a vice; I thought my eardrums would pop. I stole a glance over my shoulder. I couldn't see their truck. Couldn't see a damn thing through the fire and smoke. Bullets travel faster than gimpy legs. *Keep moving.* I turned back, slogging up the mountain, trudging toward the crack in the earth.

My feet moved but I didn't seem to be making good time—it's hard to gain traction on a glacier so steep. I had no idea where I was, how close to the edge. Flames bloodied the sky behind me but even that picture was distorted. The precipitous climb warped the atmosphere, which made gauging distance impossible. The scorching winds disoriented. Blasts of heat punctuated the subzero temperatures that froze anything not covered. One second I feared I'd burn to death, the next that I'd freeze in place. The relentless jet stream racing down the slope pummeled progress. Behind me, I heard an engine roar to life.

Huddling in the blanket, I curled my body best I could, scrunched to shrink down, condense my mass, leave the least of me exposed, blend into the landscape. I had to draw them out, lead them to the edge.

Then, like that, the fire extinguished, leaving only black smoke and smolder. I tasted the melted parts, plastic and kerosene distinct as burnt hair. That fire, besides keeping me semi-thawed, had provided my sole measuring stick, however inaccurate. I lost sight of how far I'd traveled. Now shellacked black, the darkness of Lamentation roared louder with the storm. I wouldn't have heard the Carls if they were standing on top of me. I awaited my fate in the middle of a wind tunnel.

The engine revved and I saw the headlights, which were on me fast, in seconds. Like those dumb deer I smashed into on the Turnpike, I remained frozen, hypnotized. Time both sped up and slowed down. I saw Aiden being born and my big brother being killed; I relived lazy summer days with Jenny by the water; then the cold, the ice, the inhospitable, infertile existence I'd chosen. When I snapped out of it, there was no time left to think, only react. I dove to the hard, frozen earth as the hot swoosh of diesel rushed past. Took a second, time delayed, speed of sound trapped in a bubble, satellite signal blocked by misaligned planets. It wasn't until I heard the panicked voices echoing deep in the abyss that I realized the men had driven over the cliff, plummeting into the Gorge.

Then the screams ended.

The vortex sucked me backwards, toward the pit. I slipped, dropped to a knee, digging the tips of my clawed fingers into the fruitless earth. Fighting against the drift, I scraped, scratched, crawled, dragging away from the sucking crater, pushing myself to my feet, staggering from the grips of terminal velocity.

When I looked down at my untied work boots I saw I was three feet from the edge.

I had minutes before I froze to death. I already couldn't feel my nose or fingertips, dizzied from the lack of air.

Through a refracting snowflake, a glint in the darkness. The snowmobile.

With raw, clumsy hands, I used a piece of iron mounting stripped by the explosion to rip out the ignition.

I have gone back and forth on the existence of God, and I sure as shit didn't believe in angels looking over me. But in that moment, I couldn't think of any other reason the snowmobile should've started. Forget a mickey-mouse trick I'd learned as a kid, in this cold the gasoline should've frozen in such a tiny tank, a fact I hadn't considered when I was mulling hasty getaways. The fire must've warmed the metal enough to defrost the fuel.

Crouched over the wheel, still huddled in the blanket, I shifted forward, and sped down the mountain. Squinting, turning my head to avoid the ice and rime. High speeds, trees and blindness be damned, forging my own path because I couldn't see anything resembling a road or even trampled path. I hopped frozen brush and rigid bramble, going faster and faster, my need to get to the bottom of the mountain paramount, spurring me on to ride the throttle harder. Blood chilling to near fatal levels, I was losing consciousness, felt the pull of death calling me, pulling me under . . .

I saw the closed gate in time to hit the brakes, tried to regain control of the wheel. I jerked around the pole, attempted to re-right the skis, but by now I was sliding sideways. I abandoned ship, tumbling off the seat, rolling down the hillside, rock and stump jabbing my innards, jostling my organs, smacking my already damaged ribs.

When I came to rest, I was at the bottom of the mountain, still breathing, still alive. I patted down my body. Didn't feel any blood soaking my shirt; no fractured bone fragments pierced my skin. My legs and arms were beat to shit but they moved when I commanded them to. Took a second for circulation to flow, for my extremities to come back to life. I felt terrible, of course. And though temps were still below freezing, being in the lowlands added another twenty-five degrees, making it the balmy tropics by comparison. I was ready for my bright blue drink and tiny umbrella, crank the Jimmy Buffett.

The snowmobile lay thirty yards away. Flipped on its back, its engine still purred.

I had two choices. One, I could go to Turley and the authorities. Tell them about the two men who had disappeared over the side of a mountain into an endless abyss, the only evidence of their existence: a stoned fry cook in Chevreport and the windblown ashes of the blind. I could try and explain about the toxic soil, but as soon as I mentioned the word "Lombardi," no one was taking me seriously. I didn't see how I talked my way out of this. Owen Eaton, a man I hated, was dead. Which left option number two: clean up this mess myself. Too much was at stake to put my fate in anyone else's hands. How far would Lombardi go to protect their profit margin and blood money? They had everything on their side: the law, the perfect frame job, the odds stacked against a man on his last leg.

I had the snowmobile. There was light in the flats, still overcast and murky, foggy, but light. If I could get a car or truck, I could make it to my motel before checkout. I had two grand in a shoebox. I needed to get somewhere safe and plot my revenge. By now Owen Eaton's body had been discovered, and it wouldn't take that long for them to zero in on me as a suspect. Which made my next move twice as dangerous.

Flipping the snowmobile back on its skis, I stayed hidden in the brush, tracing the backstreets of Ashton toward my apartment.

The thing ran out of gas about a quarter mile short. I hated stealing from Hank Miller. Having been his tenant most of my life, I knew where he kept the keys to the cars he was repairing. I could as easily walk up to his door, explain the situation, and he'd give me a damn car, but that would also implicate him, make him an accessory. Sometimes you have to be cruel to be kind.

The filling station wasn't open. Not uncommon after significant snowfall or during inclement weather. An old man, Hank often got a late start. I broke the window to the garage with my elbow, snatched a set of keys to a Honda sedan, and drove to my motel.

It was still witch-tit cold, overcast with slop on the streets. I slowed down, focused on my breathing, reminded myself that, for now, I was just another man on the road, grinding along, merging with the morning rush hour traffic. On the way to his job in the fields or the cubicle. I was disappeared, no different than you.

Back at the motel, I stopped in the office and explained that I'd locked my key inside by mistake. The clerk recognized me, didn't ask why my face was bashed and gashed. In my room, I washed off the blood, got my money and packed up. Didn't take long.

Next door to the motel there was a small grocery store. I paid cash for a carton of Marlboro lights and a case of Michelob. Why bother pretending?

Back in my truck, I turned up Springsteen so I didn't have to think and started driving south. A fugitive, I lit a cigarette and opened my first beer in nine months. Goddamn, it tasted good.

I was shipping off to Boston to find Bowman and that hard drive. I'd clear my name, prove Lombardi was behind it all, and nail the sonsofbitches to the wall.